GOLDEN

GOLDEN: Book One of The Golden Trilogy
Copyright © 2017 by K.M. Robinson.

Published by Crescent Sea Publishing.
www.crescentseapublishing.com

Cover designed by Reading Transforms.
Image copyright © K.M. Robinson Photography.
Interior graphics by Millennium Genesis.

GOLDEN

BOOK ONE OF THE GOLDEN TRILOGY

K.M. ROBINSON

"I fell for Dov instantly and wanted to snag him from Auluria every time they had a fight. K.M. Robinson creates incredible characters and the tension between them kept me glued to the page. I loved being in Auluria's head and can't wait for more in the series."
–Constance Roberts,
author of SIGIL IN SHADOW

DEDICATION

To those who make the right choices despite what has happened to them. You can't control what happens to you, but you do control your response to it. Well done for not turning your circumstances into excuses, but instead, choosing to make the best out of it.

The condensed version of my story is this:

*The girl with the long golden hair, or Goldilocks, as they would
eventually call me, was awakened by one of the three bears. She
had no memory of how she got there. She sat on their furniture,
ate their food and slept in their home. They found her,
talked to her, and ultimately chased her away.
That is the story they tell.*

But there are things they didn't tell you. The stories never
mention that I had been intentionally sent there
to find the Baer family's weaknesses and use them
to then destroy their group.
No one ever said that I would fall for the youngest.
Nobody talked about how he would try to save me, even
when I couldn't be saved.
And they never said my entire world would
come crashing down
around me as I tried to save him and
betray the only family I had left.

I am Auluria, and this is my real story.

Chapter 1

The first thing I smelled was sweet spices. A wave of warmth washed over me, coaxing me out of my sleep.

Someone was breathing on me.

When I opened my eyes, all I saw was blue. Blue so deep and so intense I had to blink to bring it into focus. Dark fringe fell over the blue color as it sparked and flashed, awakening me fully. Those were eyes. The most brilliant blue eyes I'd ever seen.

Then it hit me…and I panicked.

"Who are you?" I snapped, sitting up so quickly I nearly collided with the boy next to me. No, not a boy; a man.

I clutched at my collar and backed away from the figure next to me. His face fell as I scrambled away. He reached for me, but not in time to save me from falling off the far side of the small bed and landing squarely on the ground. My flailing hand slammed into a small table near the cot and sent its contents crashing to the floor beside me.

"Auluria, stop," Blue Eyes said.

"How do you know my name?" I sputtered.

"You don't remember?" he asked, concerned. He stepped quickly around the bed and stood at the foot of it, unsure if I'd accept his help. He reached out his hand but pulled it back, looking disappointed as I recoiled.

"Are you all right?" he asked gently. He knelt to the floor submissively, trying to soothe my terror.

I looked around. I had made a mess, but I hadn't broken anything. Still, I was confused...I had no idea what was going on.

"Who are you?" I asked again, softer this time.

"I'm Dov." He placed his hand over his heart as he spoke. "You know me."

Breathing heavily, I tried to calm my gasping.

"Why am I here?"

"You came here. You came with me. You don't remember?"

"No." I didn't remember anything about him.

"We only just met yesterday. You've had quite an

experience." He spoke softly to me as if trying to calm a child. "It's okay that you don't remember. You will."

He couldn't have been much older than me, maybe a year or two. The man was tall when he was standing, I could tell even from down on the floor. He had long, strong arms. Something about the way he brushed the hair back out of his eyes set me at ease.

I started to stand and he rose with me. He never took his eyes off me.

"And just how did we meet, Dov?"

"Come. Sit down and I'll tell you. Would you like something to drink? Water perhaps?"

I slowly made my way to the table at the far end of the room. I started to sink into one of the mismatched chairs.

"Actually, maybe not that one," Dov said, skirting around me and pulling out another chair. "This one is much more comfortable."

I obliged, though I didn't know why.

"Here," he said, handing me a glass of cool water. "Are you hungry? I can make you something."

Without waiting for me to respond, he walked over and started the stove. He reached for a pan and busied himself making food.

"So, why am I here?" I prompted after a few minutes of watching him cook. Once I was convinced he wasn't going to hurt me, I relaxed back into the seat and watched him work. It calmed my nerves to see him methodically creating breakfast.

"You are here, Auluria, for a great many reasons," he said dramatically, his grin making his eyes sparkle again. "One of which happens to be…"

The door flew open, interrupting him. I jumped as it crashed against the wall. Turning to look at the noise, I sent my hair cascading over the back of the chair and around to my shoulder where it hit me in the face before falling into my lap.

"Well, look who's up," a woman said, scoffing. "Sleeping Beauty."

"I can't believe you brought her back here, Dov. She's nothing but trouble," the man said. He was an older, darker version of Dov. He seemed to be plagued by something heavy. Even his steps were weighted as he moved about the room as if dragged down by some invisible chain.

"Are you hungry?" Dov asked ignoring their comments.

I watched as the woman glanced around the room. Her eyes fell on the bed. Its sheets were tangled from my fall. The man followed her gaze. They both cast Dov looks, raising their eyebrows at him. No one said anything. Suddenly, I was extremely self-conscious.

"Well, well, baby brother. Looks like you have a story

to tell." The man howled with laughter. My cheeks burned and I ducked my head.

"Enough, Berwyn," the woman said quietly. She looked aside as he cast her a disparaging glance.

"Auluria doesn't remember us." Dov sounded annoyed.

"Oh, but we remember her," Berwyn said, making it sound like a bad thing.

I couldn't figure out what I had done to these people to make them so vicious toward me. Well, not all of them. But it was clear the man and woman were not pleased to find me there.

"I thought we told you to get rid of her," he said seriously, making my stomach jump into my throat. He slammed his fist against a table, and Dov ducked as though he had been hit.

"I won't and you know why. She won't hurt us; she's more likely to help us than anything else."

"Let her stay, Berwyn. I think it would be nice to have another girl around. And besides, Dov's been alone for so long, it's nice he has someone." I couldn't tell if she was being helpful or mocking.

"It is kind of a pain that he's always a third wheel, I guess," the big man relented.

"See? I knew it would work out," the woman said, her mid-length blonde curls bouncing as she strode toward him.

I opened my mouth to speak, but Dov caught my attention and signaled me to stay quiet with a quick shake of his head.

"Come on," the man finally said, leading the woman away.

I looked back to the stove where Dov was, but he was already at my side setting down a plate.

"That's my brother, Berwyn, and his wife, Eden," he said as a matter of fact.

"They're married?" I said, shocked. "He can't be more than twenty-five."

"Twenty-four, actually."

"How old is she?"

"Eden's twenty-three," he replied. "Do you want more water?"

"Dov, why am I here?" I asked again, trying to get him to focus. I needed answers.

"Do you remember being in the forest yesterday?" he asked me.

I shook my head.

"Well, I don't know why you were in the woods, but that's where I met you. You were running through the forest and you jumped over a small stream.

"I saw you flying through the air and thought, 'What must this crazy girl be doing to be running so quickly through such a dense part of the forest?' When you landed, you took three whole steps before you came face to face with me.

"I'd never seen a more panicked look in all my life. You clutched your skirts in your hand and whipped your head from side to side. I'd never seen such long hair on a girl; when it finally settled, it ran past your waist," he said as if I didn't know how long my hair was.

"And when you looked back to me, you whispered, 'Help.' I could see in your eyes that you were in trouble." He said this with grandeur, illustrating his story with his hands. "So I took you by the waist and spun you into the trees. We ducked behind some large rocks and hid among the vines. You were breathing so loudly I thought you were going to give us away."

I wondered how the story would sound if he dropped his dramatic tone. I assumed he was using it to try to keep me engaged.

"What was I running from?" I interrupted.

"Men. There were men chasing you. You refused to tell me why." He grinned as if it were all a game. I was in no mood for games.

"Once the first group of men chasing you was gone you started off again, barely throwing a 'thank you' over your shoulder. But I couldn't let you go alone, not after what I had seen, so I walked with you."

I hoped he would get to the point, but he had more to describe in detail.

"You only tolerated me for so long until you started throwing things at me. An apple. A tree branch. Some small pebbles. I admit, it hurt my feelings a bit."

He frowned playfully, but his eyes sparked to life from under his dark hair.

"But…persist I did, and I followed you for the better part of an hour, talking at you the whole time. That is, until I was attacked. In my blind disregard for my own safety"—he waved his hand to the side, as if I should be impressed—"I hadn't realized where we had wandered. I was taken completely by surprise when those guys jumped out of the trees and landed on top of me."

He laughed, his eyes lighting up. "But you, for as surprised as you were, ran right at us and tackled Jake to the ground. He hit the dirt so hard that it knocked the wind right out of him. I'm sure he couldn't ever believe a girl would ever consider dating him, much less throwing herself at him like you did."

I felt my eyes grow wide at his teasing words. He was only joking, a play on words, but still, I would never throw myself at a man in that context. It vexed me that he would insinuate that I might.

"Once I took out Marty, we found ourselves in the clear. That didn't stop us from trying to make a fast getaway though. We almost made it, too, but somehow Jake struggled to his feet and he went after you. Just as I subdued Marty and placed him on the ground, I lifted my head and saw Jake barreling toward you.

"I couldn't make it to you in time. The sound it made when he hit you…it was almost as if I could feel it from as far away as I was." He offered me a sad look, his eyes clouding.

"If it's any consolation, I slammed his face into a tree and messed him up pretty bad. You insisted that you were fine, but you could barely stand. I scooped you up and carried you.

"We talked all the way back here. Well, mostly I did." I refrained from rolling my eyes. Of course, he had been the talkative one. "You told me your name and then you asked a few questions before deciding to stay quiet. So as of right now, all I know is that your name is Auluria. You have long hair. You're running from something and you are being chased. And you're looking for a place to belong—though I added that last part on my own."

He counted his points off on his fingers for me as he summarized what had occurred yesterday.

"And what did you tell me about yourself?"

"Well, as you know, my name is Dov. Baer is my last name. You've met my brother and his wife yesterday briefly, and again today. As you can see, my brother doesn't trust you, but don't take offense, he doesn't trust anyone.

"You can't really blame him with all that's going on," he continued. "It's hard to trust anyone these days."

"I suppose."

I looked down to my dress, covered with dirt and mud at the bottom. There were a few small holes that I assumed occurred during my fall. That's when I remembered.

I had been running. I just couldn't remember why.

I remembered meeting him though. As the men gained on me, I leapt over a river, almost directly into Dov's arms. He hid me until the men passed. I never told him of the danger I must have surely been in and he was in for being with me.

"You remember." Dov's voice changed, snapping back to the conversation.

"I remember." I nodded. "Thank you for your help yesterday."

"Anything for a pretty lady." He half bowed to me from his seat next to mine.

"Now, tell me Auluria, why were you running from those men yesterday?" He grew serious again, wanting more information from me.

"They were chasing me," I said simply.

He chuckled. "But why?"

I swallowed hard. "I don't know."

"You don't remember?"

"It picks up from where I ran into you." His eyes

narrowed intently, but soft enough to know he was concerned, not angry.

"Where do you belong, Auluria? We have to get you back to where it's safe." He took my hand in his own hands, the gesture so sudden that it shocked me into stillness. I let him hold my hand in his while his eyes searched me for answers.

"I...I don't belong anywhere." That was the truth. I never belonged there. "And do you really think going back is safe, since that's where I was coming from in the first place?"

Little flashes of memory floated through my mind. Not enough to blend together and form a picture, but pieces all the same.

"You will tell me eventually, Auluria," he said withdrawing his hand. He looked genuinely hurt that I wouldn't divulge any new information.

I didn't like that he thought I knew more than I was saying.

"You can stay here until you're ready," he added quietly, almost to himself.

I looked at him and it was as if he read my mind.

"You'll be safe here. They won't find you and Berwyn won't hurt you. I'll make sure of it."

That thought scared me. If this man was telling me I'd be safe from his brother, then what was so bad about his brother that made it potentially unsafe?

"Finished?" he interrupted my thoughts. Lifting my plate, he turned to the sink.

I watched as he washed the dishes, his shoulders rising and falling as he worked. His muscles looked stiff at times, seizing with pain. My gaze lingered on them as he worked. I watched his chest expand and shrink as he breathed.

When he turned, it startled me. Dov only raised an eyebrow and smirked. He nodded his head for me to join him in the makeshift living room, walking away from the kitchen.

Just as we started to sit, I blurted out, "What did you mean? 'Protect me from Berwyn'?"

"Oh. I see you don't remember all of yesterday after your rescue." He added apologetically, "Berwyn is just a lot to handle at times. Sometimes he gets a little too upset. At times, he says or does things without thinking. It's nothing to worry about. He won't hurt you, he's just… loud sometimes."

As if emphasizing his brother's point, at that very moment Berwyn crashed into the room and slammed the door behind him. He glared at us before stomping through the kitchen and marching out the door.

Eden appeared, rolling her eyes. She looked over to her young brother-in-law and gestured around the room.

"Baby, you need to get this taken care of." She turned on her heels and retreated the way she came.

I looked to Dov. "Baby?" I giggled.

"Oh, be quiet," he said, throwing a pillow at me as he stood, careful to avoid my face.

"Let me help you," I responded, rising to follow him, knowing that I owed him for his help the day before.

We started cleaning up the mess around the room. Bottles lay strewn about the floor. Unfolded laundry sat in a pile on a chair. It looked like there had been a celebration that someone forgot to clean up after.

"How's your head feeling?" he asked as we worked.

"It's okay," I said, feeling more secure about being alone with him. "What happened in here anyway?"

"Berwyn and Eden had a fight yesterday. It's best to get out of the house when that happens." He stooped to sweep up pieces of broken glass. "They never hurt each other, but they sure do know how to make it sound good."

"Was it about me?" I asked.

"It started out about you, but most of this is from after."

I helped him straighten the room. His eyes flitted over to me every so often, making sure I wasn't going to pass out from my injury the previous day.

The quiet that stretched between us was almost comforting. I've always liked the silence. It means that you are comfortable enough with a person that you don't feel the need to fill up the space with words. You can just exist together.

Berwyn and Eden didn't make another appearance until that evening. Dov had suggested I take a nap to help regain my strength, so after lunch, I lay on the couch under a light blanket. It really was too warm for a blanket, but I liked the protection it offered me.

I never truly drifted off to sleep. While I felt safe in that house, I knew I didn't really know these people very well and I didn't want to trust them too quickly.

"She's still here," Berwyn grumbled.

"I told you, we're not sending her back out there. She's being hunted and she can't remember by whom or why. We have to protect her."

"Stop it, Berwyn," Eden interrupted before he could say anything. "I don't like it either, but he's right. We're not sending her back out there until we have some answers. Your father started this whole thing to *help* people, so you need to *help* people. And start with *her*." I heard the edge in her voice when she talked about me. Maybe she *hadn't* been sincere about letting me stay.

"Fine," he huffed. "For now."

I kept my eyes closed, feigning sleep, and waited for

them to leave. I heard their steps creak across the floor-boards as they walked out of the room. A moment later I felt the couch arm dip slightly as someone leaned on it.

"You heard that, didn't you?" his gentle voice asked.

I opened my eyes. "Yeah," I acknowledged.

He took a deep breath and sighed. "At least he's letting you stay."

"For now," I added.

"For now," he said, worry slightly edging into his voice.

That probably wasn't their best choice.

Chapter 2

The next day I woke early. Dov had given me his cot and had taken the couch for the evening. I heard him periodically check on me throughout the night. When he discovered I was still breathing, he would lay back down and wait an hour to check again.

"Dov?" I asked the next morning, getting his attention. "I'd like to help. What can I do?"

He gave me a curious look, unsure of what I meant.

"If I'm going to stay here, I need to help. So, give me something to do."

"Umm…" He glanced around the room, pushing his

hair out of his eyes. "Well…you can help me cook. We cleaned up yesterday, so that's taken care of."

"I can cook," I assured him.

Walking into the kitchen, he led me where they kept everything. He showed me the food; clearly, they were running low.

"What if I help you get more food?" I suggested.

"You shouldn't go outside." He shook his head. "We still don't know who is looking for you."

"They have to be long gone by now. Really, who's going to find me out here? Come on, let's go."

"I really don't think…" He trailed off as I marched toward the door. "Auluria, please."

I didn't stop. I let the door go behind me. He caught it just before it slammed shut.

Dov stumbled as he pulled on his remaining shoe and hurried to catch up to me.

"You don't even know where you're going."

"So, show me," I said defiantly.

"Are you always this stubborn?" he asked.

"I wouldn't know." I grinned at him.

"Of course, you wouldn't." After a moment he grinned back. "You have an ever-convenient head injury. I bet you pull that card all the time to get your way."

"Yes, whenever I feel like someone won't do as I want, I'm sure to find a way to throw myself to the ground and get beaten up so I can use a head injury as an excuse to manipulate people. As you can see, I'm clearly a genius," I said sarcastically.

We marched through the woods, ducking under tree branches and hopping over fallen logs. The birds sang a path for us as we traveled further and further from the house. A few squirrels came out to greet us, stealing fallen nuts from their grassy beds.

"Where are we going, exactly?" I looked at my guide.

"To the storehouse. It's not much longer," he replied, glancing over at me.

The storehouse was hidden inside a cave. I wouldn't have even noticed it if Dov hadn't pointed it out to me. Inside, the cave dropped into a deep descent, pushing down into the earth.

It was cool and earthy, perfect for holding food. The walls were lit brightly, casting shadows from the crates of edible contents. People gathered around, collecting things to take with them.

"Who are all these people, Dov?"

I had never seen any place like it. Food was a scarcity in our society. There was barely enough for the people and the little they had was cause for great fighting.

The government had taken control of all food many years ago, to assuage a foreign nation. To avoid an attack, the officials took most of the society's food and resources and gave them to the enemy. The theory was to give them what they wanted and they'd leave us alone. Unfortunately, that didn't work. They came back for more. The threat became too great. Young men without high standing were sent to train for the military. Young women were encouraged to breed to get the population numbers up. Many girls disappeared—first those who wouldn't be noticed, then the rest, sent to breeding camps.

"Pick out what you like," Dov interrupted my thoughts, snapping me back to the present as he deftly evaded my question. I let the question of who all the people were rest between us, remaining unanswered. He handed me a basket and started browsing around.

"Where did all this come from?" I asked.

His eyes lit up like he was about to share a great secret, but he merely shrugged and tossed an apple into the basket.

"Here and there," he said. "Do you want some eggs?"

We filled several baskets full of food before he led me back toward the entrance.

"Good morning, Dov." A man about his age nodded to him.

"Good morning, Silas." He nodded back.

"Who's this?" the man asked curiously.

"A new friend." Dov smiled politely, refusing to tell him more.

"All right," he drawled. "But if she shows up again,

you're going to have to start answering questions," he said with a chuckle.

"You picked a good one there, Missy," he added, ducking his head to me before moving on.

Missy.

Something flashed in my mind. That word. It was familiar.

A face darted before me and left just as quickly.

He had light hair and grey eyes. His eyes sparked as if he were angry.

"You okay?" Dov pulled me back.

"Yeah." I shook my head to clear it. "I saw a face. That's all."

"Do you know who?"

"No." I knew him though; just not how or who.

As we left the storehouse, we walked in silence. I could see the house in the distance before I spoke again.

"Dov, what was that place really? There's nowhere like that around here. And I've never seen that much food in my life. Tell me what's going on."

He sighed deeply. "Auluria, you don't need to know everything right now."

"But I don't know anything. I just want to understand what is going on," I said, frustrated.

"It's a storehouse. That's all you need to know."

"Is it stolen food? Who took it?"

"It's not stolen. It's reacquired."

"Reacquired?"

He didn't answer.

Eden was in the living room when we returned, arms crossed and ready for a fight.

"What were you thinking?" she scolded. "Taking her there—it could destroy us! No outsiders—remember that, Dov? Only the group is allowed in. We don't know her! We know nothing about her! She could be a spy; she could get us killed! You know what happens when people like us get caught! You know what happened to Griz!

"What is your problem?" her rant continued. "You haven't seen enough death for one lifetime? What are we supposed to do now, huh? Keep her locked up here forever? She can't go out—you knew that! Now we can't let her leave!"

"Eden, stop!" Dov exploded. "She is no threat. I've been watching her. She's a scared girl on the run. She's just trying to survive. She's not going to betray us."

"You don't know that!" Eden screeched.

"Yes, I do!" Dov shouted back.

"No, you don't!"

"Eden, she's fine—" His words were cut short as Eden lashed out her hand and slapped him hard across the face.

I gasped as he reeled back. Anger rippled through his blue eyes, but he didn't move toward her. Eden almost looked shocked as he turned back to face her, realizing she had hit him.

"You will not touch her," he said in a low, threatening, terrifying voice.

Eden backed up. She stood watching him for a moment before shifting her gaze to me. Looking back at him, she conceded and slowly turned to leave.

Once she had retreated, Dov turned to me, hand still on his face.

"Berwyn must never know."

I nodded quickly. These people were terrifying. Something told me this wasn't the first time Dov had been hit or threatened by his family.

"Ice," I whispered.

His face softened. "What?" he asked, unable to hear me.

"Ice," I said a bit louder, but my voice was still unsteady. "Do you want ice?"

Suddenly I found myself rushing to get ice. His face must be throbbing by now. A red handprint was forming under his fingers as he tried to rub the pain away.

I stumbled back to him as he lowered himself to the

couch. He slouched in the corner and allowed the cushions to envelop him. I gently touched the ice to his cheek and he winced as it made contact.

"Are you all right?" I asked quietly, afraid to look him in the eye.

"I'm fine," he mumbled.

"This isn't the first time that's happened, is it?"

He looked me in the eye and I understood everything.

"You didn't have to do that for me."

"It's fine."

"No really, I don't want to cause any problems. I'll leave today," I offered, determined not to make the situation worse.

"You will not. Everything will be fine."

"But…"

"Auluria, you are staying. That is final. Besides, they're better behaved when you're around, so think of it like you are helping me," he tried to coax me into staying.

You are helping me.

"You are helping me," the blond man said. He had me by the shoulders and was looking deep into my eyes. "You have to do this. For me, for our family. You're the only one who can get in there," he said. I remembered nodding, agreeing, complying. I was on a mission of some kind. When I was caught. I was on a mission before I found Dov.

"You remembered something." He leaned away from me, taking the ice from my hand.

"I was on a mission when I found you. I was doing something for…someone. A man. A blond man. It had to do with…my family? I think. But I don't have a family, so how could that be?"

"No family?" he asked.

"No." I shook my head, thinking. "They…died. They died." I looked up at him. "They died. I have no parents."

"How?" he prompted softly.

"They…they…died."

"It's okay." He tapped my shoulder lightly. "You'll figure it out."

I hated not knowing. At least some of it was coming back to me. Slowly. I've always hated slowness.

Dov let me make lunch for him. As I worked, I tried to figure out why I was in the woods to begin with. *What sort of a mission was I on and who was the blond man?*

Dov wouldn't offer any further explanation for the storehouse. I didn't push him on it. The red mark slowly disappeared from his handsome face and the anger crept out of his eyes. He let me clear away his plate when he was finished, the only way I could think of to thank him for standing up for me.

"Dov?" I asked after I had cleaned up. "Why don't they like me?"

He looked at me, his usually sparkling blue eyes clouding.

"It's not you that they don't like. It's the situation. This has happened before and it didn't end well."

"What do you mean?" I pushed. I had to find out.

"We're very careful about who we let into our group. Sometimes people slip in, though, that shouldn't be here. There was a girl..."

He waited, trying to collect his thoughts.

"There was a girl, who joined us. She wanted to get away from a situation she was in, and she found us. We took her in. Some things happened and she was forced to turn against us."

"What happened?"

"She betrayed us, gave our secrets away. When the group found out, she was forced to leave."

"I understand how that would make the group nervous. I'm sure you must be wary of all new people. It would be awful if that happened to you all again."

He nodded, his dark hair falling around his eyes.

"I have another question, though," I added.

He gave a slight nod for me to go on.

"I understand why you won't let people in," I started slowly. "But...when Berwyn said to get rid of me, you said you wouldn't. You told him that he knew why. Dov...why?"

Dov moved closer to me and took my hands. Their warmth reached all the way up my arms and tingled up to my neck and cheeks. Tipping his head, he looked straight into my eyes.

"Auluria, there are people out there who want to hurt us. They don't like what we stand for and they will find any way they can to hurt us.

"That girl, she went back to her group—not by choice—and they weren't happy. She had failed in her mission. They hurt her. Eventually, it got so bad she just gave out. They made sure we knew her death was our fault.

"And it's not just the other groups out there. It's the government. The Society wants information on us too. They're still mad about everything that happened in past years. They've been looking for us, and they won't hesitate to use you to find us.

"So, I'm not just going to let you back out there. You may be new, but you need protection. I won't send you away without it." He looked sad.

"That girl. You were close with her?"

"She was a friend."

I didn't believe that. He could tell I was skeptical.

"I wasn't with her, if that's what you want to know. She was a bit younger than me, and yes, Berwyn and Eden got it in their heads that she would be a good fit for me, so they kept her close, but I never wanted her like that."

"That explains why they were so angry. Betrayal is always bad, but betrayal by someone close is so much worse," I thought aloud.

He took his hands away from mine, leaving them suddenly cold and empty.

"Don't be nervous though. We'll protect you. You're not going to be kicked out, Auluria."

It was my turn to nod.

Deciding I needed to do something to reassure the Baers about me, I was planning a good meal for dinner to make peace with Berwyn and Eden later that night. For dessert, I wanted to have fresh fruit. Dov directed me to some berry bushes a few yards into the woods. He watched me from the window for a moment but turned away once I caught him staring.

I began to fill the bowl with raspberries and blueberries, humming to myself as I worked. I barely noticed the hand slip around my waist as a second hand clasped my mouth, preventing me from calling out. I silently hated myself for causing Dov to look away from his watch post.

I struggled against my captor as he pulled me further into the tree.

"Shh!" he hissed in my ear.

I pulled out of his grip, swinging around to confront him. As I was hit by his green eyes, it all came flooding back.

"Shadoe." I relaxed.

Shadoe was my handler. And my fiancé. My cousin —*my cousin, the blond man from my flashback*—had pushed Shadoe and me together. It was never a question, it just was.

I worked with my cousin, Lowell. He was part of a resistance movement that was working to bring down the corrupt government. When my parents had died, my aunt had taken me in. When she died, Lowell brought me into his group. I was trained and given missions for them.

I was on a mission now.

"Where have you been, Lur?" he asked, a mix of annoyance and concern.

"Shadoe," I said again. I shook my head to clear it. "After he found me, we got attacked. One of the guys hit me and knocked me out. I lost my memory. I *just* got it back when I saw you right now."

"You missed the first check in."

"Clearly." Now I was the one who was annoyed.

"What did you find?" he questioned.

"Not much yet. I didn't know why I was there so I didn't know I was supposed to be looking." I paused to think. "Well, we have a complication. Berwyn is married."

Suddenly I realized what that meant for the plan. My job had been to find a way into the Baer home and to get Berwyn to trust me. Lowell had sent me because I was Berwyn's type, or so he thought.

"That's not good." He looked worried. "What about the younger brother, Dov?"

"He's the one that rescued me. He's been protecting me this whole time."

"Good. He's the one then. Go after him. Get him to fall in love with you and use it to find the information."

I then realized just how awful this mission really would be. Manipulating Berwyn would have been one thing, but Dov had been nothing but kind. I didn't want to see him hurt in the fall out of my cousin's master plan.

"What else did you learn? Anything?" he cut me off.

"Umm…there's a storehouse. I don't know exactly where it is, but it exists and it's full of food."

"Find out. We need an exact location."

I nodded, creating a mental checklist for myself.

"We need exact information so we can pull this off," he continued.

I felt the lightness leave my shoulders as I slipped back into my old persona. A seriousness washed over me that I didn't know I was missing. I could feel my rib cage constrict around my lungs, forcing the air out and pulling me down.

"We'll meet in two days," Shadoe continued, drawing me out of my thoughts. "All right, Lur?"

"All right." I nodded, raising my hand to where my neck met my shoulder. I hoped it looked like I was working out a knot, but really, I was trying to calm my heart rate down.

"At the meeting place."

"Yes. I'll try to slip away."

He nodded, picking my hand up in his and giving a light squeeze before backing away.

"You can do this. Now that you're back, you'll be incredible," he said before turning, sounding far more like Lowell than himself.

"*Destructive* is more like it," I muttered as I turned to go back inside.

I snatched a few more berries along the way. When I walked back into the house Dov was standing in the kitchen moving some pans around.

"Find any?" he asked, barely looking up.

"Yep." I offered him a weak smile and held out the bowl even though he wasn't looking.

"Good," he said, tinkering with something. "So, who

were you talking to out there?"

My heart slammed into my chest again. Apparently, it was a feeling I was going to have to get used to.

"What?" I asked, hoping my voice didn't betray my worry.

"Who were you talking to out there? You were gone an awfully long time." He laughed as if he were making a joke. Maybe he hadn't seen.

"Oh, just my…shadow," I tried to joke back.

I swept across the room with a lavish flourish and deposited the bowl of berries next to him on the table. I plucked one from the bowl and popped it into my mouth. "Mmm."

Dov looked at me and I swear he was amused.

For a moment, it flashed through my mind how easy it would be to get him to fall for me and tell me everything I needed to know. I instantly regretted that thought, ashamed that I would ever be okay with hurting someone as kind as Dov.

I reached for another berry just as he did. His hand covered mine for a brief second before I pulled away.

"Go ahead," I said, my hand still burning from where our skin touched. I felt the corners of my lips twitch up as I turned on my heels and moved further away.

Dipping down to the floor, I searched the cabinet for another bowl.

"I think I'll actually go pick some more," I added, desperate to be out of that house so I could think.

"I'll go with you," he said decidedly, scooping up yet another bowl. When he saw my hesitation, he added, "You take one side and I'll take the other."

"All right," I said softly, trying not to sound annoyed.

"Oh. I had Eden pick you up some new clothing. Now you won't have to borrow hers. They're over on the cot." He motioned to my temporary sleeping space.

"Thank you," I said, blushing. "That was so very kind of you."

Kind.

This boy was going to kill me. He was going to get us all killed.

We walked outside together and into the trees. True to his word, he stayed on his side and gave me space on mine. I deftly reached out and pulled the fruit from their bushes, listening to the birds singing, hoping for their advice.

I liked Dov. He was a good person. He didn't deserve to be hurt. I wanted to protect him. But Lowell was a good person too, and if he said this needed to be done, I had no reason to not believe him. No matter how hard I tried, I couldn't find a way to have Berwyn take the fall without involving Dov.

I couldn't.

My job was to find their weaknesses and use whatever it was against them. If I did my job right, *I* was supposed to be Dov's weakness.

But I couldn't.

My bowl was full by the time I finally settled on my only option. I had to play both sides. I would make sure Dov and I were friends but I wouldn't let him get close enough that it could hurt him. There would be no relationship, fake or otherwise. I'd get the information I could, but I'd do my best not to use Dov to get it. I'd report back to Shadoe and Lowell.

When the time came, I'd try to convince Dov to come with us. I'd tell him all about the mission and beg him to leave. Ultimately, though, my loyalty had to be to my only family, my cousin. I knew that. I had to believe that was right.

I'd keep Dov safe. I'd do whatever I could. If I was careful, I might be able to save Lowell *and* Dov. I had to try.

"You ready?" Dov asked, eyeing my full bowl.

"Yeah," I breathed. Some of the heaviness lifted from my shoulders. I could make this work.

"Wasn't that kind of her?" Dov prompted after dinner. The berries we had collected had been devoured quickly.

"Thanks," Berwyn grumbled as he stood. His gaze swept around the room, falling again to our sleeping arrangement. The clothes Eden had acquired for me sat alongside the cot, my only possessions in the world aside from what I had with me when I arrived.

"Did you get everything taken care of, little brother?" he asked, not commenting further on my temporary stay. I was grateful.

"Yes, everything is confirmed. We shouldn't have any problems." Dov nodded, walking away from the table. I rushed to clean up before Eden could start gathering dishes. I wanted to make myself useful so they wouldn't mind having me around as much.

She glared at me but allowed me to take care of them. I watched quietly as Berwyn directed Dov to the far side of the room, far enough away that I couldn't overhear. They both took turns nodding as Eden watched them from the table, fingers lightly tapping where her plate had once been. My eyes darted away as she glanced at me.

As she looked away, I studied the room from the far

side of the kitchen. Light found its way in through the windows, an almost golden glow from the setting sun peeking in through the treetops outside. It danced along the floorboards, mesmerizing me for a moment. Each second they swayed a different way as the branches outside moved in the breeze. For a fleeting moment, I had the urge to run outside, far from the cabin. It was strange to be indoors again. It had been so long since I lived in a house of any kind.

Grounding myself, I forced my feet to stay in place, unmoving and unchanging. I longed to feel the air push back my hair. Instead, my hair blew away from my face as I exhaled sharply, my eyes catching Dov's from across the room. The corners of his eyes tweaked up as he flashed me a quick smile before turning back to his brother.

Quickly looking away, I turned to focus on the dishes in front of me, hoping Eden didn't notice. She did.

I could feel her watching me, her eyes on my every move. I hadn't even felt that scrutinized when Lowell watched my training. Eden scared me. If I didn't win her over, she could be my undoing. I had to find a way to connect with her. She had been the one to finalize the decision to allow me to stay, in a moment of apparently uncharacteristic kindness, but now it was as if she was searching my very soul, ready to attack at any moment.

The room tensed. I braved a glance at my hosts, immediately wishing I hadn't. Berwyn was watching me, a hungry look in his eyes. He was waiting for me to make a mistake; he was waiting for me to give myself away. The man was like a starving animal watching his prey. I could almost hear him growl when he caught my eye.

Dov looked up as I fumbled to catch the plate that I had nearly dropped. Glaring at his brother, he forced his attention back to their conversation. Eden smirked as she looked away from the scene. For someone that looked like she should be so soft, she had an incredibly rough edge. I imagined it had been why she had survived so well in our world.

Berwyn ended the conversation abruptly and nodded for Eden to follow. Together they wandered away from the main part of the house.

Still slightly unnerved, I chose not to say anything to Dov. He stayed on his side of the house, allowing me to finish my work in peace. I tried not to glance up at him, but I couldn't help myself. Most times I found him watching me, his gaze much easier than his family's. A faint smile played at his lips as he watched me work. I could feel myself blushing and tried to let my hair hang in my face to conceal it as I worked.

Unsure of what to do when I finished, I wandered over to the cot and sat down. My eyes were firmly focused on the floor, charting each board and rug in the room.

I stopped breathing as he walked toward me. Counting the steps until he arrived at my side, I waited to see what internal battle I was about to face.

"Thanks for the berries. They were great," he said, sliding down onto the floor by my feet.

"Oh," I replied, not having expected him to bring it up again. "You're welcome."

"They may not have said it—or at least said it well—but Berwyn and Eden were grateful for your contribution as well."

"I'm sure," I muttered.

"Give them time, they'll come around," he encouraged me.

As I sank down to the floor next to him, he pulled a basket out from behind his back. Somehow, I had missed it. Setting it between us, he waited for me to investigate. When I didn't, he reached inside and withdrew its contents, handing me a pile of clothing.

"We're mending," he supplied, retrieving a needle and thread.

I had not been anticipating that turn of events and floundered for a moment. Dov laughed when I hesitated momentarily before thrusting my hand forward to collect the thread. In my overzealous actions, I knocked over a pile of the clothing, nearly toppling the basket.

He took out a second set of tools and began mending

with me, another surprise. In the past, I had taken care of Lowell and Shadoe, or if I hadn't been available, one of the women who swarmed after Lowell would see to the work. Dov was remarkably impressive.

"You don't need to do all those chores around here, you know. It's nice that you help, but you shouldn't feel like you need to earn your keep. We don't require you to do anything to find safety here."

I held up the mending work in my hands and raised my eyebrows. Dov laughed, looking down at his own work.

"Truly, Auluria, you don't have to help out here. We're happy to have you...or *I* am. Eden and Berwyn don't really count in this conversation. And as for the mending, that's just something for us to do while we talk."

"But I *want* to help," I insisted.

"I know you do, and I appreciate that," he responded, "but if you're going to do something, don't feel like you have to kill yourself working to stay here."

I couldn't help but smile.

"I know, but Dov, I truly want to help. I'm not doing it out of guilt." Well, maybe a little...or a lot, since I was deceiving his entire family and setting them up for my cousin's plan...but I wanted to help Dov out.

"You're pretty good at this," he commented, motioning to the work in my hands.

"Yes, I suppose I am fine. I am, however, thoroughly impressed with your skills," I said, assessing his work.

"Dad taught me. He thought Berwyn and I should be able to take care of ourselves should we ever need to. I suppose he never realized that would happen so soon." He paused. "Tell me, where did you learn?"

"This? Oh, I don't know. I suppose I grew up knowing. I don't remember ever not being able to do this."

My aunt had taught me at a young age to mend clothing. It was one of the ways she brought in extra money to care for us. As soon as I could, I helped her, anything I could do to support her and take part of the burden.

"I used to help mend clothing when I was younger to bring in extra money for food," I added.

"You're remembering." Dov gave me a small smile.

"Oh. Yes, I guess I am... a little," I covered. We worked in silence for a moment.

"That was kind of you. Selfless, even." Dov nodded.

"It was more about the need to eat to survive. If mending socks for people and guards was the price of living, I could handle that."

"Well, I would have suggested you sew the guards' socks *shut,* but I can't imagine that would have helped your cause," Dov snickered.

"No, I can't imagine it would have. However, sewing them shut with the guards' feet *still in them*...now *that* might have helped my cause."

Dov's head whipped around to face me. He attempted to hold back a laugh but snorted instead before bursting out into that glorious chuckle of his. I laughed along with him as he pretended to sew his own sock onto his leg, his lips quirking up into an amusing grin.

"I was right about you," he announced when he had controlled his laughter.

"How is that?" I asked, returning to my mending work.

"You're trouble." He grinned.

"*Trouble?*" I tried to quip, terrified he knew something.

"If you are willing to put needles through a guard, what else might you do?"

"Well, I *have* been known to beat up men twice my size," I said flirtatiously as if it were a joke. There was nothing humorous about it. Shadoe had trained me well.

"Have you now?"

"I'll have to show you sometime," I replied with a giggle.

"Please, just no broken bones."

No, just a broken heart, if Lowell had it his way.

"Never. I wouldn't dream of it," I said.

"Of course, not," he said, holding my gaze. "But truthfully, maybe we *should* work on your fighting skills, Auluria. It's far too dangerous for you to be out there without having any fighting skills. You need to be able to protect yourself."

If only he knew.

"I can teach you, if you'll let me," he insisted.

"Maybe," I said, trying to stall. There was a very good chance that that was a very bad idea. If I couldn't make it look like I was new to defending myself, or if at any point my reflexes and survival instincts kicked on, I would betray my own secret. He could never know just how well trained I really was.

"Are you nervous about it?" he asked.

"Yes," I answered truthfully, but not for the reasons he thought.

"Just...think about it okay. It would help me be less worried about you," he said awkwardly.

"All right," I agreed.

After a moment, he added, "It would help you to protect the people you care about too."

"Like you?" I asked absentmindedly. I froze when I realized what I had said. I rushed to cover my mistake, attempting to keep my voice calm. "I'll always take care of the people in my life, Dov, you included. I would do anything to protect my friends. Even if that means fighting. Even if it means losing. Whatever the cost is to me, I can take it. I'll take on whatever I have to if it's for the greater good." I took a breath. "You can teach me if you want, but not just yet. I'm not ready for that yet."

"But soon?" he questioned, still watching me.

"Yes, soon. I'll let you know when I'm ready," I agreed.

"You really *would* give up everything for your friends, wouldn't you, Auluria?" he questioned. "You're easy to read. I can see in your eyes and on your face that you meant that. I believe you would sacrifice yourself if it came to that. But Auluria, don't do anything stupid on my account. I can take care of myself. You don't need to worry about me. If for some reason it ever comes to it, just make sure you keep yourself safe."

My *Mission* gave me permission to put myself first. I couldn't believe where this conversation had taken me.

"I'll look out for you, the same way you look out for me, Dov," I replied. "It's nice that you want to protect me, but from where I'm sitting it looks like no one else is looking out for *you*. So, if looking out for you is up to *you and me*, I suppose we had both better do a good job of it."

"You're not going to listen to me on this, are you?"

"Well. there's always the option of sewing your lips closed so I don't have to *not listen*." I raised an eyebrow at him.

"Helping by hurting...so that's how you work then," he mused.

My head went reeling as his words hit true. *I hurt people to help other people. I hurt Dov to help Lowell.* He was absolutely right and didn't have a single clue.

"Yes, well, a lady does what she must." I forced a grin.

"A *lovely* lady at that," he flirted.

My gaze flew to my hands. I could feel myself blush.

He was making it so easy and so difficult all at once.

"Turns out I rescued a pretty special girl," he said, "if she's so willing to give up her freedom to be my friend."

"Not as special as you think, I'm afraid."

"Or perhaps more than she realizes. No one has ever done that for me before, cared enough to focus on me as a person and not me for what I could do for the group. I appreciate it, Auluria. I'm really glad you are here." His words lingered in the air as we both fell back into our work.

We sat in a comfortable silence as we worked.

"Why is your hair so long?" he asked after sitting in quiet for a while.

"What do you mean?" I asked, glancing at him.

"It's longer than most girls," he said thoughtfully. "Eden's hair is only partway down her back, but yours… it's different."

"I suppose," I replied, looking back at my work. "I just like it that way I guess. My mother always had long hair and I always thought it was so beautiful."

He nodded slowly, focusing on the fabric in his hands.

"Are you remembering anything else?"

"Some things," I admitted, trying to guard my words.

"What *do* you remember?" he asked gently.

"Bigger things," I answered. "I remember things about the Society and the government. I remember my family. I remember the way my mother used to sing to me... quietly, as if it were a secret."

I smiled, humming the tune to myself absentmindedly as I worked. Dov's voice joined mine, adding in the words. My breath caught, unbelieving that he knew the very song my mother used to sing to me.

He grinned at me. "Mine too. She used to dance all around the house to it when I was little," he added before continuing the song.

Abruptly, he pulled himself to his feet, extending his hand to me. His voice grew louder as he switched to a livelier song. Without waiting, he pulled me to my feet, causing me to drop my project. It bounced off the floor as he spun me around, respectfully holding both of my hands in his. I was grateful he hadn't tried to hold me as we danced.

I couldn't contain my laughter as he spun us around the room. I tried to shush him, worried his brother and sister-in-law would hear.

"They're out now, Auluria. We're on our own for the time being," he paused to say before singing again.

Circling around the room, we jumped in time with each other, his singing eventually cascading into an uncontainable laughter. When he finally slowed our frivolous display of dancing, my hair crashed into him, wrapping around his back and cradling his shoulder. I pulled away from him and my golden hair dripped down his chest before falling against me.

In between breaths, we laughed again, our chests rising and falling nearly at the same time. He grinned as if he had won something; proving his unspoken point.

Shaking my head, I nearly raced back to my work, throwing myself on the ground. Taking up my task once again, I waited for him to rejoin me. He settled next to me on the floor, still breathing heavily. Brushing back his hair, he picked up the fabric he had been repairing and set back to work.

"Do you dance often?" he finally asked flirtatiously.

Smiling, I gave him a patronizing look. "Oh yes, in all of my spare time, I focus on my studies in the art of dancing for my time in the high society parts of our fine country. Was it not obvious?"

"Not when you stepped on my feet," he grinned, eyes sparkling with a challenge.

"I did no such thing, and even if I had, it would have been your own fault. I had no control of our movements."

"You're saying *I* caused your missteps?" he questioned.

Yes, you are in fact causing my missteps.

"If I had had a different partner, one not tromping us all over the house, I can assure you it would have been more graceful," I said haughtily, tossing him a sly smile.

"Oh, I imagine you are always quite graceful, Auluria," he said, catching my eye. He was going to be a problem.

"Is that so?" I retorted.

"Tell me, where *did* you learn to dance?"

"A very interesting woman taught me not too long ago," I replied, my thoughts drifting back to my training before the mission. Lowell had made sure I was prepared in every way.

"She must have been a good teacher."

"I suppose so." I considered his words for a moment before demanding my thoughts turn back from my time in Lowell's watch.

"The more pressing question, Dov Baer, is where did *you* learn to dance?" I instantly regretted the question as a shadow passed over his face.

"Another story, for another time, my dear Auluria. How is your mending going?" he regained his balance.

"Almost finished. Yours?"

Before he could answer, I sucked in a harsh breath, attempting to cover my gasp.

He was at my side before the blood had time to bubble up out of my skin. I watched as it leaked out of my finger, red against my pale flesh. Dov gathered my hand in his and pressed it against the fabric in his hand. Holding me until the blood stopped, I sat frozen in place as he watched my hand intently. Neither of us spoke.

Dov removed the cloth, watching for signs of the

bleeding to stop. It ended quickly, despite feeling like it was taking an eternity. Releasing my hand, he moved back to his place a few feet away. He never acknowledged our closeness, the way his hand warmed mine as he cared for me.

"Thank you," I whispered quietly.

"Who took care of you, Auluria? Before all this. Who looked after you?" he responded quietly, no longer willing to look me in the eyes.

I looked away, unwilling, perhaps *unable*, to answer. He took my silence as my response and let the moment slip away.

"I'll look out for you, Auluria," he said quietly, making me unable to breathe yet again. "I know I have no right to, but we're friends now, since the day we met in the woods, and I'm going to look out for you."

I started to protest but he continued, cutting me off.

"I know you can care for yourself. That much is obvious, or you wouldn't have made it this far. But you can't go through life alone. It's too hard, trust me. You need people on your side, and I want to be there for you. I don't expect anything from you, but I want you to know you are safe with me. I want to look out for you."

"Dov," I started.

"You don't need to say anything, you don't even have to like it, but I want you to know I am on your side. Whatever you are going through, I am here." He finally looked up at me, convincing me with his eyes. *This man couldn't possibly be real.*

"Just don't go running away on me now, okay?" he joked, but I sensed something more, something stronger behind his words. His easy grin set off butterflies in my stomach, their wings pushing my heart into my throat.

This couldn't possibly get any worse.

This couldn't possibly get any better.

"I won't." I attempted to laugh off his comment, but deep inside I knew, despite Lowell's directives, I didn't want to stray from this man who had become my mission.

"Besides, I'm injured now," I said seriously, holding up my needle-pricked finger. "How far could I really get?"

His somber face held true for only a moment as he nodded before breaking out into a glorious, radiant smile accompanied by that strong, solid laughter I had come to know from him.

"Well, if I knew getting you to stay was that easy, I'd have had you sewing the first day!"

"That worried I'd run off, were you?" I smiled back.

"I admit, I was a little worried at first." He leaned back against the cot. "It is possible that I didn't sleep the first few nights just to make sure you weren't planning on running away in the middle of the night."

Had anyone else said those words, I may have

panicked, but I could tell he had been genuinely concerned for my wellbeing.

"I'm not frightening you, am I?" he asked, less enthusiastic. "You know I'm not trying to keep you here against your will. It's just far too dangerous for you—or anyone, really—to be out there on their own."

"Yes, I'm aware," I agreed. "And I'm not worried about your intentions, Dov. Besides, I'm starting to like it here."

"Maybe you still haven't fully recovered from your memory loss…but you *do* remember who the other occupants of this house are, don't you?"

Before I could respond, the door opened on the other side of the house. Dov's eyes darted to the far end of the room and he scooted a bit further away from me as Berwyn walked in.

The older version of Dov glanced at us, eyeing our repair work. I offered him a weak smile that was not returned. He nodded once to his brother before walking off.

"We should probably rest," Dov offered, setting the last of the repair work back in the basket.

I glanced out the window and noticed the stars had come out, peeking through the tree branches as they swayed. It seemed the higher branches always swayed in the place, constantly moving and changing shape.

I set my material down, allowing Dov to help me up. I tried not to smile when his back was turned. Controlling his emotions could have been so easy, but instead, he was controlling mine.

Settling into the cot, my head was whirring with too many thoughts. I fought to control them, willing myself to be still. Sleep, usually one to betray me, welcomed me after a brief time.

Chapter 3

"Come on, we have somewhere to be," Dov's soft voice woke me.

"But it's the middle of the night," I complained, sitting up in bed, keeping the blanket wrapped around my body. I pushed the hair out of my face and struggled to see him in the dark.

"Yeah, I know. But it doesn't change the fact that we have somewhere to be." I swear he was grinning at me, though I still hadn't adjusted enough to see in the dark.

"Fine," I grumbled, rising from the cot. "Where are we going?"

"There's a raid tonight. I have to help, which means you need to come with me."

"Why do *I* have to be involved?"

"Well, first off, I thought you'd like to see what it is we stand for. However, if you're *not* interested, you *could* stay with Berwyn and Eden. They aren't going out until tomorrow."

"What, no second point?"

"What?"

"You said 'first off' but you never had a follow-up."

"I thought that was implied," he said.

"No." I was not amused.

"Not much of a night person, are you?" he teased me.

"Catch me right before sunrise and we'll see who's functioning better, Owl," I scoffed as I found something to change into.

"Uh-huh," he retorted. "Now get a move on."

I changed behind the screen Dov had set up for me. Pulling my hair up into a ponytail, I walked around and grabbed a light overcoat. When I looked up, Dov was watching me.

"Ready?" he asked.

"Lead the way," I motioned and followed him out into the forest cloaked in darkness.

"We're collecting food," Dov explained as we neared the site. "The government has been taking food for years, leaving the people with practically nothing. We," he said, gesturing to the small group we were approaching, "reallocate it."

"Reallocate, huh?"

"Yes, Auluria. We reallocate it. That's what the storehouse is for. We share. Those that are in need can have *what* they need. Not everything there is stolen. We grow our own crops too."

We approached the group and they looked warily at me.

"This is Auluria. She's a friend. She'll be helping us tonight," Dov introduced me, challenging anyone to question him. Berwyn may have been in charge, but Dov was second in command...after Eden, of course.

"We're going in through the south entrance," a boy explained. "There's no one watching that side of the building. If we're quiet, we can sneak in one or two at a time. Everyone will fill their sacks and we'll slip out. Questions?"

He threw a collection of sacks on the ground in front of him.

"I'm on lookout," a petite girl informed us when no one spoke.

Dov nodded, casting a wicked grin at the girl. A rush

of jealousy coursed through me. I pushed it aside…I couldn't have feelings like that.

Dov turned back to me and whispered in my ear, "You'll go in with me." Now it was the girl's turn to be jealous.

He stopped and picked up two bags. He handed one to me and I slung it over my shoulder. I started to lead the way toward the entrance, but quickly realized I wasn't supposed to know how to do this, so I slowed and waited for Dov to lead me.

We slipped into the building, old and brown with age. It smelled like mildew and I wanted to cover my nose.

An older girl brushed past me. "Breathe through your mouth. It helps."

Once we were inside, we started collecting items. Some of the stronger boys lifted down heavy crates and broke into them. We took whatever we could fit in the sacks.

I took mostly food, fitting it into my bag as best I could. Then I slipped some small trinkets in around the gaps of food. It was dark inside, but while our eyes were mostly adjusted to the dim lighting from being outside, there was no moonlight inside. I could make out outlines of objects. My fingers told me more about what they were. I felt cold metal pieces a few times. Some items were smooth and others rough and damaging to my fingers.

I worked my hands around the contents of my sack, pushing and reorganizing until I couldn't fit anymore. Dov stayed by my side, brushing against me every so often to be sure we were still together. At one crate, we stood, shoulder to shoulder, foot against foot, and systematically emptied the contents into our sacks.

Just as we were leaving we heard a voice. Everyone froze, inches from the exit. We waited but heard no further noise. A young kid started out the door before we could stop him.

The noise that followed told us he hadn't suffered.

The group panicked, rushing back into the building, searching for another exit. The people outside slammed the entrance closed, blocking us in the room. I scanned the edges of the walls. I wasn't supposed to be able to function in a situation like this one according to the mission plan, but in the moment, I had no choice.

I felt along the wall. With my fingers, I found the weak spot in the wood. The building had been constructed as a temporary house for the goods. The walls had not been reinforced; they were merely pieces of wood nailed together.

I couldn't have been more grateful for the training Lowell and Shadoe had offered me than at that very moment. I may have been young, but Lowell insisted I was ready to take care of myself before I go on any missions. He wanted me working young, so he trained me from the moment he brought me into his fold.

"Here," I shouted, motioning the group over.

I stepped back, moved my skirt to the side and prepared to kick at the rotting wall.

"Wait," Dov said. "Let me."

He kicked to the side, striking the wood where I had pointed. Two other men joined him, taking turns kicking at the decaying material. It shattered. A few more blows and it was wide enough to escape through.

The group poured out into the night, the sounds of our attackers close behind as they realized we had escaped from the other side. I ran as hard as I could, hair whipping behind me as I turned to check on their advances.

I was on my own, running toward the trees. The moon lit my way, casting eerie shadows as we all moved in different directions.

"Get down!" Dov said, pulling me to the forest floor behind some bushes. He had kept his eyes on me as we ran, much to my amazement, and managed to overtake me.

We waited as the guards ran past us, shouting angrily. It wasn't until Dov put his hand on my shoulder that I realized how heavily I was breathing.

"You okay?" he asked.

I nodded. "You?"

"Yeah, I'm fine. You're sure you're okay?" he asked again, brushing a piece of fallen hair behind my ear.

My breath caught. I pulled away before I could think through it.

"Let's go," I said, standing.

He lowered his hand from where it was still resting after moving my hair, words still on his lips. Dov stood without a word and we walked back into the night.

"How could you let that happen?" Berwyn yelled.

He was even more terrifying in the stillness of the night.

"You oversaw the raid. It was your job to know!" He slammed his hand down on the table, causing everyone to jump.

"You got that boy killed tonight, do you realize that? We don't even know if the others made it back yet. How could you be so stupid?" he bellowed.

His next sentence gave me chills.

"Get up," he whispered.

Dov rose from his seat at the table slowly. I wanted to scream, to throw myself in front of him, but Eden stepped in front of me, forcing me to stay in place. They were out the door before I could say anything.

When they had gone, Eden turned to me.

"You might as well get a little rest. They won't be back for a bit." She glanced over her shoulder as she walked away and said coolly, "Just be glad it wasn't you."

It was late morning when Berwyn and Dov finally returned to the house. Berwyn walked in the door, mumbling to himself. He didn't even bother looking at Eden, but she hurried after him anyway.

After a moment, Dov made his way in. His lip was split open. I could see he was nursing several bruises on his stomach and chest as he walked across the room. He winced with every step.

"No," I breathed as my face fell. "Dov, what did he do to you?"

I raced to his side to help him in. I started to reach for him but pulled back, knowing I shouldn't touch him.

"It's fine, Auluria." He tried to push me off.

"It's anything but fine," I insisted, trying to inspect his wounds.

"It's *fine*, Auluria," he shouted. I stepped back as if I'd been the one who had been struck.

"I'm sorry. I didn't mean to yell," he said in a hushed tone.

"Why?" I asked bitterly, looking for an explanation for his injuries.

"Because that boy died last night," he said as if it explained everything.

I must have looked confused because he continued to fill in the gaps for me.

"He died. There had to be some accountability. We went to his father and Berwyn put me in my place."

"He beat you because a raid went sideways?" I couldn't believe anyone could be so cruel.

"It's better than losing a bunch of people when that father went after the people involved," he said. "It's not as bad as it looks."

"Let me at least check it," I begged.

He gave a slight nod and I approached him. I touched his chin, tilting his head up so I could see his split lip. His face was warm in my hand and suddenly I was caught in those blue eyes again as I glanced up at him.

I pulled away and nodded to his shirt. He lifted it and I watched as it revealed his chiseled body. The sight was almost as addictive as his eyes.

"Here, let me help," I said when I saw him wince.

I lifted his shirt the rest of the way, careful not to brush against him, and examined his injuries. I could barely stop myself from touching the wounded skin as I inspected them.

"Turn," I commanded softly.

He obliged and spun for me slowly, allowing me to see his sides and back.

"Well, I don't think anything is broken. You're going to be sore for a while though," I said.

"Really, do you think, Doc?" He smirked and then grimaced.

"Why don't you go rest?" I pointed to the bed. He deserved a good place to sleep now.

He sauntered over to the couch and flopped down gently. He watched me as I watched him for a moment.

I walked over and knelt beside him.

"What do you need?" I asked, concern in my voice. I was going to take care of this man, no matter how hard I tried not to, it seemed.

"Just sit with me for a bit," he said closing his eyes.

"All right," I said, leaning my back against the couch. After a few minutes, I tipped my head back and stared up at the ceiling.

He was brave, I realized. He took a beating he didn't have to take to protect the lives that could potentially be lost later. He was brave and kind and selfless.

I sat with him for two days. We talked when he wasn't

sleeping. He told me a bit more about the raids. One night he talked about his family.

"My father started our group," he blurted out. "He wanted to help people. That's why we're doing this—to help."

"What happened to him?" I asked quietly.

"Something went wrong. He tried to take us underground, but they managed to find him anyway. They tried him and hanged him."

I tried not to look horrified.

"What about your mother?" I asked.

He sighed deeply.

"You already know how the Society is fighting that war against our enemy countries. You're aware that they tried to make a deal with them—our food and supplies for our freedom from attack, but those foreign countries took our food and supplies and threaten to attack us anyway. So, the Society takes all our food and supplies to try to appease them, but they still want to get out from under their thumb." I nodded, knowing all this already.

"Well, they want to raise our population numbers, so we can eventually fight against them. Often, the Society takes young boys—not the ones from rich families, mind you—but they take the boys and send them to training camps. Then they ship them off to the military.

"They take young girls and use them as breeders and

then when they're done with them, they, too, end up fighting.

"What you may not know, is not all of the Taken are young. Sometimes, if they find women on their own, they take them too."

I had heard rumors of this but never had any proof.

"They found my mother one day, isolated her, and tried to take her. She fought back and they killed her for it."

"Oh, Dov, I'm so sorry. I shouldn't have asked," I said as a single tear threatened to slip down his cheek. I wanted to reach out and wipe it away, but I forced my hands steady at my sides.

He nodded for a moment, regaining his composure.

"What about your family?

"My parents died in a raid when I was little. I barely remember them. My aunt raised me."

"And is she…?"

"She died, too," I said sadly. "She died so she could take care of me and my older cousin."

"Where's your cousin now?" he asked.

"We were never particularly close." I didn't lie; Lowell and I were never close. I just did what he told me because he was the only family I had left and I was young. I *had* to trust him.

"So. Orphans, then."

"Orphans," I agreed. I almost mentioned that he still

had his brother, but then I realized he'd probably be better off without him.

"You're awake," Dov announced a few hours later, the moonlight barely hinting at his face from his place on the couch.

"Yes," I whispered back. "I see you can't sleep either."

"No, I suppose not."

"Why not?" I asked. I knew I had a lot on my mind, but what would be keeping him up?

He shifted uncomfortably, grimacing.

"Oh. You're in pain," I said quietly.

"I'm all right, Auluria," he insisted.

Untangling myself from my blanket I crossed the cool floor and lowered myself by his side. He watched my every move.

"What are you doing?" he asked as I settled myself beside him.

"Making sure you're okay," I answered.

"I'm fine, Auluria. I told you that." He studied me.

"I'm aware of what you said," I replied, staring back at him.

"And yet you're still over here," he observed, leading me to speaking again.

"I know what you said, Dov, but I can also read you. You put on a brave face, but you're hurting. You shouldn't have to hurt alone."

"I can survive on my own." His voice took a harsh turn. I didn't like the hurt in his words.

"I'm sure you can, Dov. But the point is that you don't *have* to." I stopped short of saying more. I wanted to tell him that I would be there for him, that he could depend on me, but the truth was that he *couldn't*. He could never trust me.

He smiled at me as I repeated the sentiments he had not so long ago expressed to me, forcing me to look away. My eyes darted to the floor, the table, the door, the window…anything to avoid connecting with him.

"Tell me, Auluria, where did you come from and how do you know so much?" His words might have scared me if his voice hadn't been so sincere.

"I came from the woods, and I only know enough to survive," I teased. I looked up and saw his eyes drifting to my lips, teasing me in a completely different way.

As I shook my head to look away, a strand of hair fell into my face. I reached up to move it back, but my hand brushed instead against the warm flesh of Dov's hand. Locking eyes with me, he pushed back the fallen lock, taking his hand away slowly.

"How *have* you survived?" he asked quietly, concern flowing from him.

"I...I don't know," I replied. In truth, I had no idea how I had survived a life without someone like Dov Baer in it.

"Tell me more about your family," he prompted, his hand playing with the blanket that lay over him.

Taking my own piece of the blanket in my hand, mindful to stay as far from his hand as possible, I thought of what possible answer I could give. I refused to outright lie to him; I simply couldn't bring myself to do it. I could have talked my way around the subject—I had been trained to easily do that—but my best option was to avoid it all together.

"Tell me about your mother," I countered.

He looked at me quizzically. His eyebrows quirked up in the moonlight, his face covered in shadows.

"She was kind," he said, keeping his eyes on me. "She was very observant...like you. And she always knew the right thing to say. She was good at keeping Berwyn calm."

"And here I thought no one could keep him in check." I smiled.

"Oh, *she* could. So could my father for that matter. It was only after we'd lost both that...well...you know." He looked away. Staring out the window, he added, "She was quiet, my mother. Always noticing things...noticing people. She knew everything; at least I always thought so.

"She always focused on doing the right thing, even if

it was uncomfortable, even if it was hard. She always put us first."

"I don't remember much about my parents," I said, shocked I was allowing myself to speak so freely, "but according to my aunt, they were very much like that too. Selfless."

"What was your aunt like? She mostly raised you, didn't she?" he encouraged me to speak.

Being with Dov was like being given a freedom you didn't know you were missing. He was easy to be near, easy to talk to. His whole presence made me want to trust him. He, simply by existing, made me want to tell him everything, knowing he would care for me once I had finished crying.

I couldn't though. I couldn't tell him the truth. No one could ever forgive me for that. Not even someone as strong as Dov Baer could forgive a betrayal so deep and so calculated.

Still, something inside of me gave me permission to speak. It was as if the window had been thrown open, letting in the warm breeze that forced the words from my mouth.

"But she was strong. She did what she had to do to protect us. She gave up her life to make sure I had enough to survive. She kept me safe from the Society. My aunt always made sure I knew about my parents, though I don't know much and I remember even less. She was a good woman, much like I assume my mother would have been."

"She raised a strong woman…a good person, Auluria. Your parents and your aunt would be proud of you. You have a good heart."

A sharp stabbing pain in my chest nearly forced me to double over at his words. I tightened my grip on the blanket edge. He noticed my change in demeanor and reached for my hand. I dropped it in my lap, tangling it in my hair as it rested against my leg.

"Auluria, do you really not see how special you are?"

"*I'm* special?" I shook my head. "I do believe, Dov, that *you* are the one who voluntarily took a beating to prevent more bloodshed and death. If I'm correct, this isn't the first time either."

I could tell his eyes had grown wide, even with the dark shadows dancing across his face.

"Why, Dov? Why must you always take his wrath?"

"It's not wrath exactly." He chose his words carefully. "Sometimes he is mad, and sometimes he takes it out on me. Other times it's more of a sacrificial thing; a price must be paid and instead of *someone else* paying it, it's better if I do."

"But must it always be *you*?" I asked.

"Better me than them," he replied, tipping his head to the side slightly.

"You're a good man," I replied, but Lowell's words

crept into my thoughts, forcing me to wonder just how honest the conversation really was and how one's actions were changed by perception.

"You've done nothing but care for us since you've been here," he redirected the conversation. The moonlight sparkled in his blue eyes. "You've been nothing but selfless."

Selfless? Perhaps selfish, but never selfless.

"Regardless of what it meant for you personally, you've done whatever you could to help the people with you. You've been wonderful."

I supposed, if I stretched the meaning of his words, what I was doing was an act for someone other than myself. Everything I had done and was doing was for Lowell and his cause. And to save Dov.

I was uncomfortable with the attention and praise he was offering me. Lowell would have been furious I had not latched onto it like I had been trained to do.

"*You're* the selfless one, Dov," I murmured.

"Maybe we're more alike than we think," he mused, grimacing. His hand floated to his stomach.

"You should rest," I whispered.

"Goodnight, Auluria." He grinned wickedly, eyes following me as I walked backward away from where he rested.

"Goodnight, Dov."

"You have no idea how…" His whisper drifted off as he chose to keep the rest to himself.

Sleep. Going back to sleep was nothing short of a miraculous occurrence.

"You need to eat," I said the next morning as he stirred on the couch.

I brought a dark bowl over to him. The steam trailed behind me.

"What is it?" he asked.

"It's porridge," I replied. He looked at it skeptically.

"I know, it's not the greatest breakfast. I don't particularly care for it. But it's warm and it will fill you up. You need to get some strength back. Please…just try it."

"It's hot," he protested as I walked away.

"Well, then, let it cool down. Just don't wait too long, or it will get cold."

He looked at me with puppy dog eyes. I sighed and walked back over to the couch, kneeling next to him. I reached out and placed my hand on the rim of the bowl, careful not to touch him. He moved the bowl toward me as I bent down and blew carefully over the steaming food.

I could see him watching me, but I refused to look up.

His eyes traced over my hair that fell around my chin, my shoulders, my waist and pooled in my lap in front of me.

"There," I said softly. "Just right."

His eyes flitted back to mine and he gave me a small smile of thanks.

Eden watched me that afternoon as I swept the house. Her eyes followed me every time I hurried to Dov's side when he had trouble breathing or if he asked for something. She allowed me to do the laundry for her.

Berwyn continued to glare at me whenever he walked through the house. I tried to pretend I didn't notice. I needed to be in their favor, whether it was to betray them or to save them.

The next day I heard something fall outside. I looked out the window to see a pile of wood toppled over. When I walked outside to recreate the tower, I found myself being abducted once again.

Shadoe's hand clamped over my mouth and he shushed me as he dragged me away.

"You missed the meeting," he said angrily.

"Something came up."

"You can't just decide to skip a meeting, Lur." He pulled me forward, away from the house. "Lowell wants to see you. *Now.*"

Having no choice, we raced through the woods to where I was summoned. I was grateful Dov was sleeping and hadn't seen me running away. He would have tried to save me and he was still in too much pain for that.

"Auluria," Lowell greeted me, his usual well-mannered demeanor gone.

"Lowell," I greeted him.

Looking at Shadoe, he dismissed him. Shadoe retreated a few steps to the far side of the room we stood in.

"Want to explain to me what's been going on?" he asked.

I raised my eyebrows at him, asking what he meant.

"You've been missing your check-ins. You've barely gathered any intelligence. I know you hit your head, but come on Auluria, give me *something* to work with," he demanded.

"I already told Shadoe about the storehouse," I huffed. "I witnessed a raid the other night, but we were caught. A kid died. I'll have more information after the next one on how they operate though. They trust me." I neglected to tell him it was only Dov who trusted me.

"I need you to do better than that. Usually, you are exceptional at finding information for us. Why can't you now?"

I was silent.

"Oh," he drawled. "Now I see. It's that boy. Dov. You *like* him." He grinned. It made me shiver.

"He's a decent person," I started.

"No, he's not. He's playing you Auluria. I told you he would. *They all do*. You'll see. You know what they did—how they killed all those people years ago. You'll see how they really are." He paced around me in a circle.

"Get your head around him, Auluria, and do your job. We must bring these people down. We are taking down the Society and *those people* are going down with it. Don't get attached. I would hate to lose you at the end of this." He glared at me. "And besides, *Missy*, Shadoe is so devoted to you. Would you really do that to him?"

Shadoe was less devoted to me than to Lowell, but Lowell had paired us together, and Shadoe took that seriously.

"Let me be very clear here, Cousin. I see you need some motivation." He looked me up and down. I didn't like this intimidating side of him. He was never warm toward me, but even in his coolness, he had been respectful.

"Either you pull it together, or Shadoe will become very aware of Dov distracting you. Once Shadoe sets to mind to do something, well, you know how good he is at finishing a mission. I bet that boy won't last the day." His words were jarring.

"And really, while we're pinning this on the Baer family, it doesn't matter *which of them* takes the brunt of it. I was planning on it being Berwyn, but the kid will do just fine."

I could feel myself panicking but I kept my face still and my voice steady.

"That won't be necessary, Lowell, I'll take care of it."

"Good." He nodded in approval. "Now, go make him fall in love with you and then get the information we need. Run along now."

He turned his back on me and left. Shadoe returned to my side and escorted me back through the woods.

My cousin's threatening words followed me all the way back to the house.

I was too aware of Shadoe's presence on the journey back to the Bears' home. When Lowell released me, Shadoe had slipped alongside me, moving in our usual silent way. Since I had first met Shadoe I had felt many different emotions toward him, mostly angry ones, but in all our time together I had come to understand him.

I breathed a sigh of relief when he left me to return to Lowell. He still had other missions to oversee, but Lowell was making sure I was kept in line.

I pulled my dress skirt up to my knees and raced through the forest, having learned the layout of the route on the way to Lowell's meeting place. The small cabin had been abandoned, just the way Lowell liked it to appear. I imagined it had been rarely used, if ever.

I used my time to think of ways to protect Dov from Lowell and Shadoe. I had to make sure Shadoe didn't think Dov was going to be a problem, or he really *would* take care of him. In the time I had spent with Dov, I had learned he was quite capable of taking care of himself, but until I found out the true extent of his training I had no way of knowing if he was a match for my handler and former mentor. Shadoe, on the other hand, I knew to be deadly.

I became hyper aware of everything around me, even more so than I had already been. Every snapping branch seemed louder. Each inhale seemed too vicious and needy. Every exhale promised to give me away.

Certain areas of the woods were light and alive with dancing color as the sun's rays shifted through the branches. Still, other parts bore a darkness that seemed to conceal too many secrets, none of which I could unravel. Though the darkness concealed my movements, the light seemed to force my intentions out into the open.

I moved in the illuminated areas, hoping they would force me to realize my own purposes.

I slowed when I neared the Baers' home, stabilizing my breath, ensuring they had no reason to question me. The final minutes of walking toward my temporary housing were almost as painful as if I had ripped each hair from my head in one-by-one strands of gold.

Chapter 4

"Where were you?" Eden asked as I walked in the door.

"Out walking," I said, brushing past her.

I knew she didn't know how long I had been gone and I didn't offer to tell her. She gave me a skeptical look but dropped it. I was grateful she had no idea how long I'd really been gone.

"Hey," Dov mumbled as I lowered myself to the floor by the couch, making sure to stay further back than usual. He opened his eyes, still heavy from sleep.

"Hey," I greeted him back. "How are you feeling?"

"Better. A lot better. In fact, I think it's time for me to

get outside and move around. Want to come along?" he asked, sitting up.

"Sure," I said, as monotone as I could.

I wanted to go with him. I also desperately wanted to avoid him. He would get hurt because of me and I wanted to stay as far away as I could. I also didn't know what Lowell and Shadoe had planned for him. I decided the best plan of action was to go with him, to protect him, but stay distant.

"Do I smell or something?" Dov chuckled as we walked.

"What?"

"You're walking all the way over there." He waved his hand at me.

"Oh." I paused. "We're just walking, it's not a big deal."

I hopped over a fallen tree trunk. I could hear the roar of the frogs as we neared a small lake. Cattails sprung up all around the water, concealing it unless you were standing right next to it.

Dov grinned at me mischievously.

"Come on," he said and quickened his stride to the water's edge.

I realized where he was headed.

"Dov! We can't go swimming *now.*" The water looked inviting. But I knew if we went swimming we'd have to leave our clothes on the bank and I couldn't bear to see him shirtless again without staring. Whatever I did, I had to keep him from seeing me stare at him.

Since he had been hurt, once I was sure he was asleep, I'd watch him in the dark. His masculine features rose and fell as he breathed. He slept with his lips open just a touch. They looked so inviting. His dark hair fell in his face, and he would reach up and brush it back as he dreamed; I wanted to reach out and touch his silky locks. Dov's eyelashes were so long and perfect I was jealous. I felt the constant tug of wanting to run my hand along his cheekbones and chin. He could never know I studied his face, his arms, his chest. He could never know how much I wanted to care.

"We're not, only sticking our feet in," he said.

I followed him to a rock near the edge of the water. He rolled up his pant legs and I lifted my blue skirt above my knees. We silently slipped our legs into the cool water.

The ripples flowed out gracefully from where we disturbed the glossy surface. The frogs stopped their calling for a few moments as they watched our approach. When they were certain we weren't a threat, the chorus started again, loudly scolding us for bothering their sanctuary.

"Very few people know about this pond," Dov said. "I've never seen anyone else here. Once I even rigged it by wrapping string around the cattails to see if anyone would disturb it. No one ever did. I like to hide out here sometimes."

"It's a good place to think," I supplied.

I could feel his arm stiffen next to mine. Out of the corner of my eye, I saw his hand deftly move toward mine. The electric buzz pulsed around the back of my hand and wrist. I sucked in a quick breath and froze for only a moment before I leaned forward and dipped my hand into the water.

I saw him pull back, looking hurt, but I pretended not to notice.

"The water feels so refreshing. Do you swim here often?" I asked, still leaning forward, moving my hand in the water.

"Yeah, sometimes," he answered, regaining his composure.

I leaned back and kicked my feet, splashing the water around us. I smiled. It was one of the few things I remember doing with my mother when I was little.

"Well. That was fun," I said after a few minutes. "But we should get going."

I stood, leaving him on the rock. He followed behind me, brushing the water off his legs as he moved. We left our clothing pulled up for a few minutes as we walked so we could air dry.

"We need to stop by the storehouse on the way back. I'm supposed to meet one of the guys there about something," he said, changing direction from the path we were on.

Each step away brought me closer to the path Lowell set me on.

The storehouse was crowded as we entered. A cheer of greeting rose when they saw Dov. Most people ignored me, but some continued to glare at me suspiciously. I was still an outsider.

"Silas," Dov called, waving. He turned to me. "You can look around if you like. See if you want anything."

He walked away from me abruptly, leaving me standing alone in the middle of the walkway.

"Look out, dearie," an older woman croaked as she walked past me.

"Sorry," I mumbled after her.

I watched Dov talk to Silas from a distance. I'd walked down the aisle and pretended to inspect the items, but my mind was about fifty feet away from where I stood, next to a tall, dark-haired man.

"Do you want that?" a voice asked next to me.

I looked down at my hand, realizing I was holding a trinket. I was absentmindedly turning it over, trying to make it look as if I weren't watching Dov and Silas.

"No, you can have it." I handed it over to them, catching a glimpse of their face before they turned and shouted thanks over their shoulder.

A loud sound rocked the floor of the storehouse. Food tumbled from their precarious piles on the tables. Weapons and supplies clattered to the ground. A bright flash blinded us.

I blinked, but couldn't refocus my sight. Stumbling around, I tried to find something familiar. As my vision came back into focus, I saw men rushing into the storehouse.

They yelled and pushed people. The storehouse was being attacked. The old woman from a few minutes ago was pushed to the ground, leaving her in a heap. I rushed to her side and helped her up.

The invaders attacked anyone they could find. They started taking food and supplies. The young men from the storehouse ran at them, trying to defend the building. Dov charged at a man, forgetting his injuries, and knocked him unconscious.

The older people were trying to help the group escape from the invaders. They blocked the exits and only let their own run through, preventing thieves from following.

I ran to help several more people. Pulling them from the floor, I guided them to the door that led to freedom. The attackers ran past me, but never once touched me.

That's when I caught a glimpse of a man charging through the storehouse. I knew who it was immediately, even though his face was covered. Shadoe.

He must have been following me, convinced I couldn't do my job. He had summoned one of his groups and they attacked the storehouse.

"Auluria, get out!" Dov's voice pierced through the noise and reached me.

My head shot up, searching for him. I saw him struggle as a man punched his shoulder near his neck.

My legs moved before I commanded them to. I raced to his side, throwing a punch at the man I didn't recognize. I saw Shadoe's eyes through the opening in his mask when my fist connected. They flashed horror, anger, and finally approval. I was doing as he asked and making the Baers think I was one of them.

The man lost his conviction to ignore me and whipped his hand back, ready to strike. Dov, though injured, lifted his hand, taking the blow for me. I punched the man in the stomach, stomping on his foot, and grabbed the nearest heavy object I could find to send it colliding into his head.

The man fell, unconscious at our feet.

"Come on!" Dov grabbed my arm and wheeled me around toward an exit.

Somewhere, someone had started a fire; they would not let their storehouse be lost to invaders. They would rather burn it to the ground than let them have the upper hand.

The fire crackled, licking up the wooden tables. Smoke filled the room. It became so dense so quickly that we could barely see to escape.

The fresh air felt good on our lungs and we gasped for more of it. The sky was bright blue, not a cloud to be seen. Crickets chirped and birds sang as they flew overhead. Only the sound of the chaos inside ruined the picture.

A voice called loudly from inside the burning storehouse.

"That's not one of ours," Silas said as he came up beside us.

Dov looked at him and then back at me.

"Stay here," he commanded. He was back inside the building before I could process what he said.

"No!" I yelped. Silas held me back.

"He'd want you to wait here. He wants you safe," he said, trying to calm me.

I wouldn't be calmed though. I struggled against him,

but he held on tighter. I hadn't been prepared for him to grab me, so he had the upper hand.

"Settle down, miss," he insisted, wrestling me in place.

After what seemed like an eternity, Dov reemerged, a young man walking next to him with his arm slung over his shoulder. Dov practically carried him outside.

I audibly breathed a sigh of relief.

Dov had saved that boy *knowing* he was the opposition. He had run back into a burning underground building to save someone he didn't know. He could have died and all he was worried about was keeping me safe and helping someone in trouble.

Lowell was wrong. Dov didn't deserve what we were doing to him.

Dov coughed as he released the boy. The boy took off, running for his life.

"Let him go," Dov coughed, signaling for his friends to stay put. "He's a kid."

Mercy. In that moment, I realized just how *merciful* the man before me was. He showed kindness and mercy. And *I* was trying to destroy him. No more…I wouldn't.

"We need to separate," Silas announced for Dov who was still having trouble catching his breath. "Go!"

Everyone scattered. I took my place under Dov's arm and helped guide him away from the blazing underground hideaway. His breathing steadied as we moved deeper into the covering of trees.

"What's going to happen now that the storehouse was destroyed?" I asked. I had been hyperaware of watching for anyone following us. Shadoe had been too busy trying to salvage the storehouse to notice my departure.

"There are more storehouses. We only lost that one," he said. "We'll be okay." He gave me a small smile and lifted some of the weight off my shoulders until his arm was simply lying across them.

This would have been nice, walking through the forest with Dov, under ordinary circumstances.

"Dov?" I meant to tell him everything, but when I opened my mouth, I said, "Why did you do that? Run back in?"

"He needed help." He looked confused.

"You didn't know who he was, only that he was trying to hurt us. But you ran in anyway," I said, looking to the ground.

"Auluria, it's about doing what is right. Yes, he was fighting against us, but that doesn't mean he should die."

"It doesn't mean you should die *for* him either," I protested angrily, stopping in my tracks.

I hadn't realized how upset I was that he just risked his life like that.

"*I'm fine*, Auluria," he tried to convince me.

When I didn't speak, he turned to look at me. His face was serious, voice dropping to a tone so low I could barely hear him.

"Auluria…why did you brush me away earlier?"

No answer. I looked at my feet.

"Auluria, why have you been avoiding me?" He stepped closer.

I looked away.

Silence.

Then I felt myself being pushed backward several steps until I landed against a large tree trunk. Dov had my left shoulder in his hand. He stretched his other hand up the trunk above my head and leaned in toward me, his eyes searching mine as he drew close. *Too close.*

He lingered there, inches away from me. The silence made my heartbeats stretch apart.

"Tell me to stop," he breathed and inched his face closer to mine.

I gasped and watched him move. I tore my gaze away.

"Hmm," I whimpered, barely audible. I felt myself breathing heavily. I was desperate for air.

"Tell me to stop," he repeated, his voice low and husky. He moved closer.

"Hmm," I mumbled more forcefully, keeping my sight glued to the fallen leaves on the forest floor. I could feel him grin as I blushed and fought to keep the smile from my lips.

"Look at me," he said softly. A smile played at his lips as he moved closer and repeated in a loud whisper, full of longing, "Tell me to stop."

His words forced me to look at him. His lips hovered above mine. All I had to do was tip my head up and they would connect. I couldn't breathe.

"Tell me to stop," he whispered one last time, his breath moving a few stray hairs across my face, tickling me.

I felt my tongue dancing behind my lips, desperate to say the words that would end this torture and keep me true to my word to protect him, but they stuck behind my teeth. I prayed he would stop, even though I wanted anything *but* for him to stop, for I knew the second he touched me, I would lose indefinitely.

"Don't stop."

He closed the space between us, his lips touching mine. Fire raced through me. He smelled of smoke and his face was smudged with soot, but as he let go of my arm and reached around my waist, clutching my back, all I could think of was how right it felt to be held by him.

His hand ran down the trunk of the tree, scraping against the bark until his hand was tangled in my hair. He cradled the back of my head, pulling me toward him and deepening the kiss.

I slowly raised my limp hands from my side, skimming the sides of his waist before I ran them up his chest and to his collar where I clung desperately to him, holding him against me. I leaned back into the tree and Dov leaned into me. His kisses became more desperate with each passing moment. In that moment, I was desperate too.

He kissed me until we had to pull away for air—though I admit, I thought about letting it end right then and there, allowing us to die happy.

He pulled back just enough that we could catch our breath. I still clung to his collar, clutching it in my nervous hands. He kept his strong arm wrapped around my body, brushing my hair repeatedly with his free hand. He pulled my hair in front of me, wrapping it around his fist. He let it go and untangled it before pushing it back over my shoulder, then pulled it back between us once more.

His eyes danced as he smiled at me, revealing the most gorgeous dimples I had ever seen in my life. His breathing forced my hair back in puffs. I was happy.

He grinned at me and laughed. I laughed too.

"I've been wanting to do that since the day I met you," he said breathlessly.

I laughed again. So, this was what joy was like.

"And tell me, was it worth it?" I asked. Lowell would

have been so proud of me for flirting with him, had I not been serious about it.

"Oh, it was worth it." He nodded enthusiastically. He closed his eyes and bent his head, nuzzling my hands still clutching at his collar with his strong chin.

I sighed.

He whipped his head up to look at me when he heard me.

He stared so deeply at me, like he could see everything inside of me. He leaned forward and kissed me three more times. Twice forcefully and passionately, the last time tenderly and slow.

"You're beautiful," he sighed, pulling back slightly.

Suddenly embarrassed, I turned my head and gave a short laugh.

"You are, Auluria. You're beautiful."

"Dov…" I started to protest.

He took my chin in his fingers and forced me to look at him. Biting his lip, he looked harder into my eyes. It made me melt. I knew I was blushing.

He stayed there for a moment, frozen in time, watching me. Finally, he pulled back, releasing me from his manmade prison against the tree. My hands released his collar and momentarily dragged down his strong chest, feeling everything under his shirt. I nearly stumbled when he let go of me.

"Let's go," he said softly and waited for me to take my place under his waiting arm.

I slipped under his shoulder and held myself to his side. I watched him as we walked, letting him guide me as we moved. The smudges on his face even looked handsome.

We stopped by a stream so he could wash off the soot. Dov dipped his hands in and splashed the water on his face. Noticing he had missed some of the dark smudges, I cupped my hands and guided the water to his face, wiping off as much as I could. I tried to be gentle, knowing he was still injured, a thought that didn't occur to me when I was kissing his split lips only minutes before.

Dov reached up and caught my hand as I worked, fastening on to my gaze. I felt myself blush again. This time I didn't look away. I had never felt this way with Shadoe.

He let me finish and took me back under his arm. It was soothing, listening to the birds' chatter as we walked by. All too soon we found our way back to the house.

Chapter 5

"Berwyn?" Dov called as we entered the house.

"What?" he answered from around back.

"There was a bit of a situation today," Dov called back. "One of the other groups found the storehouse today. We all got out, but we had to torch the place."

"Good," he said coolly. He seemed more relaxed today and less violent. "How much did we lose?"

"I'll check in with Silas tomorrow. We had only just arrived and I didn't get a good look," Dov reported.

Berwyn nodded before turning to me.

"Still want to stay with us, little girl?"

"Well, I don't want to leave," I replied.

"Suit yourself." He shrugged before walking away.

"That was different," I said quietly, looking at Dov out of the corner of my eye as I watched his brother walk away.

"It happens sometimes. He gets angry, but usually he's pretty good at keeping it in check."

"And beating you is 'keeping it in check'?"

"There was a reason behind that, Auluria, you know that."

"And did he have good reasons for the other times too?" I baited him.

I struck a nerve, but he didn't lash out at me. "It's not as bad as you think it was, Auluria. Can we drop it, please?

"Fine," I agreed. "So now what?"

"Now we find out who it was that broke in," he stated.

Another day, another secret to keep from him.

I knew who it was. I wanted desperately to tell him right there on the spot. He trusted me and I wanted to earn that trust. But I also knew that secret was deadly. I needed to wait until I was sure it was safe.

"You know what we need? Something fun," Dov announced, pulling me back to the present.

I gave him a questioning look as he started across the room. He stooped to pick something up, ducking behind the row of cabinets and out of sight.

"Dov?" Berwyn said, entering the room again.

"Yeah?" He popped back up from behind the wall.

"Come on," Berwyn said, motioning as he walked out the door.

Dov started to say something, disappointment spreading throughout his face. He sighed, shoulders sagging.

"I'm sorry," he whispered as he moved past me toward the door. "I promise we'll do it later."

Now *I* was disappointed. I didn't like seeing him go. And I wanted to know what he had planned for us.

I walked around the house for a bit. Finally, I sank onto the couch and curled my feet up under me. I tipped my head to the side and rested my arms on the couch's arm. If I breathed deeply I could smell Dov on his pillow.

I used the solitude to try to make up my mind about what to tell Dov. I needed to figure out how and when to tell him. I prayed he wouldn't be too angry.

Eventually, I fell asleep on the couch, waiting for his return.

Two more days passed before he resurfaced. I was starting to worry, but Eden told me everything was fine. At first, she avoided me, but by the end of the first full day, she came around. By the second day, she tolerated me spending time with her.

"What's your story, Eden? How did you end up here?"

"Same as you, I suppose." She cast me a disparaging glance.

"Meaning?" I pushed, waiting for an answer. She didn't respond.

"Either *you* can tell me, or someone else can," I said casually.

"Fine," she grumbled.

"A few years ago, I was taken from my home. I was there alone and these men broke in and dragged me out. I fought, but I wasn't strong enough. They were going to take me to the camps.

"Some men saw and tried to help me. It gave me enough time to sneak away while they were fighting.

"Unfortunately, not too long after I escaped, the black-market traders found me. Turns out, they were the ones who had freed me. They tracked me down and took me to the underground markets."

I must have looked confused.

"You don't know about the underground markets, then, I see," she continued. "They do all sorts of selling down there, but there's a big market for illegal brides.

They find girls and auction them off to be hidden wives. Some of the rich men pay for extra wives because they want more children.

"You know how the higher-ranking officials are deemed more worthy if they have more heirs because it 'leads the way for the people to do that same and rebuild the population,'" she quoted the Society.

"A lot of the time, the rich men don't go themselves, they send discreet workers on their behalf. That, however, makes it easier for unwelcome people to slip in." She grinned.

"One of the men who works with Berwyn got a hold of me and another girl. He told us he was helping us and brought us to a meeting at the storehouse. They questioned us, which was terrifying, but eventually they cleared us.

"Berwyn was one of the men to question us." Now it made sense.

"He took a liking to me after I had been cleared. He tried to help me.

"One of the women took me in, but it only lasted a few months before Berwyn and I were married. He trained me to fight alongside of him. I mirror him in every way, though he's much stronger than me."

"Why do you do this, Eden? You could be happy living your life with Berwyn. Why fight?"

"We're working to help people. And if you hadn't

noticed I have a bit of a temper. This is a positive way of letting it out.

"And anyway, there's a lot we can *accomplish*," she said bitterly.

She might have been right about it being a productive outlet for her anger, but I could see more anger than she was referring to just boiling right under the surface. She was still holding a grudge and with each day it was growing stronger.

"I can see you want to help people, but there's something else," I said. "You want revenge."

"If I can get revenge for what happened to me, then yes, I'll take it. It's not my main goal, but I won't turn it down if the opportunity presents itself either," she confided.

"I don't blame you," I said, finding a new appreciation for Lowell's cause. He had a mission too.

"Honestly, I'd like to burn those camps to the ground, close the illegal trading markets, and hang all of the men who forced people there," she said mostly to herself.

"What about Berwyn? What's his story?" I asked.

"He's recovering from the loss of his father. Griz started the group years ago. He peacefully helped so many people. Then one day an operation went sideways," she started.

"What does that mean?" I asked, brushing back my hair.

The door opened and Berwyn and Dov walked in. Eden stopped talking.

"Hungry, boys?" she asked, back to her cool self.

We made dinner for the group. It was mostly silent as we ate. Dov sat next to me, occasionally, reaching below the table to find my hand. He would brush his hand against mine, tickling my skin, before he pulled away.

It was getting dark when we went our separate ways.

"Dov?" I said when we were alone. "Can I ask you something?"

"Sure," he said, taking a seat near me on the couch.

"Eden and I were talking."

"You what?" he interrupted.

"Eden and I were talking."

"Eden *talked* to you?" he interrupted again, surprise in his voice.

"Yes," I confirmed.

"Well…now you're stuck here forever. You're going to have to *marry* me," he joked, "if *Eden* likes you. I don't think you have any choice," he chuckled.

I smiled, unsure of what to do with myself.

"Go on," he prompted, growing serious again.

"She told me her story," I regained my balance.

"*Ahh*, the kidnapped and out for revenge while simultaneously doing good story. I know it well. She probably left out a few details about her temper and slightly violent tendencies though. You have to watch those."

"Uh-huh. Anyway, she was about to tell me more about Berwyn and what happened to your dad when you walked in."

"I see. Berwyn doesn't like talking about it."

"So, what happened? I know something went wrong, but what was it?" I asked, leaning against his shoulder. I wrapped my fingers around his muscular arm and waited.

He sighed, giving in.

"There was this kid who joined the group. His father died and he wanted to be a part of bringing down the Society. He was good, smart, and he rose in the ranks. My father really liked him and put him in leadership.

"But the kid was bent on a more dramatic type of revenge. He tried to talk Dad into being more violent, causing some 'real' destruction, but Dad wouldn't have any of it. He *thought* the kid was under control.

"Then one day, one of the missions got a little violent. The kid liked it and made the situation worse. Dad reamed him out for it. Secretly, the guy formed a small alliance within the group of people who wanted to perpetuate the problem.

"They sabotaged a mission and people died. Dad tried

to take everyone underground, but the guy made sure the Society knew it was Dad's group.

"Eventually they found him, tried him and hanged him, even though it had nothing to do with him.

"He kept the rest of the group safe though," he added.

"And then Berwyn took over."

"Yes, Berwyn took over."

"What happened to the kid?" I asked.

"He disappeared. Formed his own group." He shook his head.

"Do you know where he is?"

"He's around somewhere. We run into his guys from time to time," he offered.

"Dov, I have something to tell you," I started.

"Oh hey! We never had our first date," he suddenly realized, grinning at me mischievously.

"First date?" I asked curiously. "That's what you were doing before you left?"

"We can do it now. I promised you we would."

"It's dark," I protested.

"Then it will be a moonlight picnic," he said, crossing the room and pulling a basket out from a cabinet.

My heart started fluttering. Shadoe had never taken me on a date. Shadoe had never done anything but work with me. Missions hardly counted as dates.

We walked back to the pond, only the crickets serenading us. Dov set out a large blanket near the water. The moon sparkled off the glimmering pond.

Fireflies blinked around us, swirling as we set out our food. A heron swooped down from a tree and glided into the water gracefully.

"What would you like, Auluria?" Dov asked kindly, motioning to the spread before us.

I reached for the strawberries. "Would you like one?" I asked, holding one out for him.

He took it from me, intentionally keeping from touching my skin. He sat back a distance away and leaned back on his hands as he ate. He was tempting me.

I watched his chest rise and fall under his dark blue shirt. Even in the darkness with only the moonlight, his eyes shone a radiant blue color. He offered me bits of other foods and we ate quietly together.

"Why are you so far away?" I finally asked.

"Don't like it?" He raised his eyebrow to me. "Do something about it," he said slyly.

I stared at him for a moment before rising to my knees and crawling toward him. He waited, unmoving, as I tucked myself against his chest. He shifted his arm just slightly so it was covering my shoulder.

He rested on his free hand and I leaned into him.

"I need to tell you something Dov," I finally forced myself to say. I hated that I was about to ruin this moment.

"Okay," he said. He leaned back, falling to the blanket, dragging me with him so we were lying side by side looking up at the moon and stars.

I had always felt secure under the stars. The way they sparkled and came out of hiding every night, it just comforted me.

I breathed him in. I tried to will myself to speak. He waited for me.

After what seemed like an eternity, I spoke.

"I haven't told you everything," I said so quietly I wasn't sure if he heard me.

After a minute, I felt his hand squeeze my hip. He was waiting.

"I," I started, "I'm really glad you found me that day." I chickened out.

He smiled and it pierced my soul.

"Me too," he whispered, nuzzling my hair.

Chapter 6

We had slipped back into the house unnoticed a few hours after we left. We just stared at the sky until we nearly fell asleep. He roused me and half carried me back to the house.

I barely slept once we got back. I couldn't stop playing that moment over in my head.

I should have told him. It was my chance…my chance to be honest, and I was selfish instead, wanting to keep him all to myself.

I promised myself I would find a way to tell him.

"Auluria!" Berwyn said loudly as he walked into the room.

I nearly dropped the glass I was washing. He had never used my name before.

"Yes?" I asked, trading a look with Dov.

"Come with me," he said and walked toward the door.

I looked to Dov; he stared wide-eyed at me. I saw Eden nod her head to me. Dov turned to look at her and when she nodded to him, he indicated that I should go.

I set the glass down and followed him outside.

We walked in silence for a very long time. I fidgeted with my clothing as we walked.

"You like my brother," he stated, catching me off guard.

"He's a good man," I said, unsure of how to reply.

"You will be the death of him." I reeled back as if he struck me. *How had he found out?*

"He's going to be in a situation where he has to choose between himself and you and he'll choose you. Or even worse, you and the group, and he will, in the end, choose you. You're going to get him, or all of us, killed."

He didn't know.

"That's not my intention, Berwyn," I started, but he cut me off.

"If he wants to be with you, I can't stop him, but I can tell you that I will not let you be the destruction of him. He's the only family I have left, and even though it may not seem like it, I *do* look out for him."

"I know you do." Then I added quietly, "In your own way."

He glared at me but said nothing.

"If you're going to be staying here, you are going to have to learn a few things," he said, quickening his pace.

"You'll have to learn how to protect yourself. It may not seem like it, but even Dov knows how to fight properly.

"You'll also be given a job. You'll have to contribute if you want to stay with us.

"The group must vote you in, so you'll need to start making a good impression now. You'll need to be helpful. Today you'll be meeting our leadership—minus Dov, of course."

So, *that's* where we were going.

"We have a stop to make first," he announced. "Do you know where we're going?"

I thought for a moment before it hit me, remembering Eden's words.

"I have to be interrogated," I said as calmly as I could.

"Smart girl," he answered. "Here."

He handed me a dark sack.

"Put it over your face. You can't see around you, but

you'll be able to see directly down so you don't trip," he supplied.

I obliged, lifting the foul-smelling sack over my head. We walked for much longer than I expected. Berwyn guided me around trees, walking directly in front of me. I followed the sounds of his steps. He warned me whenever dangers lay in my path.

Taking my arm, he guided me into what I imagined must be a smaller version of a storehouse. The underground room was cool and damp. The smell of soil was strong and earthy as it assaulted my senses.

The light was dim in the room but my eyes adjusted quickly when he removed the hood. Two men stood before me. Berwyn nodded as he left.

Silas stood against the wall, leaning against his shoulder. He watched me closely, never smiling. The other man was bigger, older. He strode confidently toward me.

"I hear you lost your memory, Auluria. May I ask if you've gained it back?"

"Yes," I said, slightly unsure of myself. Shadoe had practiced interrogations with me. I could confidently answer any question these men asked me, but I knew it was better to come off as being unsure and intimidated by them.

"Good. I'm glad to hear that," he said, a cold edge in his voice.

He placed his hand on the table and leaned on it. After

a moment, he pulled out a chair and sat facing me. Watching me, he waited. Silas stayed in his spot against the wall.

"Tell me, Auluria, how did you come to find us?"

"Umm…well, I was out in the woods. I was being chased. Dov found me and he hid me from the men who were following me."

"I see. And who were those men following you, Auluria?"

I didn't like how he kept using my name. Over and over, with every sentence. *Auluria. Auluria.*

"Guards," I answered, casting my eyes downward in shame. I needed him to believe they wanted to take me to one of the camps.

"And what did they want, Auluria?" *My name again.*

"To take me to the camps, I think," I replied, still looking down.

"But you outran them?"

"No, Dov found me. He hid me."

"How did you get so far in the woods before he found you, Auluria?" he questioned, trying to pull apart my story.

"I hid a few times and they ran past me. I went in a different direction, but they managed to catch up to me."

"Where specifically did you come from, Auluria?"

"I lived in town. My parents died when I was young and my aunt took me in. I lived with her until she died."

"Then where did you go?"

"I stayed in her house until it was too dangerous. I did small jobs around the town in exchange for food." It was true enough. I just left out the part about Lowell.

"And then the black-market traders found you?" he tried to trick me.

"No. There were no black-market traders. It was the officials who tried to take me." I frowned.

"Yes, the officials." He nodded.

I saw Silas twitch. The change was about to happen.

The man before me threw his fist against the table, rocking it.

"Who do you work for, Auluria?" he shouted at me, rising out of his chair.

I widened my eyes and sunk backward into my seat.

"Tell me!" he demanded.

I shook my head, choosing not to speak.

I cast my eyes over to Silas as he uneasily stood by the wall. He lifted himself a few inches toward me, but stayed relatively put. As I watched him, I saw the conflicted look in his eyes. Dov was his friend. He wanted to believe in me because he believed in Dov, but he also wanted Dov to be safe and he didn't know if he could trust me.

"Please," I silently mouthed to Silas.

His lips formed a tight line and he almost imperceivably shook his head no.

I looked back to my interrogator.

"Look at me when I talk to you," he yelled. I shook my head up and down.

"You didn't find us by chance, so why are you here?" he asked through clenched teeth.

Somehow, I imagined this would all be more intimidating if it were Berwyn doing the yelling. It might be a challenge for me.

The man stood and walked around the table. He grasped the chair around me and spun me to face him.

"If you ever want to leave this room, start talking," he hissed at me.

"Enough," Silas said, tearing himself away from the wall.

The man set my chair back down and walked to the doorway. I could see his shadow as he waited, just out of sight.

"Auluria," Silas said, cautiously asking me to look at him.

"Silas," I said glumly, not quite making eye contact.

"You remember me then," he stated.

"Yes."

"Then you know I'm friends with Dov. You need to understand I want what is best for him. If that's you, then I'm happy for him. But if you're trying to hurt him, I won't hesitate to take you out of the picture. Do you understand?"

"You're a good friend," I said, finally looking him in the eye. I meant it.

"You need to talk to me."

"I tried to talk to that other man, but he didn't want to listen," I said.

"He wants the truth."

"I gave him the truth. I think you know that."

He smiled, the corners of his mouth just barely tugging up.

"All right, so let's try this again."

He went through all the questions again. Where did I come from? Why was I here? How did I find them? What did I want?

I repeated each of my answers.

Finally, the man walked back in, knife in his hand. Silas glanced at him, eyes large. He shook his head no, but the man jutted his chin out, forcing him back to the sidelines.

I breathed heavily as I watched him. I knew he wouldn't hurt me, but I had to show fear.

He circled the table, walking behind me out of my line of sight. I locked eyes with Silas. The man dragged a finger along my hair, pulling it around to the side. I shivered for real.

The knife felt cold against my neck. The dull edge was pressed against my throat, but to someone who wasn't aware of this tactic, it would have been frightening. He inched it along my skin, making me wince.

Dragging the blade down my shoulder he started speaking.

"If you are lying to me, Auluria, you will feel such pain as you have never known. You see, the Baers are family to me, and if you hurt them, no one will be able to find the pieces of your body." He grinned.

"I'm not trying to hurt them," I said bravely.

"I don't believe you." He knelt in front of me.

He used the tip of the knife to lift my chin to look at him. His icy eyes greeted me. At that point, I had enough of the accusations. Lifting my foot, I kicked his chest hard, knocking him into the table. He cursed and started toward me, fist in the air.

Silas raced forward and caught his hand, forcing him to stop. I scooted the chair back as far as it could go and jumped to my feet.

"Berwyn!" I shouted, hoping he was nearby.

He stomped into the room, looking from me to the men.

"She's cleared, Berwyn. She's cleared," Silas shouted, still holding the man back.

I hurried to Berwyn's side, hoping for protection.

He fixed his gaze on the man, still trembling with anger. After a moment, Berwyn relaxed and nodded to Silas.

I breathed a sigh of relief. I had made it.

"Calm down. She's been cleared," he announced.

Silas watched me as I left. His eyes offered an apology as I walked away.

"That was cruel," I said as I staggered away from the underground interrogation room.

"Everyone has to go through that," he stated simply.

"With a *knife?*" I demanded.

"No, most don't have to be threatened with weapons."

"So, why did *I?*" I asked angrily. I folded my arms over my chest as we walked.

"Because of Dov."

My head snapped up to look at him. My glare demanded more information.

"You're going to get him killed. And if that was your intent, I wasn't going to make it easy for you," was the only explanation he'd offer.

"You will not tell Dov about this," he instructed.

He told me a bit about each of the leaders as we walked to meet them. I tried to remember names when I could—not to help Lowell, though I should have, but to make a good impression when I met them.

I was so lost in my attempts to memorize facts that I didn't see when we were approaching a public area. We had at some point walked out of the woods and into the outskirts of a town.

Many people that worked with the Baers lived in town to keep up appearances. A few of the people that worked for Lowell did as well, though they were mostly spies and contacts.

People bustled about, and suddenly I realized where we were. Many times, I had come to that very spot, often with Shadoe by my side. This was a place for the rebels and the misfits to hide and trade and plan while blending in with the lower classes of Society.

We darted in and out of the walking masses. I followed closely behind Berwyn as he skillfully maneuvered the streets.

"Well, look who we have here," a voice bellowed from behind us.

Berwyn froze and turned slowly on his heels, seething.

"Lowell," he growled.

"And hello to you too, Berwyn," Lowell grinned, stepping toward us.

Berwyn reached in front of me, wrapping his arm around me, and shoved me behind him. I realized he was trying to protect me. I peeked around his strong arms at my cousin facing him down.

"Get out of here Lowell, before I do something I'll regret."

"And scare the little lady? I don't think so, Berwyn." He motioned to me.

"She is none of your concern!" He glowered. "Leave her be."

"Berwyn," I said quietly.

"Stay back," he said in a rough, hushed voice.

"You never did quite manage to figure out how to protect people, did you, Baer?" Lowell laughed maliciously.

I held on to Berwyn's arm, forcing him to stay in place. He tried to shrug me off, but I held tight until Lowell walked away.

"See you 'round, Berwyn." He waved over his shoulder, still laughing.

"Berwyn…" I started.

"You are never to go near that man, Auluria. Do you understand me?"

I looked at him, horrified. "Why?"

"He killed our father."

Chapter 7

The reality of his words sank into me, sending a chill down my spine. The kid that had worked with Griz's team, the one that went violent and turned against him…that was my cousin.

He had lied to me. The Baers didn't cause those deaths, Lowell did.

My head spun as the pieces fell into place. No wonder Lowell wanted the blame on the Baers. He blamed them for kicking him out. It all made sense.

I thought back and remembered bits and pieces from my childhood when my aunt was still alive. As I thought back, I could finally understand the changes I had seen in my cousin over those years. I watched a man break and then break again.

I saw him come to leadership and form his own group. And then he brought me into his fold. He trained me. He *used me* for this. But he never counted on me questioning him.

I could barely focus as I met the leadership with Berwyn. He kept a close eye out for signs of my cousin, though he was long gone. I knew Lowell had purposely stepped into our path. It was a reminder not only to Berwyn, but to me.

Dov knew something was wrong as soon as he saw us approaching the house. He met me on the path and led me away, leaving his brother to finish his work after he announced I had been cleared.

"What's wrong?" he asked when we were far enough away.

"You didn't tell me about Lowell," I spat out.

"Yes, I did." He looked confused. "Wait, I didn't tell you his name…"

"He was in town today. I thought Berwyn was going to attack him, I had to hold him back."

"Auluria, Lowell is a very bad man. You can't go near him ever again. Do you understand me?" He sounded concerned.

"*You* don't understand *me*," I pleaded with him to listen. "Dov, Lowell is my *cousin*."

The color drained from his face as he processed what I said. He released his grip on my arms and took a step back.

"What?" he asked, shaking his head.

Then he mumbled, "The blond man from your flashback."

"Dov," I said, stepping toward him, "I didn't know."

He pulled away from me.

"How could you not have known?" he gaped.

"He didn't tell me…" I pleaded.

"*Tell* you? *Tell you?*" he shouted, scaring me.

"What *did* he tell you? *Huh?* What did he tell you?" He moved toward me and I stepped back, stumbling.

Tripping over a rock, I fell hard, still looking up at him, never taking my eyes off him.

"Dov, I didn't know. I had no idea, please, believe me," I begged, tears springing to my eyes.

"You are going to tell me everything," he said in a low,

quiet voice that sent more fear into me than when he yelled.

I nodded ferociously.

"I tried to tell you. I just…I couldn't bring myself to do it," I whimpered.

I told him everything. How Lowell was the cousin who cared for me when I had no one left. How he took me in and trained me. How I worked for him, knowing no other life. How I thought I was doing the right thing because he was family. How I didn't know anyone had been hurt.

I told him of Lowell's plot to overtake the Society and pin it on his family. That I was supposed to find my way into their lives and get Berwyn to trust me. When we discovered he had been married, I was to target Dov, but I found the good in him and couldn't. I told him how I tried to push him away but he pulled me back in. How I couldn't escape him. I told him of my promise to protect him.

He didn't scoff when I told him how he made me feel, but I saw the brightness in his eyes dim. He didn't believe me. He thought my tears were an act.

"Dov, please," I begged, sobbing. "I never wanted to hurt you. I tried to tell you."

"When, Auluria? When you were kissing me? When you were making me fall for you? *When* were you going to tell me?"

"Last night," I said softly.

"When you said you had something to tell me," he mused softly.

I nodded.

"I just...I didn't want to destroy that. I wanted that moment...for us."

"There is no *us,* Auluria. You lied to me." His words crushed me.

I felt my chest cave in on itself. I couldn't face him. I looked away, tears slipping down my face.

"So now what? You report back to your cousin?" he asked, walking closer.

"No. I have no intention of helping Lowell, especially after finding out what he did to your family already," I said, suddenly feeling stronger.

I stood up and pushed my hair back.

"Then where are you going?" he asked.

He had banished me.

"I'll find somewhere," I said quietly.

"It's dangerous out there," he said quietly, still not able to look me in the eye.

"I'll be okay," I said. "Dov...I'm so sorry."

I stood and turned to go. I wanted to run as far and as fast as I could. I wanted to escape my heart breaking. I tried to leave with the little dignity I had left after throwing myself at his mercy. I walked ten steps before I heard him following me.

"It's dangerous. You shouldn't be out here alone," he said.

He kept ten paces behind me. We didn't speak again.

He despised me and what I'd done to him, but he was a gentleman to the end.

The birds I had loved listening to on our walk only the day before now seemed to be playing a dirge. Their sad and lonely songs filled up the newly opened space in my heart.

I walked without direction, simply moving along until I found somewhere to go.

"You don't have to follow me," I said without looking back—*unable* to look back. "I'll be fine from here."

"Hush," he said quickly.

I turned and started to speak, but the look on his face forced my silence. I listened as he looked around the woods.

A twig snapped and we turned to face it.

The silence was eerie. They rushed forward from all sides, surrounding us. Three men ran at Dov, the remaining two toward me. My hands flew to my face to protect myself as the attack came.

"Run!" Dov shouted, but it was too late.

I heard the sickening thuds, but one of the men had wrenched me around so I couldn't see it. He tried to get my arms pinned behind my back, but I wriggled free. I landed a punch to his face, sending him backward.

The second man kicked my feet out and I toppled to the ground. I kicked back hard, causing the man to curse and backhand me. A scream escaped my lips as he connected.

I heard a loud grunt as Dov lifted a man off his feet and pummeled him to the ground. He hit hard and the air rushed from his lungs. Dov punched one of the men—I recognized him as Jake, from the first day I met Dov.

The man I had hit was back on his feet, coming toward me. Before he could reach me, Dov was by his side. He reached around his neck, cutting off his air supply. The man fell to the ground, unconscious.

Dov wrenched around to face the man holding me. I tried to get away, but he held fast. Dov ran at him, tackling him to the ground. I went down with them, but could roll away as they tumbled over one another. Dov straddled him and slammed his fist into his face, blood splattering with each blow.

"Dov!" I screamed as I watched Marty lower himself and run full force at Dov.

He looked up, but I was already in motion, running as fast as I could toward the man targeting Dov. I crashed into him from the side, sending us both toppling over. He rolled on top of me, pinning me to the ground. He looked at me, wrapping his hand around my throat, and then looked to Dov.

"Don't move," he commanded.

"Marty, let her go," Dov said, hands raised in the air.

"I don't think I will, Dov." He moved his hands around my throat, applying enough pressure to scare me.

"Marty, stop!" Dov begged.

"Get back!" Marty yelped.

Dov retreated, locking his terrified eyes with me.

It was hard to breathe with Marty on my chest.

Marty looked back to me, keeping Dov in his peripheral vision. His eyes traced my hair, my cheek, and settled on my lips. He smirked viciously.

Taking one hand away from my throat, he traced the line his eyes had followed. His hands crept through my hair, over my temple, and along my cheek. He grinned when he reached my mouth, but continued dragging his rough fingers along my chin, across my neck and out onto my shoulder.

A burst of air escaped his nose as he latched onto my collar and ripped it, exposing my shoulder.

"No!" I heard Dov say, but his voice was so far away as panic set in. At some point, my gaze had drifted to the man straddling me and I watched as he looked hungrily at my exposed skin.

"Marty, you leave her alone, or I'll…"

"What?" Marty looked up and shouted. "You'll do what? Because I will kill her before I let you have her back."

Dov stopped, sinking deeply onto his heels. I could see he was fighting everything within him to not run to us. He looked terrified and angry and wild.

"A *golden girl*," he said stroking my hair, "for a *golden boy*."

He looked to Dov to make sure he was watching.

"Get up, darling," he bent low to my ear and whispered.

He started to stand, pulling a knife out from his belt. He held it to my throat as I rose to my feet. I saw Dov suck in a breath of air. I could feel the anger radiating off him even from far away.

"Now don't get any ideas about being a hero, Dov. If I even *think* you're following us, I will kill her." He grinned. "Come along now, darling," he said to me.

We walked backward, away from Dov. I watched him breathing heavily, trying to contain himself. I prayed he would stay put and not come after me, and he did. Marty would surely kill him if he ever saw Dov again.

I stumbled as we walked, the knife at my throat making it hard to move. We trekked through the woods, and Marty whispered cruel things in my ear.

"Looks like it's just us now, darling," he growled

quietly. "You and I are going to have a great time together."

He had to be around Dov's age, but he seemed so much older and more menacing to me in those moments.

He breathed heavily into my ear as we walked. "However, do you get your skin so soft, darling?" he cooed.

I cringed with every word. I wished for some rescue. Dov. Shadoe. Even Lowell or Berwyn. But I was alone.

I fought to find a way to get the upper hand without him slicing into my neck. I tried to reposition myself as we walked, hoping to find a more protected angle.

I considered trying to play along but knew that wouldn't end well for me. I let him guide me through the trees and hoped for an opening to escape.

We hadn't been gone more than a few minutes, but there, being subjected to the torture of knowing what was coming, it seemed like a lifetime. I felt myself panicking and tried to calm myself.

I fell fast. Something had crashed into us and sent us careening toward the earth. The knife landed in the soft ground, protruding like it had been jabbed into a heart.

The hand released me, trying to get up and find the weapon, but Dov had him pinned to the ground.

"Go!" he shouted and I ran several paces away.

The two struggled on the ground.

"Don't you *ever* touch her again!" Dov screamed as he hit Marty's face.

He grabbed the man's collar and lifted his head off the ground just enough to slam it back down into it.

"If you ever come anywhere near her *ever* again I will kill you, do you understand me?" He released his anger until the boy stopped struggling.

Marty managed to find the knife with his hand and raised it toward Dov. Dov snatched up a rock and connected with the side of Marty's head. He lay motionless on the ground. Dov felt for a pulse.

"He's alive. For now," he said quietly, taking the knife and turning toward me.

For a moment, he stood there facing me. His shoulders sagged up and down with each labored breath. His mouth hung open, craving oxygen. The knife lay limp in his hand at his side. His feet were spread apart, his stance forcing him to stay upright.

Then he crumpled toward me, caving in on himself and running as fast as he could to me. He crushed me in his arms. He buried himself in my hair and I could feel the tears work their way through my golden strands.

Finally, he pulled back just enough to breathe. "Are you all right?" he asked, his voice thick with emotion.

I held him, trying to be strong.

"I'm safe," I said.

When he didn't let go, I clung to him.

"Are you okay?" he asked in a coarse whisper.

"Dov," I whispered back.

He released his grip on me, pulling his face away. He bent and rested his forehead on mine and breathed me in.

He found his voice again.

"Did he hurt you?" he asked in a strong voice.

"No, you got here in time," I said, realizing he must have run the long way around and looped back on us to have surprised us like that.

"Are *you* hurt?" I asked, suddenly concerned.

"I'm fine. It's you I'm worried about."

"I see that," I stated. "Dov. Why did you protect me? After everything, why did you save me, knowing I could still hurt you?"

"I would never let anyone hurt you," he said, still not looking at me.

"Why did you protect me so fiercely?"

"Because I care about you fiercely." His words filled my soul.

"Why do you care?" I asked softly, needing to know.

"Because you are worth it," he whispered, finally looking at me.

We walked back to the house, standing near each other but not touching. He would need time to heal from my betrayal, but I had the promise that he would soon come to terms with it.

He didn't tell Berwyn about what happened.

Chapter 8

As the days went by, he resigned himself to tolerate my presence. Had he not been forced to confront his feelings for me when he saved me, he may have let me go. He always kept me in his sights but held me at arm's length.

Eventually, he warmed up to me again, though cautiously. I gave him his space. I didn't want to push him away.

"Auluria, we need to talk," he said one day.

"Okay," I replied.

We sat down at the table once he was sure Eden and Berwyn were gone. The space between us felt like a hundred miles. I wanted desperately to reach across and take his hand, but I held back.

"We need to figure out what we're going to do," he said.

"We can be friends for now, if that's what you want," I said quietly, casting my eyes downward.

"I meant about telling Berwyn," he said and I blushed, realizing my mistake.

"You do kind of work for the enemy here, Auluria," he followed up. "But that too, I suppose."

Great, not only had I assumed he would want to talk about our relationship, but I had also neglected the real problem and most likely sabotaged any chance I had of fixing the situation.

"I'll tell him," I offered.

"No, we'll do it together. But we're going to have to come up with a plan to fix it first. If you're not willing to work with us and betray your cousin, we need to get you out of here. Now."

"I have no real connection to Lowell. Apparently, I never did. I don't want to see him hurt, but I'm not going to let him hurt you either," I said, determined to make it true.

"All right then," he said thoughtfully. "We need to find out exactly what he's planning. We could feed him some false information. What were you trying to find out?"

"Locations, meetings, but mostly"—I hesitated—"your weaknesses."

"And did you find those out?" he said coolly.

"No. I don't know them."

"But *I* was supposed to be easy, right? My weakness was supposed to be you." He took my silence as confirmation.

"All right. Then we should make it look like it's working. So, in public, we'll be a couple. We'll make sure they see us together. We'll figure out something for Berwyn."

I hated knowing that'd he'd be touching me, holding my hand, walking with his arm around me, and it would only be for show. That he no longer had feelings for me. But I didn't have a choice.

We discussed the rest of the details and planned our speech for Berwyn.

I was surprised with how well Berwyn took the news. I expected fury and injury. Instead, he had flipped a table and broken some items from around the house.

Eden calmed him down and helped show him the good parts of our plans. Once he settled, he agreed to play along. Discovering he could use me against Lowell made him glow.

Over the next few days, Berwyn sent us out on several missions. These were mostly created so we would be seen together, solidifying our fake relationship.

I made every deadline with Shadoe and gave him the information Berwyn fed to me. Dov had insisted one of them follow me, watching from a safe distance, but I knew better. Shadoe would pick them out instantly, so I was alone when I snuck out to meet my handler.

I made it look like I snuck away from a food gathering trip during one of our meetings. Shadoe held me there an alarmingly long time.

"Have you found anything we can use yet? Something you can take without them noticing?" Shadoe prompted. Lowell had wanted something that belonged to each of the Baers, but in my original search, I hadn't found anything I could easily sneak out. Now that the Baers were aware, they needed me to stall.

"They notice everything, Shadoe, it's not as easy as it sounds."

"You've been able to locate things before. There must be something hidden somewhere." He sounded agitated.

"There's nothing, I searched the house," I confirmed, hoping he believed me. In truth, I never had found anything that would have helped us even before I decided to side with Lowell's enemy.

"We saw you with Dov. You've been swaying his attention?"

"Yes." I nodded.

"Good. Do you have his trust?" he questioned.

"I believe I do."

"He'll follow you then?" His rough voice irritated me. I wished he would release me so I could get back.

"He will," I replied. "He believes I have his best interest at heart. He'd never have any idea I was working with you."

Dov had always thought kindly of me until I told him of my deceptions. He had believed the best in me. Never would he have suspected I had been sent to infiltrate and destroy his group had I not told him of my cause.

"Make sure you keep it that way. We need him to do everything you say without questioning it. He needs to be absolutely devoted to you."

"He is incredibly devoted, Shadoe. Not just to me but to everything he does. Once he commits to something, he devotes himself fully to it and sees nothing other than it. He won't be a problem." I assured him.

"You're not getting too close to him, are you?" he asked, putting his hand on my arm. It was strange to have him touch me so familiarly. Shadoe rarely touched me in our time together, even after Lowell had committed us to each other. In public, he would touch me only to show his claim to me, and in private we were rarely close.

I shrugged him off, letting my anger bubble up slightly. He let his hand fall as I bristled.

"I am very aware of my place with him," I snapped. *There was nothing real between me and Dov, no matter how much I wanted it.*

"Good. You've been trained well. Lowell knows how strong you are. We know we can depend on you to see this through. Your role in your cousin's plan is critical. Without you, this entire operation would fall apart."

I weighed his words. If I simply disappeared, everything would fall apart. I couldn't, of course. I had to help the Baers fight back against Lowell.

"I know my place, Shadoe," I affirmed.

"You and I will help lead together someday, Auluria. This is how we get there."

"We're Lowell's right hands. I know," I sighed.

I refrained from glancing over my shoulder as he continued to speak, far too aware of the passing time. Everything in me screamed to leave and run back to the house tucked far away in the depths of the woods before I was caught. Instead, I stayed planted to the spot, tolerating Shadoe's insistence on running over details of the missions Lowell was running. None of them, however, were helpful to the Baers.

Each minute that passed caused me greater worry. Each minute was one more minute that something could go wrong with my plan. When my mentor finally released me, I ran as quickly as I could, praying I could make up the time.

When I finally made it back, the Baers were just walking back toward their home.

I could feel it the instant we walked in. Something was different. It didn't appear the others noticed, but something made my hair stand on end. I couldn't place what it was. I examined the room carefully, but couldn't see anything out of place. I mentioned it, but they assured me nothing had been displaced.

A smell, maybe?

I wasn't sure what it was.

I kept my eyes open the rest of the day.

"Why did Marty attack us *again*?" I asked Dov, the silence surrounding us in the house so deafening.

"What?"

"He keeps attacking you. Why?"

He shrugged. "They just do that sort of thing."

"That wasn't just for fun, Dov." He still winced every time I spoke his name. "That was personal."

"Fine," he relented. "Do you remember that girl I told you about? The one that betrayed us?"

He spat out the word *betrayed* like it was something bitter in his mouth.

"She was Marty and Jake's friend. They both had feelings for her, but she was sent off to seduce *me*." He looked at me when he said 'seduce', comparing *our* feelings to a directive.

"They hated me for it. But when she was kicked out and sent back, she was interrogated. She stopped giving them information on us, and they weren't happy. She failed, and they weren't happy. Like I said, her body gave out. They blamed us for her death, but Marty and Jake blamed *me*."

"Did you love her, Dov?" I wanted anything but to hear his answer.

"No. I never loved her. She wasn't like…" He stopped and my breath caught.

"Will they ever leave you be?"

"Probably not." He kicked at something invisible on the floor.

"You should be careful, though. Marty was going to hurt you to get to me. He thinks we're together, so he'll be targeting you. He'll do whatever he can to take you away from me."

"Too bad he doesn't know it's all a cover," I said sadly.

"Too bad," he agreed, twisting the knife in my heart.

Dov held my hand as we walked through the crowded streets. I followed along behind him. The town was busy that day. Berwyn and Eden walked in front of us, stopping to look at different items along the way.

I knew we'd see Lowell that day. That was the entire purpose of the trip. Berwyn wanted Lowell to see me with Dov.

I spotted him out of the corner of my eye as he veered out from an alleyway. He strode purposefully over to us, walking paces behind us until Berwyn finally turned around.

"Get out of here, Lowell," Berwyn growled.

"Hello again, Berwyn. And look, the wife and kids," he grinned.

"Back off, Lowell," Dov snapped as Lowell reached for me. He stepped in front of me and shielded me from my cousin.

"A bit overprotective, aren't we, Dov?" Lowell said. "I just wanted to meet the new girls properly." His gaze lingered on me a moment before turning to Eden. "And what about this pretty lady?"

Eden looked as if she had been slapped. For a moment, something flashed in Lowell's eyes. He smiled again and pulled his hand back.

"Dov, get them out of here," Berwyn commanded.

Dov stood for a moment longer, challenging Lowell. He pushed me back and walked a few steps backward before turning around and walking Eden and I away from the scene.

Dov escorted us back to the tree line. I could see Berwyn and Lowell arguing. Eden stood off to the side, watching her husband and enemy. I had turned to watch the scene but Dov kept moving me backward until I found myself against a tree.

He lifted his hand to my face and buried it in my hair behind my head. He rested his other hand on my far hip as he leaned into me and pressed his lips to mine.

Stiffly he kissed me, and I wished he meant those kisses. They were harsh and foreign and obligated. Just when I thought he would pull back all the way, he lingered. He rocked forward and kissed me again. I'm sure it was to make sure we would be seen, but I could almost swear his kisses changed. They no longer seemed calculated and forceful, but desperate and full of desire and heartbreak.

"I think that's enough," Eden commented, but he didn't stop.

A moment later he leaned away, pulling me from the tree. He wrapped me in a tight embrace, pulling me to his chest tightly. He couldn't even look at me. *This must disgust him,* I thought painfully.

I wanted to run my hands along his chest and up into his hair, forcing him to look at me. I wanted him to talk to me, even if it was to yell at me. I hated the cold silence that often followed us.

Before the conversation came to blows, Lowell walked away from Berwyn. Dov's brother joined us at the tree line.

"Did he see?" I asked.

"He saw," Berwyn confirmed.

At least something was going right.

I silently cried myself to sleep that night. As soon as we were safely in the woods Dov had ripped his arm from around me. He fell back and worked his way to the other side of his family, separating us by what seemed like hundreds of miles as we walked.

He wouldn't take dinner with us. Dov refused to talk to me. He wouldn't look at me. Even Berwyn noticed something was wrong.

The last time I had cried like that was when Lowell told me I would eventually be marrying Shadoe. It wasn't that I didn't like him—he was a nice enough person, very cordial and friendly—but I didn't love him and I never would. We worked well together, but we were better partners than *partners.*

He accepted our fate better than I did. Or if he didn't, he never said anything to me. He had a blind faith in my cousin, though. *That,* I imagine, caused him to not even question the directive.

Dov was different. He cared for me as more than someone to complete a mission. At least, he *had.* Shadoe had kissed me a few times since Lowell had committed us, but they were dry, chaste kisses. There was no passion or feeling like there was with Dov.

Of everyone in the universe, I had to betray Dov. I would never forgive myself for messing that up.

I had nightmares during the little sleep that I did have that night.

Her hair was long, with beautiful curls. She was almost elegant, despite being so young.

I could only see the back of her head as she sat on a bench with my cousin. I watched as they talked, Lowell leading the conversation. She nodded appropriately and waited her turn to speak.

She pulled her hand away as he took it in his, clearly upset at what he had said. He tried to calm her, but she stood, preparing to leave. His next words forced her to stay in place. It took time, but he convinced her to sit again. She crossed her arms and looked away.

"Who is that?" I asked my aunt that cold afternoon.

"That is a friend of Lowell's. Come over here and help me fold these," my aunt chastised.

"Why are they arguing?" I questioned, retreating to her side to assist her.

"People argue sometimes. Lowell fixed it; he's very good at fixing things. Now, don't you be so worried about what your cousin is doing." She waved her hand in my direction, refocusing me to the task at hand.

"Today, I have to go into town. You need to stay here. Don't leave the house," my aunt continued.

"I won't," I replied, setting down the sheet we had folded. I knew better than to leave the house alone. It was far too dangerous outside.

The young girl with Lowell stood, less frustrated, and left. Lowell watched her walk away, clearly no longer as upset as he had been.

He walked away in the opposite direction, not bothering to say goodbye to his mother.

When we had finished, my aunt left to go into town. I knew she was having trouble affording food and we had spent the entire morning looking for items around the house to sell or trade.

The dream jumped ahead several days and I found myself

sitting at the table as Lowell burst into the room, yelling something about someone being gone. The blonde girl.

I woke up confused, but with a haunting sense of familiarity. I had forgotten about the blonde girl that day. I knew Lowell had been angry about her, but I never did know why. Something about the girl wouldn't leave my thoughts. I never saw her face, but the dream continued to nag me. She was important to Lowell, I could tell. He never treated any of the girls in his fold like that; had never reacted to them that way. It was such a strange dream. I wondered if it had been only that…a dream I made up and not something I saw once. Perhaps I would never be sure.

I eventually fell back into a restless sleep. When I woke up in the morning, it was with the faint remembering of something long ago. Everything was fuzzy as if I were still in a dream. I pictured something just out of view, not quite yet in focus. I tried to pull myself together enough to decipher it.

I was still puzzling it out when Berwyn stepped into the room, Eden following on his heels. Dov refused to look at any of us when we sat down to eat, instead keeping his eyes focused on his plate.

As we were cleaning up I gasped.

"That's it!"

Everyone stopped to look at me, even Dov.

"I figured it out. I knew something was wrong the other day. When we walked in and I said something was wrong…" I tried to remind them.

"It was a smell. I knew that smell. It was one of my handlers' trainees. He always had a specific scent to him. I hardly ever saw him, that's why it took me so long to place it." They looked at me.

"He was here," I connected the dots.

"But nothing was missing."

"Something must be, Eden. He was *here,*" I insisted.

"Fine, we'll check again." It was the first thing Dov had said since yesterday in town.

A knock pounded on the door.

"Dov!" a voice shouted.

"Silas?" Dov stood and went to the door.

Silas pushed past him. "Berwyn, good. You're both here. Something's happened."

"What is it, Silas? Berwyn asked.

"In the towns," he said. "Something is happening in the towns. We should go."

The men stalked toward the door.

"Wait!" I shouted. "It could be a trap."

"We have to go, Auluria! People might need help," Dov said bitingly.

"Fine, I'm coming too."

"No, stay here," he commanded. I continued walking toward them.

"She's not going to let you stop her, Dov," Berwyn warned. Dov stopped fighting.

We ran through the trees. I could barely keep up with the strong men in front of me. Eden ran with me and we reached the clearing a few moments after the boys did.

What we saw was horrifying.

Chapter 9

There was smoke everywhere as buildings burned in the center of the town. I knew at once it must be the government buildings. This had to be Lowell.

People ran, screaming as they tried to escape. Loud explosions ripped through the air and shook the ground. Although, I barely heard it through my labored breathing and pounding of my heart.

We ran into the center of the chaos, splitting up and looking for ways to help. People ran past us, pushing us out of their way. I stumbled and fell into the side of a building. Berwyn lifted me upright and continued.

The government workers were being attacked from

all sides. Their uniforms made them stand out, creating easy targets.

"For Griz!" A cheer went up in the crowd. Fists pumped in the air.

These people weren't working for Griz's group though. They used his name to create violence and chaos and place blame on the family that had taken me in.

I ran to the men I used to work with, begging them to stop. They only laughed at me or called me a traitor. They said Lowell would be furious, but I didn't care.

I ran from group to group looking for someone I could trust, or convince, or get information from. As soon as they discovered I wasn't helping them, they turned on me. No one dare lay a finger on me for fear of retribution from Lowell, but they refused to help me.

I watched as men poured out of a building, fire creeping up its walls. Shadoe ducked around the corner. I followed as quickly as I could.

"What are you doing here?" he hissed when he saw me.

"Shadoe, this is wrong. You have to stop," I insisted.

"Stop? This is just the beginning, Lur, you know that."

"Lur?" a new voice questioned.

"Well, if it isn't the *target*," Shadoe challenged, dropping the act. He pulled me behind him, standing between me and Dov.

"Shadoe, let go." I tried to wrench away, but his grip held firm.

"Let her go," Dov demanded.

"She's not yours, lover boy," he said cruelly.

Realization crept into Dov's devastatingly handsome face as it dawned on him that Shadoe was more than just a handler. He looked betrayed all over again and the conviction nearly caused me to crumble.

"Let her go," he repeated in a steady, strong voice.

"She was never one of you, Dov."

"She was never *yours either*," he spat back at him.

The metallic scent of blood was in the air, mixed with smoke and burning flesh. Everything seemed so still as the two men faced each other down despite the violence going on around us.

I leaned forward and whispered quickly into Shadoe's ear. "Long con."

I kicked the back of his knee, knowing if he thought I was playing Dov, he'd let me leave with him. He hit the ground and stayed there, giving us enough time to escape. He would find out about my betrayal soon enough.

I launched myself at Dov and we careened around the corner of the building. We ran until he stopped me, pulling me tightly against a wall.

"No!" A piercing scream filled the air. Eden.

Dov moved faster than I could and was around the

building first. Eden was still screaming as she raced toward a falling building.

"He's in there!" she screeched to Dov.

He overtook her and raced into the flames. She stopped before she reached the door, unable to see inside. I took her arm and moved her several paces back. We searched through the orange-lit smoke, but saw no signs of them.

Eden clung to my arm, tears streaming down her face. I realized I was crying as well. She shouted her husband's name repeatedly.

An eternity passed. People ran around us; we didn't notice any of them. Eden and I looked up just in time to see something fly through a window above us. We pulled away as a chair crashed where we had been standing.

Two figures immediately followed, landing hard on the ground. Eden ran to their sides. I was too shocked to move. I had been trained to escape situations like that, but I'd never thought I'd have to jump from a second story window. I couldn't imagine Dov or Berwyn had been trained to take that kind of fall.

I ran to help Eden as she pulled Berwyn to his feet. I caught Dov's hand just as he lifted himself off the ground. He gave me a grateful look that quickly transformed into something hard and cold when he realized he was holding my hand.

Fire licked up the wall from the window they had just

vacated. It crackled and hissed and suddenly the cacophony of the fight erupted around us once again.

Eden and I each supported one side of Berwyn as we fled. Dov hobbled along on his own, leading the way. I looked back just in time to see one of the masked men catch my gaze. If Lowell didn't know already, he would know soon.

"The Society sent in more guards. They killed some of the rebels and took others for interrogation," Silas informed them the next day.

Berwyn and Dov had been committed to the couch since their fall. Eden and I hovered, trying to help.

"They're blaming us," Berwyn said angrily.

"It's not confirmed, but yes, sir, they are."

"This was all a part of his plan. Your cousin…" he growled at me.

"This wasn't *her* fault, Berwyn," Eden snapped at him, cutting off his tirade.

"I'm so sorry," I said, shame filling my voice.

"You didn't do this, Auluria," Dov said without emotion.

My eyes bounced to him. It was the first time I felt

like I wasn't being blamed for everything going wrong. Relief washed over me.

"They'll be coming for us," Berwyn said. "We have to move."

Eden sighed and placed a tender hand on Berwyn's shoulder. I'd never seen her so gentle before.

"Where do we go?" Silas asked.

Berwyn shook his head. "This is just like before," he muttered.

"We go underground. For now. We're better prepared this time," he said resolutely.

"We go underground," Lowell had said. I thought back to several months earlier.

"We go under just long enough for them to blame the Baers. Then we come back, stronger than ever, and take out the Society. Or what's left of the Society after the Baers are done fighting back.

"If they think they crushed the people responsible, they won't be looking when we attack and we'll catch them unprepared. We'll have the upper hand and we'll emerge victorious."

"What does it mean, to go underground?" I had asked.

"We have safe houses. We'll stay there. People won't know to look for us there. We just need to have the right evidence to

point the Society toward Berwyn and his people. After all they've done, everyone is better off to have them out of the way."

"What did they do, Lowell?" I questioned in my blind ignorance.

"They betrayed us, Auluria. They're the reason so many plans went wrong. They're the reason people died. They've been destroying lives for years. They refuse to listen to people who know what they are talking about, and everything has fallen apart because of them," Lowell seethed.

"Good riddance. They must go. You see that, don't you?" he guided.

Chapter 10

Eden and I packed as quickly as we could. We took only what we thought we'd need the most. Silas put the word out for everyone to gather at the safe houses. Most of the group lived in town and blended in with the rest of society. It would be more dangerous for them to escape. Those whose identities were safe enough to keep were instructed to temporarily cut ties and stay put.

Berwyn leaned on Eden as we walked through the forest to our new hiding place. Eventually Dov dropped back with me, keeping an eye on me.

"You were with him, weren't you?" The agony in his voice nearly froze me in place.

"Not the way you think," I said. "I never chose to be with Shadoe. Lowell said it was to be, so it was. Shadoe trained me, we were partners on missions, but we were barely even friends."

"Did he kiss you?" He sounded afraid to ask.

"Only a few times, but none of them were real. Not like how we kissed."

His jaw clenched and I saw his body freeze up. I wanted to turn to him, but I knew he would only push me away.

"I never wanted him, Dov," I added quietly. "I only ever wanted you."

He slowly inched away from me, not saying anything else. I couldn't blame him.

The safe house was small. Berwyn said there were dozens of them placed among the woods. Most were larger, made to accommodate large groups of people. Since Berwyn was the leader and would be the target of the search efforts, he was isolated, and by extension, so were we.

There was a large mattress and two small mattresses placed on the floor. Dov bent and dragged one to the far wall when we entered the room. I was on the opposite side, a chasm of mistrust placed deep between us.

There was a fully stocked storeroom just off the main room. When we arrived, we found they had stored enough for at least two weeks of coverage.

Even so, Berwyn decided we needed to get as much as possible before the Society decided the attack was the Baers' fault and came looking. We only had a small window of time to move if we needed to.

The four of us crept out of our hidden space. Dov was forced to walk with me as Berwyn and Eden went to a second location. Growing up I had loved silence. I even loved being silent with Dov, knowing we could exist together without needing to talk, but in that moment, I hated it.

The new storehouse wasn't too far off. We silently descended into the earthy room. Silas was waiting for us.

Dov waved me off and turned to talk to his friend. I focused this time on finding supplies. We had brought extra sacks with us to transport our goods in. Once I filled a bag, I slung it over my shoulder. Eventually, there were too many to fit, so I held them on my arm, weighing me down heavily to one side.

As I reached for some dried meats, I felt the weight lifting off my left arm. Silas stood next to me, handing some of the packs to Dov, helping him put them on. He was still recovering from his second story fall.

I felt the corners of my mouth tug up in a half-hearted smile of thanks. Silas had a strange look in his eyes. Disappointment? Kindness? Pride? Realization that I wasn't who he thought I was? Anger?

I didn't know. But I knew Dov had told him of my confession.

"You know," I said.

"I know," he replied.

"I'm sorry I misled you," I offered meekly.

"I trusted you," he said bitterly.

"I know." My voice came out a whisper. Dov still didn't turn to me.

"But you're with us now?" Silas asked.

I looked up at him. "Yes," I said decidedly. "I won't help Lowell knowing what he did."

"Okay."

"Okay?" I said taken aback.

"Okay."

"That's it?" I questioned.

"That's it."

That was it. No questions. No comments. Just acceptance.

Whether it was for my sake or just for Dov's, I didn't care. This man would not hold my transgressions against me.

"Thank you."

The walk back to the safe house took much longer with our heavy packs. Every snapping twig, every rustling leaf seemed louder.

"Auluria…" Dov's unexpected voice startled me. I looked over as we walked.

"Silas told me about the interrogation," he said. "I'm sorry they threatened you like that. They never should have scared you with that knife." The dark-haired boy seemed genuinely concerned over what they had done.

"They didn't scare me, Dov," I said as gently as possible "I knew it was coming."

"Oh," he said, unprepared for my words. Then he realized. "They trained you."

"It might have…scared me…but I knew they wouldn't hurt me, Dov. I knew they wouldn't hurt me because you wouldn't have let them. They were testing me to protect you, but they knew if they hurt me, they'd have to deal with you. You would never let them get away with actually hurting me, so they'd never even try," I said, trying to explain how it was my faith in him that spared me that fear.

"I knew they'd never hurt me, because I knew you'd never *let* them. Because that's the kind of man you are.

You're kind and selfless and merciful. You're a good man. You're an incredible man," I concluded.

His eyes softened a bit as I spoke, though he said nothing. But it gave me hope. Hope that maybe someday he'd come back around and give me another chance.

"Dov," I said after a bit, "I know you can't now, but someday, will you…be able to forgive me?"

He stopped walking and looked at me.

"I *do* forgive you. I know why you did what you did, Auluria. You were trying to protect your family. I get that."

"Then why can't you look at me? Why can't you stand to be near me?" I pleaded more than I meant to.

"Because you hurt me. I don't want to go through that again, Auluria. I *can't* go through that again. Not with you." His voice broke on the last word.

"I won't hurt you again," I tried. "I don't ever want to hurt you."

I tried not to cry. I wiped the tears that fell away quickly, hoping he hadn't seen them.

"I know," he whispered.

"You deserve so much better than I gave you. Dov, I'm so sorry." I tried to keep my voice under control, but it was a losing battle. I stopped before I was defeated.

"You deserve better too, Auluria," he said softly after a moment. "Better than I could give you."

Every step, every snap, every rustle was painfully loud.

"I could never find anyone better than you," I finally said.

He closed his eyes but continued walking.

"Just...just tell me that someday we can at least be friends again." I breathed.

"We can be friends again," he answered.

His words made my heart swell and break at the same time.

Chapter 11

We dropped the supplies off at the safe house before going back out. Berwyn and Eden were waiting when we arrived. Their location was the closer of the two, giving Berwyn the shorter route to walk. Eden was organizing the room as we left for our second trip out to gather supplies.

Berwyn sent us to collect more water. We had several containers roped over our arms. Despite being light, they stayed quiet when they bumped together.

Dov made an effort to smile at me when he looked to make sure I was okay. True to his word, he was going to try to get to a place where we could be friends again.

We both perked up when we heard a loud noise

several yards away. The noises kept coming closer. Before we could move, a young boy stepped out from behind a bank of trees. He saw us before we could move.

"Run!" Dov said, dropping the containers.

He grasped my hand and pulled me away, jumping over tree stumps and roots. The boy turned and yelled behind him.

The chorus of noises rose louder as a group of men joined him. Several of the men rode large horses, their hooves stamping as they stood waiting for instructions.

I heard the dogs barking before I saw them. Their masters followed them, clinging to their leashes. The crowd saw us, focusing on our movements.

Dov's head whipped back and forth as he monitored the men and where we were running. We were far enough away that we wouldn't lead the guards back to the safe house, but in the middle of nowhere, we were trapped.

The dogs came first, howling and barking at us. I knew if they reached us, it would only be moments before they tore into our flesh. I clutched Dov's hand tighter, willing us to disappear into the leaf-covered forest floor.

He lifted my hand and stretched it across his chest until I found it resting in his far hand. As he released me into his distant hand, he wrapped his inside arm around my waist and pulled me along, gripping me tightly.

Despite the terror surrounding us, I felt safe in his strong arms.

We ran as quickly as we could, the green leaves blurring around us as we ran. The sunlight filtered through the trees, casting a dappled shadow on every place our feet touched.

Dov lifted me as I slipped on the moss of a rock we were climbing. I shrieked as I felt myself fall. His grip kept me securely at his side though, and he righted me, pulling me forward.

As if we had found our way back to the day we met, Dov and I found ourselves face to face in front of a wide stream. Without hesitation, he ran for it. Our feet left the ground at the same time and we sailed through the air. The wind whipped my hair back, in what I imagine must have been a gloriously golden arc; a banner waving and leading the guards on behind us.

We landed on the other bank, barely making it. Dov and I stumbled and fell, rolling before coming to an abrupt halt. I heard the dogs whining on the opposite shore. They did not follow us.

We stood and began to run. I checked behind us just in time to see the horsemen approaching.

"The horses," I shouted to Dov. He nodded and moved us faster.

Soon the horses had made the leap across the water. Their feet pounded behind us over the uneven terrain.

Their beats synced with my heart rate, moving faster with every moment.

The horses approached us from behind. I felt them drawing nearer until they were right behind us. One scooted up alongside of me, the man reaching down and pulling me from Dov's arms. He dragged me across his lap, pinning me in front of him. The man used one arm to restrain me and the other to direct his horse.

I expected him to slow, but instead, he kept charging forward, eventually circling off to the side. I heard Dov yelling in the distance.

The other horses had not been as fast as the beast beneath me. Under normal circumstances, I would have thought him extraordinary, but when he refused to respond to my gestures, I knew how well he really had been trained.

I prayed the other horses were not fast enough to catch Dov as he ducked under branches and wove through the small spaces between the trees.

The man slowed the horse, still using great force to keep me in place.

"Let me go!" I pleaded. "You're hurting me."

"Too bad, princess. We don't take kindly to traitors." His nose tickled my ear uncomfortably.

"Neither do we," I heard Dov's voice say, followed by a loud thud. Once again, I marveled at how Dov had known exactly where to cut us off and catch us.

The man wrenched to the side, his grip slipping on me. Dov's aim was true and the rock hit the man on the side of the head giving me enough time to elbow him. Between the force of the rock and my elbow, he fell, foot tangling in the stirrup.

Dov launched himself in the air, occupying the remaining foothold. He kicked the animal's side and it leapt forward, his master trailing behind him.

We rode for several minutes, the man eventually untangling himself and falling behind. When we reached a large cliff, we dismounted and sent the horse running off into the distance. Dov and I heard the other horses somewhere behind us.

Together we scrambled up the cliff, the rocks biting into us as we moved along. We reached the top only to find a second, taller cliff stretching out before us, hidden by the trees. Dov offered me his hand and boosted me up. He followed along behind me.

I pulled myself over the edge and waited for him to join me. Glancing around, I looked for the best direction to go in. I heard a gasp of air and ran to the edge.

Dov was hanging from one hand, the rocks under his feet giving out. Dangling precariously, he looked up to me and shouted, "Keep going."

He was insane if he thought I'd leave him there. He tried to swing his body up to catch another handhold but his feet slipped as he tried to find a stable place to push himself up.

"Hold on!" I yelled.

The trees that had blocked our view now offered us the protection of concealment. If I could find a way to get Dov over the edge, we might have a chance at escape.

A broken tree branch looked like the best option. I dragged it over to the edge and lowered it down, warning him to be careful.

"It will pull you down. No," he said, refusing to take it.

"No, it won't, now take it."

"I will not have you getting hurt because of me."

"Dov, you've broken my heart, I really don't think there's too much else you can do to me," I said without thinking. I instantly wished I could take it back.

"And anyway, I'm trained, so come on!" I didn't mention my training had never included anything like this.

He swung his arm up and caught the branch. He pulled back and pushed up with his feet. Though he slipped, the branch was enough leverage to start his ascent. He climbed and I pulled. Together, we worked his way up until he sat on the ground beside me.

"Thank you," he said when he caught his breath.

"We need to go," I answered, pulling him to his feet.

We ran as far as we could, knowing they were coming after us. I prayed they wouldn't think we'd be able to climb the dangerous cliffs. When no one approached us, I decided they had gone another way.

"Dov, stop." I stumbled, pitching forward. "I can't breathe."

As I gasped, he slowed us and lowered me onto a large boulder. He sat beside me, arm still wrapped around my waist.

"Are you okay?" he asked.

I nodded, out of breath.

"How are we going to get back?" I asked.

He shook his head.

"Do we even know where we are?"

"No, I don't think so," he responded.

"What do we do?"

"We find shelter. Those men will give up in a few hours and then we can try to find our way back," he suggested.

He rose to his feet. I must have looked terrified because he came back to me.

"I'm just going to look around. I won't leave your line of sight," he said, trying to comfort me.

I nodded, but I didn't want to.

He moved around in a large circle. He studied the ground, the trees, anything he could find.

"I think we should go this way." He pointed.

I stood and followed him, letting him guide us over the decaying surface. We walked for another few minutes before finding a large overgrown mass of a bush. The leaves were dense. The stems and branches formed a barricade around us, opening in the middle, almost like a little nest just for us.

"You did really good out there today," he said as we settled.

"You too."

He sighed and leaned back on his elbows. I did too and we looked up at the bits of light twinkling through the moving leaves.

"We're going to get through this," he said.

I didn't know if he meant being chased or if he meant *us*.

It was nearly dark before we came out of our hiding place. We took turns resting, the other keeping watch. I told him not to, but I know Dov let me sleep longer than he was supposed to.

The trees were so dense we couldn't see the stars. Only a fraction of the moonlight filtered down to us as we walked. Crickets chirped loudly as we moved. A few fireflies danced around us as we snuck through the night.

Dov helped me across a small creek, its glassy moving water shining where the moonlight hit it. He no longer held me now that we weren't running. The sound of his breathing comforted me and I relaxed as we got closer to our hiding place.

Eventually, Dov had figured out where we were and he could guide us back. We signaled before we walked in so we didn't frighten Eden and Berwyn.

"Where were you?" Eden snapped. "We heard the guards."

"They passed right over us, but they didn't find us," Berwyn informed us.

"Thank goodness," I said.

Dov explained how we had been spotted while we were out. We never had accomplished our goal of gathering more supplies. As he lowered himself onto his mattress I could see he was in pain.

I looked at him, hoping he'd let me help, but he shook his head. I stayed on my own side, giving him space.

"Are you okay?" Eden whispered, coming to sit by me. Her skirt rustled against mine.

"Yeah," I sighed, looking away.

"I'm impressed you pulled him up. That was smart to use a branch and not just reach down."

"Thanks," I said, dejection in my voice.

"He's taking longer than you'd like to come back around, huh?"

Eden was observant.

"Yeah."

"Give it time. He'll get over it," she said, touching my knee.

Eden wasn't ordinarily this kind, and never to me. But she had warmed up to me enough to speak civilly to me, and now the almost kindness she was showing restored some faith in her humanity.

"I'm not so sure. He forgave me, but I don't think we'll ever be okay again," I lamented.

"Auluria." She looked at me. "He is head over heels for you. You messed up and you hurt him, you just have to give him a little time."

"I thought I did."

"You crushed him. So what if he needs a bit more time? Don't you owe him that?"

"I owe him everything."

"So then, stop sulking," she chastised me, the switch throwing me off. "Figure out how to deal with it and let him be. When he's ready he'll come back to you. But until then, knock it off."

She stood and walked back to Berwyn who was sleeping in the corner.

I stared at her as she left, shocked.

Eden was a complicated and confusing woman.

Chapter 12

After four days of being locked up in that tiny space, we all started to go crazy. Berwyn and Eden fought every day. If we had had anything breakable to spare, I'm convinced it would have been shattered.

Dov sat in his corner, scribbling away at something. He rarely looked up, even during the worst part of the fighting. I waited out each verbal storm, braiding and unbraiding sections of my hair.

We hadn't heard the guards again since the first night. Eden and I stayed inside while the men cautiously checked the area. Once they had cleared it, we all stepped outside for fresh air.

It felt good to see the sunlight again. Though it barely peeked through the boughs of the trees, its spotted warmth felt good on my skin. The days were getting cooler as summer ended. I longed to be back at Dov's pond, sitting by the dancing waters with him.

It rained the day before and I could still feel the moisture in the air. It clung to my body and clothes. It invaded my golden locks and refreshed my face. I breathed deeply, letting it reach my very soul.

I wanted to touch everything, to feel the freedom the plants so carefully retained. The bark of a tree felt revitalizing under my hand. Fallen leaves sunk beneath my feet, still wet from the rainfall and the morning dew. I tickled the flowers that grew a few feet from the safe house entrance, running my hands along their undersides causing them to bounce and dance in the glorious morning.

When I turned around, I saw Dov watching me out of the corner of my eye. I couldn't bear to see him turn away, so I was careful not to let him know I saw as I continued my greetings of the environment I found myself in.

The wind picked up and blew my hair in my face, preventing me from being able to see. I struggled to tame it down. The more I tried, the more entangled I became. I was certain I heard Dov smirk. I finally managed to pull my face clear and triumphantly pushed my hair back down. It swung around my waist, hitting my opposite side before resting. I turned into the breeze and it forced my hair back for me.

I picked up my skirt and continued walking on, no longer caring who was watching. I walked as far as I dared, knowing they would call me back and be cross if I strayed too far. I gathered a few blossoms before my return.

Once we stepped out of the wind and into our shelter, I tucked the flowers in my hair. If I was to be condemned to that hole, I at least wanted a little life around me.

Eden raised her eyebrow at me but held her thoughts to herself. I still didn't want to anger her, but I think she was finally starting to get used to me.

On the fifth morning, I woke up and looked around the small room. Eden was sleeping in the corner. Berwyn was in the other room. Dov, however, was nowhere to be found.

"Dov?" I whispered.

I tried again louder, hoping he just hadn't heard me.

"Dov?"

"He's not here," Berwyn said quietly, trying not to wake his wife.

"Where is he?" I couldn't hide the horror in my voice.

"He had something to do. He's fine."

"If he's out there *alone* then he certainly isn't *fine*," I spat back.

"Go back to sleep, Auluria. He'll be back soon."

"Where did he go?" I demanded.

He glared at me, but I wouldn't stop.

"Where is he?"

Eden started to stir and Berwyn came at me fast. I wrenched backward, eyes wide.

"Do not wake her," he commanded, but didn't touch me.

"Where is he?" I whispered.

"Meeting someone."

"Who?" I inquired forcefully.

"It doesn't matter. Leave it be."

"I'm going to find him," I said, standing up and walking toward the exit.

"Oh, no you're not!" He lashed out his arm and caught my hip, dragging me back to the corner. He flung me onto my mattress and pointed his finger in my face.

"If you go out there, you will get yourself killed. You're never going to find him, and in the off chance you happen to catch him coming back while the Society is dragging you away, you know what will happen. So, sit down, shut up, and mind your own business."

I fumed in my corner.

He was right. I had no idea where Dov was. I didn't know when he left. He refused to tell me whom he was meeting, though if I had to guess, I'd bet it was Silas, which offered me a small amount of comfort. I didn't even know how long ago he had left or what direction he was traveling.

Still, waking up to find one of our team members missing was horrifying. I wished Dov had talked to me about it first, just so it wouldn't scare me so. I suppose I forfeited the right to know those things a long time ago, but still, I was there and I should have known.

Waiting has always been a hard thing for me. I'm not good at being patient. After an hour, I was frustrated. Two hours I was furious. Six hours and I was terrified. By nightfall, I was sick with worry. Even Berwyn and Eden were apprehensive.

The knock startled us all. Dov came back in, motioning us to hurry.

"We have to move," he informed us.

"It's bad?" Berwyn asked, pulling sacks from the other room out and handing them to us.

"It's bad," Dov confirmed. "They found a few of us. Lowell's men, the ones that were captured, led them to us, like we knew they would. There have been hangings. The bodies are still swaying from the trees as a warning."

We ran outside into the cool night. Dov and Berwyn led the way.

"It's not just us they are after. They've put a reward out for any rebel. They aren't even asking questions. They interrogate them and then they hang them, guilty or not. Unless they think they're better off sending them to the camps." He glanced back at Eden and me.

He gave Berwyn the names of a few of their group members who had been caught. There was a resolute hardness in his voice, though I know it pained him to talk about it.

After an hour of jogging through the trees, we came to our new resting place. Instead of a small hole in the ground, we found ourselves in one of the other storehouses. Groups of people populated the large space. Families grouped together, huddled in corners.

"We need to be with them to plan," Dov said briefly, the only explanation for the change in venues.

Berwyn and Eden settled in, finding a space on the outer edges for themselves. Dov sat near Silas and a few other young men. I looked around for a place to call my own.

When I found an empty spot near some young girls, I walked over and greeted them.

"Hi," I said tentatively. "I'm Auluria. I need a place to camp out, do you mind if I join you?"

One of the girls looked at me skeptically. The others seemed more friendly.

"Sure," one girl replied to me, moving her blanket to

make room for me, "I'm Reyla. This is Katarina, Maylin, and the unwelcoming one is Sharone." She waved her hand at the girl on the end.

"Thanks," I said gratefully.

"So, you're Dov's new girl, huh?" Reyla asked.

"Something like that," I mumbled.

"Well, it's nice to meet you. Have you all been doing okay since this all happened? I know they like to keep Berwyn and Dov separated."

"We've been all right. We all made it here." I tried to be optimistic.

"So how long have you been with Dov? News doesn't always get around as fast as we'd like." The girls giggled.

"Umm...well, we're not really together right now. I've known him for a bit though. He kind of rescued me while I was being chased." I neglected to mention it had been my own people chasing me as part of a plan to force me into the Baers' lives.

"How romantic," Maylin cooed.

"Only if you count being thrown into some bushes, running around a bunch of trees and then being attacked, yet again, by a couple of thugs, as being *romantic.*"

They all laughed.

"I bet he's a good kisser though, right?" Reyla asked glancing over at him.

Before I could come up with a way to avoid answering, she added, "Is there a particular reason he's *way* over there and you're *way* over here?"

"We had a bit of a fight," I answered, hoping to end the conversation.

"And he let you get away?" She clicked her tongue. "Stupid men, they never know what they have until the girl has moved on."

"Well, there's two ways to handle that," Katarina spoke up. "Either make yourself irresistible and he'll come running to beg for forgiveness."

"I don't think that will work."

"Then make him jealous," Katarina said slyly. "Watch this."

She raised herself up and searched the room before calling out a few names. She waved the boys over to us and they obliged, coming quickly to her side.

As they walked across the room I caught a glimpse of the petite girl from the first raid. She was glaring at me across the room. Her head bobbed back and forth between watching me and watching Dov talk to Silas. When she caught my eye, she grinned wickedly at me and intentionally looked to Dov. I didn't like that girl.

"What's up with Gloria?" Maylin asked.

The girls secretly glanced in the direction of the girl who was trying to murder me with her eyes.

"She likes Dov. And she apparently doesn't like me," I supplied.

"Ahh." It made sense.

The boys sat beside us.

"Auluria, this is Ben, Carter, Gregory, and Henry. Boys, this is Auluria. She's new here."

They all greeted me politely, leaning in as they spoke. They kept their eyes fixed on me as they started asking us questions. Gregory told a joke and we all laughed causing the people around us to stare.

When they suggested we play a game, I attempted to just watch, but they would have none of it. I was forced to take part in their fun and soon I forgot where I was or why I was so sad.

"So, tell us, Auluria, how long have you been with our little group?" Gregory asked, moving a card in his hand.

"Not long. Yourself?" I retorted from across the circle.

"Always." He smiled easily and waited for Katarina to put her card down.

"Most of us grew up in the group," she added, glancing at me. "Some of our families joined more recently, like Carter's family, but we all belong here."

"Your hair is incredibly long," Ben pointed out, his eyes sparkling with mischief. "Was that how you found your way in so easily? Because it caught people's attention?"

"Of course not," I snapped before grinning. "I used it as rope to tie the Baers up and force my way in."

Gregory was the first to erupt in laughter after I winked, betraying my joke. The others joined in.

"It looks like gold, could it possibly be that you're wearing a wig made from spun gold?" Gregory asked, placing another card down and disrupting the balance of the game.

"Yes," I said as sincerely as I could. Again, they erupted with laughter.

"We should cut some of it and sell to the Magistrates," Henry added, "Then we could afford an *above ground* hiding place! And maybe some pretty things for the ladies as well."

I watched as he snuck a glance at Katarina, who had purposely looked away. She truly was good at keeping men guessing.

"Oh, don't listen to them," Maylin said. "Men love girls with long hair. I wish mine was half as pretty as your, Auluria."

"Thank you, Maylin, that's so sweet of you to say." I looked down, fighting the urge to brush my hair back out of my face. "Your hair is lovely too."

She tucked her dark brown locks behind her ear and smiled.

"Tell us more about yourself, Auluria," Ben redirected us.

"Well," I said, laying down my card. "I was raised by my aunt. My parents died when I was young."

"Did you have a good childhood?" he asked, setting down his own game piece.

"It was sheltered," I replied. "Tell me more about all of you. Did you enjoy growing up a part of the group?"

"We grew up learning to fight," Gregory said triumphantly as he won the hand we were playing. "That's why I've always been able to beat these guys. I've learned all their secrets."

"Secrets?" I said pleasantly. "Well, now I need to know *everything* you know!"

"*No!*" Henry shouted, glancing up quickly at us. The girls all giggled as he tried to recover.

"Don't forget, Gregory, we have information on you too that you might not want the lady knowing," Carter challenged him.

"Yeah? Like what? Like the time, I fell down the ravine because I was trying to get that flower for Gloria?" He paused, turning toward me. "Yeah, that's how great of a man I am...I risked my life to get her that flower."

My horror for his accidental attempt to take his own life to impress a girl was washed away as he threw me an over exaggerated wink.

"Oh, be serious, Gregory," Reyla interjected, "it was barely a dip in the ground."

"And he *still* managed to nearly break his ankle," Sharone added with a sarcastic laugh. "All for a girl who wasn't even interested in his attempts to get her attention."

She realized she had brought up the fact that Gloria was still eyeing Dov, despite me being there.

"A dip, huh?" I asked, trying to move on from the heaviness that overtook the group.

"It was a chasm," Gregory said, picking up the conversation. "Don't let them fool you. A *chasm*."

"A *chasm* is what's between your ears, buddy," Henry said, forcing even Gregory to double over with laughter.

"When we were children," Henry began, "Griz used to let us go out on missions. Nothing dangerous, mind you, but he'd send us to collect firewood or food from time to time. After the incident happened, all this changed, of course, but back then we were more free."

I tried to keep from cringing when he referred to Dov's father's death. He continued, not noticing.

"We were out working one day when we stumbled across this guy." He pointed to Carter, who nodded his head. "*Gregory* was on another one of his missions to get a girl's attention…who was it that time, Reyla? Katarina?"

"Reyla," Gregory grinned at her before swinging back to look at me as I listened.

"He nearly broke his neck that time too."

"That was my fault," Carter admitted, a toothy grin plastered across his face. "I thought they were a threat so I attacked. I won."

"You did nothing of the sort!" Gregory bellowed good-naturedly.

"Yes, he did," Henry corrected. "You may have started it, but he whooped you good. I had the good sense to stay out of it in case there were more people with him. When there weren't, I propped Gregory up and found out what was really going on. That's how Carter and his family joined us."

"I had the good sense to use my words before threatening a guy over a handful of berries."

"Could I help it if they were her favorite and only grow up on that crest?" he retorted.

"You like giving gifts, huh?" I questioned.

"All women like gifts, Auluria." He wiggled his eyebrows at me.

"Don't mind him." Reyla swatted at him. "The point is that Carter joined us. And a welcome addition, might I add, since before he came along our options were Gregory or running away from home."

I burst out laughing at the thought of these quiet, kind girls running away from the likes of Gregory trying to pursue them.

"How often would you go on these missions?" I asked.

"Every few days they would send us out in groups. Usually, the older boys had to keep an eye on us because even while it wasn't as dangerous as it is now, it was still something the adults worried about," Henry added.

"Once Griz died, everyone became more serious about our training. We were all younger when it happened. Some of us, those higher up like Dov and Silas, were trained from younger ages. The rest of us started seriously training when everything changed," Ben continued.

"Even the girls know how to defend themselves," Sharone said proudly. "We just all have our places when things happen. Mostly the men fight, though there are some women who have stronger training that work with them. We mostly defend the storehouses and safe houses."

"The battles come to us; the men go to the fights," Maylin summarized.

"I see." It was so different than Lowell's flock.

"We've been exceptional at defending ourselves though. We can get quite creative at finding ways to protect our homes and families." Reyla said proudly. I could imagine Reyla being a strong and inventive leader.

"Like the time Reyla and Katarina thought we were breaking in," Gregory started.

"You *were* breaking in," Reyla corrected.

"It was a training exercise," he threw back at her. "They were making sure the girls knew what to do and had us act as if we were attacking them. At first, they thought it was real."

"It was terrifying," Katarina chimed in.

"But then they realized it was us and it was only training."

I saw both girls smile. I really did like those girls.

"It wouldn't have been any fun if we hadn't played along." Katarina said innocently, tossing a look to Henry. He couldn't take his eyes from her.

"We may have been a little *forceful* with our defense." Reyla shrugged and put her card down.

"*May* have?" Carter nearly yelled, voice raising unnaturally high.

"Really, Carter, you shouldn't take it so personally. It's not like you took the brunt of it," Reyla retorted.

"What did you do?" I asked, unable to keep the excitement from my voice. I leaned forward, dying to know.

"It may have involved warm water."

"*Scalding,*" Gregory interjected.

"*Warm,*" Reyla repeated, "We took it off the fire once we knew it was you."

She rolled her eyes and we laughed.

"You threw water at them?" I giggled.

Katarina and Reyla looked at each other conspiratorially.

"What else did you do?" I was already starting to be able to read these girls.

"It is possible that we had a few buckets of pine sap sitting in the house—" Reyla started.

"The weather was turning," Katarina supplied.

"—and Katarina ran out the back for some leaves and pine needles."

"It was incredible," Katarina added.

"You tarred and feathered them?" I asked incredulously.

"It was marvelous," Maylin laughed. "It took them all day to get it off them. I had to help Ben get it out of his hair and I worked on it for over an hour."

"And then they had to cut the sap out," Sharone finished.

"I wish I had seen that!" I chuckled.

"It couldn't have been better if we had known about it in advance. Dov and Silas had the good sense to stay back and just send these fools in after us," Katarina laughed.

"And they truly deserved it. You should have seen what they had planned for us. They were trying to terrify us," Reyla said.

"When was this?" I questioned, picturing a young Dov and Silas standing back and watching the hilarity.

"A few years ago," Reyla said, before adding quietly, "He was just as handsome back then."

She smiled, knowingly.

"Back when it happened, I thought we were going to lose Berwyn and Dov. We all did. Dov really held Berwyn together. Of course, Berwyn used that anger of his to rally everyone and protect them, but Dov was the one that kept him from destroying everyone in his path."

And took most of Berwyn's wrath.

"He was never particularly close with any of us, but we all know he's a good man. I don't know what happened between you, but I can see neither of you are happy about it," she added quietly.

I sighed, my attention jerked back to the group as they roared with laughter over the way the boys had looked after their encounter with the tree sap. Gregory slapped a card down, proclaiming himself the winner yet again.

"You've got to do better than that if you want to beat me," Gregory roared.

I glanced around at the group, the girls not happy over being defeated again by the boys. I grinned and picked up my cards. I hadn't been focused on winning but I decided it was time I put some effort into the game. I won the next two rounds without contest. Gregory, Carter, Ben, and Henry looked shocked. The girls grinned at me triumphantly. Shrugging my shoulders, I gave them the most innocent look I could.

"This is such a fun game, I only wish I knew of it earlier."

Reyla and Katarina tried to suppress their giggles. Maylin was in wonder of me while Sharone smirked. If Henry hadn't been so busy watching Katarina and grinning, he might have looked as shocked as the other boys.

"Beginners luck," Gregory taunted.

"Of course," I drawled, grinning as I picked up a new set of cards.

I made sure Maylin won the next round. She glowed triumphantly when she laid down her final card.

We continued playing, loudly telling outlandish stories to each other that the group members all shot down noisily. I listened and laughed along with my new friends.

I looked up from the cards I was holding in my hands just in time to see Dov duck his head as if he wasn't looking at the group of us along the far wall. Gloria continued to glower at me silently.

The game went on and on. We played so many times we were surprised when we had to stop to eat. The boys kindly told us not to get up. They brought the food right to us, a picnic on the hard floor of a large storehouse.

Katarina shrieked when Henry knocked over his water container. She clutched at her blankets, keeping them dry. Henry and Carter cleaned up the mess, laughing and making fun of her for yelping. Eventually, she laughed with them and settled back on the floor a few inches closer to Henry.

The next time I looked across the storehouse to where Dov was sitting, he was facing me, leaning against a wall. He turned to Silas, but Silas was watching me too. He gave me a look I couldn't quite read. He never looked away from me, but he leaned over and elbowed Dov. I couldn't read his lips that far away, but he pointed at us. Dov shook his head to him, but then looked at me for just a moment before I looked away.

"Don't look now," Reyla leaned over to me and whispered, "but somebody's looking a little jealous."

I refused to look at him. If he wanted to stare, let him. He made the choice not to sit with me, so I would have fun with my new friends and if he wanted to join us, he could.

The card games ran into the night. Once the groups started settling down we had to disband so we didn't keep them up. We decided to play again the next day if circumstances allowed. By the end of the night, even Sharone seemed to accept me.

The next morning, we all lined up for breakfast. We walked the aisles on the near side of the storehouse where everything had been moved and condensed.

I felt someone sidle up next to me, but I didn't look up as I reached for some fruit far across the table. A hand rose in the air next to me, holding an apple to me. As I turned I saw Dov standing beside me, elbow pinned to his side, hand by my shoulder, offering me the fruit he knew I so enjoyed.

He didn't look at me, he didn't even turn, but he held it out to me and I graciously took it from him. I smiled even though I wasn't sure he could see me. He moved on, going his separate way as I went mine.

The boys joined us again on the floor to share breakfast. Ben and Carter regaled us with stories from their heroic past missions. Henry found his way to Katarina's side once again.

"Pst," Reyla whispered and motioned me to lean closer.

I leaned in, tucking myself to her side. She moved my hair off my shoulder and rested her chin on it as she whispered to me.

"Some of the boys want to know what's going on with you and Dov." Her green eyes sparkled as she pulled back to see my reaction.

"You know, I don't know how to answer that," I responded.

"Well, you might want to figure it out soon, because there is some interest." She waited for me to say something. When I didn't, she leaned back in. "Figure it out, or I'll ask Dov *for* you."

She giggled as I swatted at her. I knew she would never actually talk to Dov, but she did so love to tease me about it.

"What about you? Which of these nice boys is going to end up on your arm?" I asked mischievously.

"None of them," she said proudly.

"Oh? And why is that?" I raised my eyebrows to her.

"I already have a man, thank you very much. He's just not here in the storehouse."

"Now I simply *must* know," I giggled, grabbing her arm.

It was nice having female friends. I was orphaned so young and my aunt kept a very protective watch over me. Even though Lowell had women in his group that flitted throughout my life, I mostly spent time with Lowell or Shadoe in training. I talked to some of the girls, but never about anything fun or social. Lowell had his throngs of obsessed girls coming and going, but he never had anyone serious in his life, so I didn't even have those examples to see.

Reyla told me about a boy named Peter that she had known her entire life. He was tall with brown hair and green eyes like hers. He was kind to her and took care of her, but their families were separated when we went into hiding. Everyone was assigned different locations. He sounded wonderful and I was excited to meet him one day.

Some of the younger children wandered over to us when they heard us laughing that morning. Gregory's stories became more amusing each time he told them. The children sat in our laps and played with our hair. They were particularly fascinated with my long locks.

"What's your name?" I asked the little girl raking her fingers through my mane behind me.

"Jaseleen," she said softly, grinning at the ground. "I think you're beautiful."

"Well, thank you, Jaseleen. I think you're beautiful too." I thought for a moment. "Jaseleen, would you like me to do your hair?"

The young girl nodded quickly and came to sit in front of me. I brushed my fingers through her light blonde hair. I forgot how soft children's hair could be. I hummed to her as I worked, letting my fingers take a relaxing pace. I twisted little pieces back and added some small braids, creating an intricate design.

After a while, several other small girls joined us and my new friends took turns dedicating their experience to each girls' hair. The girls squealed with delight as they sat before us. Their mothers offered us silent thanks for the break we were giving them.

Silas nearly scared me when he walked up alongside of me. He placed a large pile of flower blossoms next to me.

"Special delivery," he said quietly.

I looked down to see the flowers on the floor next to me. Catching his eye, I must have looked inquisitive because he offered me a further explanation.

"He thought you might like these for the girls."

I couldn't hide my smile.

Silas grinned back. He stood to leave, but knelt back down.

"You know you're driving him crazy, right?"

"What do you mean?" I asked.

"He's been watching you since you arrived at the storehouse. He can't stop talking about you. I know he's the one keeping you apart, but just go talk to him and tell him to get over it. He wants you back."

Silas stood and threw a wink over his shoulder before he left.

"You're so lucky you get to marry Dov," said a slightly older girl who was sitting in front of Reyla.

My jaw dropped open as I turned to look at her. Before I could stay anything, Reyla jumped in, "Yes, she is."

The two giggled as I shook my head. I finished Jaseleen's hair and tucked several flowers in it. She skipped off to show her mother who waved at me from across the storehouse.

When I turned my attention back to Reyla and her charge, I found them discussing the magnetic draw of Dov's masculine features. Somehow, I had managed to tune them out while I was working and now I was even more embarrassed to reenter the conversation.

I scooped up the flowers next to Reyla and started tucking them in the young girl's hair.

"This one really brings out your eyes," I said placing it behind her ear. "Tell me, do you have a special boy?"

She shook her head and giggled. "I'm too little, silly."

Reyla finished her hair and sent her back to her family.

"It was kind of Dov and Silas to send the flowers over," she mentioned. "What do you think made them think of that?"

"I wore flowers the other day. I suppose Dov noticed."

She lightly bumped into me with her shoulder. I bumped her back, rolling my eyes, and smiled happily.

Chapter 13

Berwyn called a meeting that afternoon. All the men joined him on one side of the room. The women, even those who fought alongside the men, were left to care for the children and straighten up the storehouse. Once a plan had been decided on, the women would be brought into the conversation.

I walked with the girls around the tables filled with food and supplies. We organized and straightened every pile. Any food that was going bad was discarded.

The men stopped for dinner, putting their conversation on hold. I found Dov off to the side, waiting for his group to get their food first. I took a deep breath and walked up to him.

"Thank you for the flowers this morning. The girls really loved them.

"No problem," he said and offered me a genuine, lazy smile. His eyes told me he was telling the truth.

I wanted to hug him; to thank him for noticing. I almost restrained myself. Almost.

I closed the distance between us and wrapped my arms around his waist, pressing the side of my face against his chest. I only held him for a heartbeat, but it was enough time for him to freeze just slightly before giving in and wrapping his arms around me. I pulled back first, not wanting to press my luck.

I smiled again and turned to leave. I caught Silas's face from the food line. His smile twisted into a smirk, but his eyes cast a questioning look at one of us. He sighed and looked back down at the food table, shrugging heavily.

Silas had a lot to say to one of us.

"Silas wants to know if you did what he asked you to do yet," Maylin ran up to me after dinner.

"Silas needs to take care of *himself*," I replied. She looked as if I had struck her.

"I'm sorry, Maylin. I'm just a little frustrated with Silas right now. He's not exactly being helpful."

She looked unsure.

"He's waiting for you to go back, isn't he?"

She nodded.

"Tell him I did not and that I'm not going to do what he asked of me."

She sighed, shoulders sagging. She clearly didn't want to deliver the bad news. She walked back to him. I turned so I didn't have to watch.

"She likes him," Reyla wandered up beside me.

"Yes, I saw that." I felt myself smile a bit.

With our backs to them, we talked.

"Why doesn't he ask her out?" I asked.

"He's a lot like Dov. They don't just date to date. They flirt with all the girls, but they never commit to any of them. It takes a lot to win those two over. We were all actually pretty surprised when you did it so quickly."

I ignored her.

"How long have they been friends? Dov and Silas?"

"For as long as I can remember," Reyla answered.

"They're good together."

"They are," she agreed.

"Well, come on," I said, turning on my heels. Maylin had stepped away from Silas and I marched us in his direction.

"Where are we going?" she protested.

"To set Silas straight." I grinned.

We marched up to Silas and I halted right in front of him.

"Auluria?" he asked curiously.

"Silas. We need to talk."

"Oh, good. I've been waiting to talk to you." He grabbed my arm and spun me to the side, leading me away.

I motioned Reyla to follow us, Silas looked a bit surprised to see her when he stopped. I cut him off before he could speak.

"You should ask Maylin out," I stated. "She's lovely and she would be very good for you."

"I'm not interested in Maylin," he said. "I am, however, very interested in you and Dov. Or rather, I'm interested in getting you back together so he can focus again."

"Dov's focusing just fine," I retorted. "*You*, however, need to find something to occupy your time. If it's not Maylin, then who is it going to be?"

I started looking around the room trying to find an alternate solution.

"Auluria, we're not talking about me."

"Well, I'm done talking about me. So, choose or I'll do it for you," I said, frustration in my voice.

He shook his head, clearly annoyed with me, and started to walk away. He froze in his tracks when a shout rose near the entrance.

"The southern storehouse has been discovered!" a boy shouted. "They've taken them."

The room was so still for a moment that I could almost hear the breeze moving as the announcer moved further into the room. Someone dropped something that bounced and rolled across the floor. A collective gasp filled the air as everyone remembered to breathe again.

"No one move," Berwyn commanded as he walked quickly to the center of the room. His face was alive with checked fury. As he turned away from me, hiding his face, he looked exactly like an older, slightly taller version his younger brother.

I glanced around looking for Dov. He stood along the sidewall, looking like he was itching to join his brother. He waited to be motioned over. An angry glare from Berwyn told us both he should have followed. Silas quickly joined him at Berwyn's side along with a few of the other men in leadership I had met.

"We're going to rescue them. Most of the men will come with us and some of the women. There will be a small group of men staying here. These men will be responsible for taking care of the storehouse and the people still here. They will also be the second wave if we fail. Most of the women will stay here. All young children will remain in the storehouse. Do not argue with where you are assigned."

"Men, over here," Berwyn motioned them to the far corner. "Women, we will come find you if you have been selected to join us. You can say no if you want, we won't hold it against you."

I watched as Berwyn separated the men. He held a small group out, the group to defend the storehouse. I watched as several of the men walked away from the group going to find the women that would be involved. None of the selected women were small or young. They were clearly well trained and knew what they were doing.

"Dov." I reached out and pulled on his arm as he passed me. "I want to go."

"It's too dangerous," he said, shrugging me off.

"No, it's not. I'm trained for this, remember? Besides, this is Lowell's fault, I have to do something."

"You're right. It's Lowell's fault. But that doesn't make it your responsibility." He shook me off again and walked away.

Silas was only a few steps behind him and had heard the entire conversation.

"I'm going," I told him as he slowed near me. I forced him to stop.

"Find me something else to wear," I said, shaking my dress skirt, "or I will."

He said nothing as he walked away, but I knew he

would do that for me. I knew he would do it because he had no choice. I was going whether he or Dov wanted it or not, and if he didn't help me, Dov wouldn't be happy to find I had died because I was tangled in my dress.

Twenty minutes later a pair of trousers and a shirt appeared next to my blankets. Reyla and the girls provided cover for me as I changed.

"I want to come too," Reyla announced, leaning close to my ear.

"No, Reyla, the only reason I'm going is because I'm actually trained. It's dangerous out there and there's a very high likelihood it won't end well."

"Why are you doing this, Auluria? For Dov? He'll be fine, he can take care of himself. You need to stay safe."

"Reyla." I took her elbows in my hand. "I'm not doing this for Dov. He can take care of himself. I'm doing this because Lowell is my cousin and he got us into this mess. I have to try to fix what he did."

"Lowell is your cousin?" She sounded horrified.

"Yes," I confirmed.

I could see her trying to process the information.

"What Lowell did is awful, but I have to try to stop it, or at least help," I said. "I can't let people get hurt because Lowell framed you all. So, I'm going. And if I died, no one will miss *Lowell's cousin* here," I said, trying to ease her mind.

"I will," she announced. "I will miss you." She threw her arms around me in a tight embrace.

"Thank you, Reyla. I'll miss you too," I said, hugging her back. She was my first real friend.

"Now, you girls have to help me get to the door when it's time," I said a bit louder.

I couldn't allow Dov to see me follow them out. Once I got to the door, I could blend in with the crowd. It was night, so the world would be dark. If I kept away from him, he'd never know. I just had to make it to the door without him knowing. The second he saw me wearing anything but my dress he would know and he'd force me to stay. I knew I'd never catch up if they left before me.

As the departure drew near, the girls quietly slipped toward the doorway. It took half an hour just to cross the room without anyone being suspicious. We stood near the exit, just far enough back to not be noticed.

I felt someone behind me as I waited. He pressed something into my hand before leaving my side. Two cold knives lay in my palm. I slipped one in my belt and the other in my boot.

The men departed. I saw Dov search the crowd for me. I hid myself behind my friends, using their dresses to cover my clothing. They all waved goodbye. When Dov couldn't find me, he stalled, hovering at the doorframe.

"She's there," I heard a sad, defeated voice said. I

looked across the people-formed walkway to find Gloria pointing me out to Dov.

He caught my eye and was visibly relieved to see me. He gave me a small smile and a nod before walking away. Before he left, he mouthed the words "I'm sorry" to me.

As the last few men walked out of the room, the girls pulled back and let me escape out with them. No one noticed as I ran alongside the men.

The group moved quickly, led by Berwyn. A scout ran ahead. I could see Silas searching for me but he hadn't found me yet. Dov had no idea I was among the crowd.

My plan had only extended as far as finding a way out of the storehouse, and so far, I had succeeded beautifully. If only Lowell and Shadoe could have seen my plan come together. They surely would have been impressed.

I hated that I still wanted to impress them.

No one seemed to notice as I filtered my way through the crowd, settling somewhere in the middle of the pack. We stopped at a rendezvous point where we were greeted by one of the early scouts Berwyn sent out.

The man shared his information with the group and Berwyn and Dov formed a plan. A few men had joined us from one of the other storehouses, but Berwyn had ordered most of the people to stay in place.

Berwyn walked around, separating us into groups. I prayed he couldn't see faces in the dim moonlight. He lingered in front of me and I knew he noticed. He paused only slightly, deciding what to do, before adding me to a group. I breathed a sigh of relief.

Silas was in my group and I was silently grateful I knew at least one of the people with whom I'd be fighting. Silas'ss group and Berwyn's groups were responsible for breaching the facility where they were holding our people. Dov's group and a few others would then follow behind to free the captives. I was grateful to be among the first wave. It was the deadliest of the jobs, and if someone had to die for Lowell's mistakes, it was better that it would be me.

I stayed hidden behind my groupmates. Whenever Dov came near, I ducked my head, hiding my long hair from him. He wasn't anticipating that I be there, so he wasn't looking for me. If I could blend in, he was unlikely to know.

"Did you tell her?" I overheard Silas ask.

"No," Dov said, sadness in his voice.

"Why didn't you say anything before we left?" he asked, a harshness in his voice. Silas knew I was there—he was doing this on purpose.

"I was leaving her...again. I couldn't do that to her. It

will be a miracle if we come back from this, you know that. I couldn't put her through that." I wanted to run to him, but I held my ground.

"You care about her. You didn't even say goodbye."

"She knows I care about her." His voice was ragged.

"What if we don't make it back? What then?"

"She'll be okay. She's strong. She's the strongest person I know," Dov said. Silas waited, making Dov fill the empty space.

"Auluria is amazing, for all her faults, she has handled this entire situation incredibly. She helped us, she warned us, and she's trying to make things right. I haven't made that any easier on her."

"You were hurt," Silas supplied.

"But I shouldn't be ignoring her like I am. She deserves better. I just…I didn't want to go through that again, not with her. I couldn't lose her again. I couldn't survive if I lost her."

"So, what are you going to do about it?" Silas prompted. I didn't like that Dov didn't know I could hear him, but Silas was trying to make a point. I shouldn't do anything stupid.

"I don't know," he paused. "What if I can't get back to her? What if I can't tell her how sorry I am. I never should have let it get this far. What if she never knows?"

"She knows," Silas assured him.

Morning was approaching. The sky turned its tender

grey color before the world was alight with color. The early morning birds started their trilling notes, piercing the sky. Soon it would be light and soon I would be discovered.

Dov and Silas walked off a few feet before splitting apart. We continued our journey into the town. The sun was just rising as we crossed over into our enemy's hands.

Chapter 14

Despite my best efforts, I found myself at the back of my group as we started toward the facility. I tried to blend in, but there's only so many ways to hide my long hair.

"No," I heard a loud whisper as we walked away.

Without thinking I looked back. Dov was staring at me, horrified. "No!" he shouted.

He rose from his hiding place to follow, but the man next to him—my former interrogator—slammed him back down, holding him in place.

I nodded to him as he struggled, letting him know it was okay. I had resigned myself to my fate, already having made peace with losing him, and gave him a small placid smile to reassure him it was the right choice.

"It's too late," I heard the man say as I turned to run.

I stopped thinking in that moment and focused only on my movements. Left foot, right foot. Watch that rock. Turn down the street. Head up. Check ahead. No one behind. Move forward. Speed up. Lift feet. Don't stop. Twenty yards. Ten yards. Ten feet. Breech the door. Wait, take out the guard.

A man ran at me, weapon in hand. I reached for my knife resting in my belt. I grabbed for his wrist with my free hand, blocking the knife from coming down on me. Before I could move, a man next to me had pierced the guard. He fell to the ground, blood pouring from his chest wound.

I stepped around him and moved closer to the entrance. A woman sidled up next to me. We stood back to back, protecting each other. "Dov's girl?" she asked. I nodded and she nodded back.

I elbowed a man in the face as he ran at us. He stumbled back as another, taller man approached. He lashed out with his foot, kicking me in the thigh. I crumpled in front of him. The woman was ripped from my side.

Alone, I found myself on the ground, reeling from a second kick to the abdomen. I groaned, trying to roll over. Amazingly I kept the knife firmly pressed into my hand.

I tried to right myself as a third blow was coming, but

it never connected. Silas had tackled the man and they rolled on the dirt ground. I moved closer to help, pulling the man away from him. The man turned on me, giving Silas enough time to escape. He took him out with a knife to the back. I watched the life go out of his cold eyes.

I heard the group breaking through the entrance. I saw a guard running to the sound and I took off after him. Silas missed my arm to hold me back. I raced toward him and leapt at him. Landing against his back, I knocked the man to the ground. My fist connected with the side of his face with a sickening thud.

He rolled over on top of me, but I kept the momentum going and straddled him. The large man reached for my throat, but my knife caught his wrists. I held his neck long enough to knock him out.

I watched as the men breeched the door. I hesitated before entering. The early morning sun made everything glow golden as I cast my gaze around the scene outside. I saw the woman who had once stood with me, now dead on the ground, her eyes still open. We had lost a vast part of our small force that morning and we had only just begun.

Inside the facility, we encountered more guards. Our

second wave had followed behind us and we spread out. One of the groups waited outside for the guards that would surely be coming to stop the chaos.

Some of the captives were Lowell's men. I recognized them from my training. Others I had never seen before. They all screamed to us, begging for help. Men and women reached through the bars of their cells, praying for rescue.

I searched the body of a guard for keys but came up empty-handed.

"Silas, how do we get them out?" I asked.

He looked frantically around the room.

"Auluria!" a deep, frightened voice shouted.

I turned to see a red-haired boy gesturing to me.

"Pick the lock!" he demanded, pointing to his cell lock.

"What?" I questioned.

"Pick it. Didn't Shadoe ever show you how to pick a lock?" Lowell's soldier asked incredulously.

Shadoe had never taught me, but I had seen him do it before. I looked around for something to use. When I finally found the small pieces of metal I rushed to a cell and tried to open it.

"This isn't working," Silas said after a few minutes, stress filling his usually even voice.

"Almost," I said.

Click.

The door opened.

The people ran out. Silas directed them to the exit where the runner group was waiting to escort them to the woods. I moved on to the next door. Silas was standing at the next cell trying to take the bars off their hinges.

After what seemed to be an eternity, we had set an entire room free. Someone found a key and Silas managed to open several of the other cells. People ran for their lives as we worked to free more people; ours, Lowell's and other unfortunate souls who were trapped there.

The fighting that erupted nearly caused me to jump. I heard the click and stepped back, releasing the prisoners. Silas looked to me and we both knew: they were coming.

The guards rushed into the room, seizing Silas and me. They wrenched our arms behind our back and restrained us. The more we struggled the more painful it became.

We were marched through the building. With every step, my captor held me tighter.

"The camps are lovely this time of year. I have a feeling that you won't find out though. You're going to die pretty, little, lady. But don't worry, we have a special demise for lovely young things like you."

As if to prove his point, I felt a sharp pain in my arm. Blood trickled down my flesh, inching its way toward my wrist. He blew air against the hair on my neck, moving it slowly up and down my skin, making me cringe.

Every muscle in my body tensed. This coming interrogation would be worse than the last one I went through and these people wouldn't hesitate to hurt me.

"Don't you touch her!" Silas struggled, overhearing the conversation.

They hit him between his shoulder and neck, forcing him to stumble.

"No!" I shouted, fighting to get to him.

"Let her go, she's a girl, she has no idea what we forced her to do," he tried again.

"Don't," I said, warning him to stop.

I had chosen to do this. Nothing was going to stop them anyway.

The guards formed a barrier around us. The fighting continued around us, but they wanted at least a few captives alive to be examples. Our people couldn't reach through their barrier of bodies as they made their way through the building.

As we reached the outside, I discovered the sun higher in the sky. The days were cooling down, but it was still warm enough to be nice out. The sun felt good on my skin and I arched up into it, knowing it would probably be for the last time.

I heard footsteps running behind us but I couldn't see what was happening. Silas locked eyes with me, silently telling me how sorry he was that he couldn't protect me. *I was the one who was sorry I couldn't protect him.*

A small explosion rocked the ground behind us. Several of the guards with us were injured. Silas moved into action faster than I did. His elbow cut into his captor's face, forcing him back. I stepped as hard as I could on my captor's foot and threw my elbow into his stomach. As I whipped around, I slammed the heel of my palm into his nose. Then I jerked back, punching him one more time. Silas took his man out and latched on to mine, throwing him to the ground.

He reached around my waist, pulling me protectively behind him. I watched for only a moment before I collected myself and turned my back to him.

"They really *did* train you well," he shouted to me above the chaos.

"I told you I could handle it," I replied.

We fought off a few more offenders before running. Several more explosions rocked around us and I couldn't help but think they were meant to aid us.

Silas hid me behind him once again as we were attacked by more guards. With our backs to the woods, if we could just rid ourselves of the men before us, we could easily disappear.

The man closest to us was suddenly flying through the air.

"Go!" Dov shouted as he tackled the man.

I tried to rush forward to help Dov, but Silas shoved me back. I watched as Dov wrestled with the man.

"Dov!" I shrieked when the man pulled the knife. Silas was stronger than I was and he shoved me toward the trees.

"Go!" he demanded, pushing me one last time before running to help his friend.

I ran toward the trees several steps before doubling back. I knew if either of them saw me, they'd try to stop me before helping each other. I kept myself hidden, waiting. Only a moment later, I launched myself toward them, striking at the man closest to me. My spare blade was in my hand, no longer hidden in my boot. He wasn't expecting me and he went down easily.

"You need to go!" Dov struggled to speak. A guard was clutching at his throat.

I picked up a large rock and brought it down to the man's skull. He rolled off Dov and I helped him to his feet.

"I'm not leaving you," I said defiantly.

Dov pulled the man away from Silas. He fell to the ground, unmoving. Silas and Dov fought off the last two men. One ran, unwilling to challenge us.

We turned toward the woods, carnage in our wake.

Chapter 15

"What were you thinking?" Dov demanded when we were far enough away.

"I needed to help," I replied as coolly as I could. He was looking for a fight.

"You could have died."

"Better *me* than someone Lowell set up," I snapped, suddenly angry.

"He *did* set you up, Auluria, don't you see that?"

"Of course I see that, but it doesn't change the fact that it's my responsibility to fix his mess. I'm sorry it's yours too, but it shouldn't have to be. He did this, not you."

"Not you either," Silas interjected, but at our snapping glares, he retreated a few steps.

"Thank you for protecting her," Dov quieted, turning to his friend.

"She saved me too," he said. "You should have seen her, Dov, she set a lot of those people free. She picked the cell locks. If it weren't for her, half of them would still be in there."

The group had scattered. When the prisoners were set free, they were escorted to the woods where they ran for safety. Those that survived the attempt to rescue our people also scattered. Eventually we were to meet back at the storehouse if we weren't followed. Many of our people died.

Dov dragged his hands across his eyes. He was frustrated, grateful, worried and angry.

"It was the right choice, Dov, and you know that," I said.

He didn't respond.

We moved in silence for a few minutes.

"I heard you," I finally said. "Before the rescue. I heard what you said about me."

The realization that Silas had known washed over him.

"You knew. And you didn't tell me," he said quietly, angrily.

"I had to keep you both safe. She was coming whether

we liked it or not. I knew keeping you separated was the only way of keeping you both alive."

"And he also knew making me listen to you would keep me from being reckless," I added. "Don't be mad at him. I forced his hand. He was right, we all would have died if you had tried to stop me and I came anyway."

We had successfully reasoned with him. He didn't fight us on it anymore.

We walked in silence again. After a bit, Dov let out a loud, long, ragged breath before lurching his body around and snatching me into his arms.

He pressed his forehead to mine and closed his eyes tightly.

"I can't lose you, Auluria. I can't."

He held me tightly, frozen in time.

I reached up and stroked his temple. Wrapping my free arm around him, I pulled him close.

"I know," I whispered.

He moved one hand up my back until his was touching my neck and shoulder. He pulled me into the hollow of his neck, leaning down to place his head in mine. He hugged me as a child would hug his mother after being away from her for a long time. Dov clung to me, clutching me closer still. The weight of his entire body was on me, giving all his worry, stress and terror to me. I took it gladly.

I cradled him in my arms, my broken love.

"We need to keep moving." Silas broke us apart.

Dov breathed in, remembering himself, and lifted himself away from me. He kept me tucked between him and Silas as we walked, protecting me from any oncoming dangers.

At some point, he noticed the cut on the fleshy part of my forearm. The long, shallow slice had since stopped bleeding and was now crusted over with deep red. Both Silas and I kept quiet about how it came to exist. I was grateful he spared me that conversation.

Every noise alerted us as we walked back to the store-house. We didn't know who had survived the rescue attempt. None of us had seen Berwyn after the initial assault.

Dov heard the change in the environment first. He stiffened beside me, listening. Silas and I heard it at the same time and turned to look.

"Run!" a voice called to us. A tall blond man came crashing out of the bushes toward us.

He tackled something in a bush at our sides. A guard fell beneath him, tumbling from his hiding place. We had walked into an ambush. The man wrestled with the guard, a blur of motion I could barely follow.

Silas ran to his aid as Dov scooped me behind him, scanning the entire area, pinning me against his back. A fist collided with a face, but I couldn't tell whose because Dov had turned me around in his effort to secure the perimeter.

When I was finally facing the attacker once again, both he and the man lay lifeless, draped over the tangled roots of a large tree. Silas stood, closing his friend's eyes and joining us again.

"Who was he?"

"His name was Peter," Silas said quietly.

That blond boy, tall and strong and brave, had saved us. He had given his life to protect us, something he didn't have to do.

"Wait," I gasped.

Both boys looked at me. "Was he dating Reyla?"

"Oh, Auluria, I'm sorry. Reyla is your friend," Dov sighed as he realized the connection.

"Oh no," I breathed, stepping backward.

My heart broke for my new friend. The man she loved was dead. She was alone and she didn't even know it yet. She was alone, and it was partly my fault.

All I ever brought was misery.

"This was not your fault," Dov said as if reading my mind.

"I know." I was unconvincing.

"He saved us all. He would have done it for anyone. Peter was a good man."

"Auluria," Silas interjected, "we'll help you tell her. She won't blame you for this."

"I know she won't. That almost makes it worse," I said quietly.

I walked over to Peter's still form. I sank gently to my knees by his side. It was easier to function in the trousers Silas had procured for me than in one of my dresses. I reached gently around his neck and unclasped the medallion that lay crooked on his chest. I placed in it my pocket for Reyla.

"Thank you," I whispered. "She'll know what you did."

An even more oppressive air hung around us as we continued moving toward the storehouse. Peter's death had cast a lingering shadow over our escape. We all knew we had lost people in the rescue attempt, but this was more directly personal to us all.

It was nearly dark when we finally found ourselves nearing the storehouse. I was exhausted from the trek, and so were the boys. My arms hung lifelessly at my sides, weighing me down.

Silas led us in, Dov following after me. The entire

storehouse fell silent. A collective sigh rang out, several people rushing toward us. I let someone slip a blanket around my shoulders and lead me down the incline into the main area.

I felt myself being guided to the floor and I didn't resist. My legs gave out below me as I settled onto a blanket. Dov and Silas rested next to me. Several others who had left with us had already returned and were waiting with us. The group surrounded us, asking for answers, wanting information, and offering their assistance.

We all needed time. The three of us sat silently, remembering the details of the day. Many of the rescued were among us, resting quietly on the floor. The little girl, Jaseleen, ran up to me and threw herself in my arms. She let my tears fall in her hair as she clung to my neck. I stroked her locks and rocked her until she was nearly asleep.

Slowly my tears ceased and I found Eden by my side. Jaseleen awoke and ran back to her mother after petting my arm one last time.

"Berwyn's okay," she said quietly. "He's just not here. He had to help another group."

I could see the relief on Dov's handsome face. I was grateful too. He might not treat Dov the way he should, but Dov loved him.

Eden lifted my arm from my lap, inspecting my wound.

"Later," I said quietly, indicating I would explain at some point.

People still straggled in, having escaped the guards and made their way back. Silas and Dov relayed the information we could give the group. They told us what they knew. Once the group had given us some space, I motioned Reyla over.

"Are you okay?" she asked, worry written on her face.

"I have something to tell you," I said, tears threatening to break once again.

She sat in front of me and let me take her hands in mine.

"Reyla, something happened." My voice broke.

She studied my eyes, processing what she saw. Confusion, questioning, understanding, realization.

"Peter," she whispered.

I nodded, tears rolling down my face. Reyla's green eyes filled and poured over. I reached for her and held her as she sobbed. Once we calmed, Silas filled in the missing information. She held me tighter. Dov and Silas watched us, pity in their eyes.

I gave her Peter's necklace and she held it tightly in her hand. We fell asleep next to each other, still crying together over the loss. The last thing I saw was Dov placing a blanket over me.

Chapter 16

Everything felt fuzzy when I awoke. I found myself curled around a tangled blanket. I was facing Reyla, her face still wet with tears, though her breathing was deep.

I moved to untangle myself from my cloth confines only to find my hand pinned behind me. Dov's hand was placed in mine, our fingers woven together. I smiled, pain coursing through my facial muscles.

When I successfully freed myself, I crept away from the people I cared about. Making my way over to where Eden slept, I knelt by her.

She opened her eyes as I gently touched her shoulder.

"Eden?" I whispered. She inhaled deeply and sat up, nodding.

We scooted away from as many people as we could, trying not to disrupt their sleep.

"So, what happened to your arm?" she asked, turning my wrist in her hand.

"A guard got me. Silas and I were caught and they decided they wanted to frighten me. It's nothing."

She gave me a skeptical look but kept quiet.

"Dov saved us."

"You're lucky. If they had succeeded, you would have been in a lot of trouble. Getting caught is always bad, but being a pretty young girl is much worse, especially if they think you're a leader."

"They think I'm a leader?"

"You set all those people free. You were one of the few women there." Eden cocked her head at me. "They think you're a leader. And if they ever find out you're connected to Dov or Berwyn or even me, it's going to be bad for you."

"I suppose you're right," I replied, considering her words.

"I'm impressed you're still wearing *those*," she commented, gesturing to my clothing.

"Oh," I said, glancing down. "I was so tired I didn't even notice."

"Makes it easier to work in, doesn't it?"

"It really does," I replied. "I take it you've tried it?"

"On more than one occasion." She looked around the room at the people starting to wake. "You might want to change before they notice."

I took her advice, preferring my long flowing dress to the trousers anyway. Walking back to my resting place on the floor, I procured a bowl full of food for us to eat. I settled my skirt around me and set the bowl down just as Reyla and the boys were opening their eyes.

"Thanks, Auluria," Silas mumbled, rubbing his eyes.

Dov reached out and took an apple from the bowl.

"Reyla, you have to eat," I said soothingly. "Please?"

I forced her to eat, though she clearly didn't want to. Katarina, Maylin, and Sharone came and brought her back to her place by them. They sat soothing her, rubbing her back and murmuring soft words to their mourning friend.

"You handled that very well last night, Auluria," Silas assured me.

Dov offered me a kind smile and I felt more at ease.

"Do we have a plan yet?" I asked.

They turned to look at me, unsure of what I meant.

"We got our people back." I paused. "Well, some of them, but what are we going to do now? The Society is coming for us and they aren't happy."

Just as I finished speaking, Berwyn walked in, two men flanking him.

"Dov, Silas." He called, motioning them.

I stood with them. Instinctively Dov reached for my hand and pulled me along.

"No," Berwyn said when he saw me.

"Yes," Dov insisted. "She's lived with us, ate our food, slept in our house, she's fought with us, and she's protected us. She is a part of this and she stays."

They stared each other down, Berwyn giving Dov that terrifying look. I was so afraid he might strike him that I nearly started trembling. In the end, Dov won.

"We know what Lowell planted. You were right, Auluria." Berwyn turned to me. "They were in the house that day."

Dov looked to me apologetically.

"They stole some of your father's belongings. The ones you had hidden away in your house," one of the men said to Dov.

"We didn't think to check the hidden compartments," Dov murmured. "Nothing else was out of place or missing."

"Griz's paw," Silas said.

"His what?" I was confused.

"Dad always wore a chain around his neck with a medallion on it. It was a bear paw...because his name was Griz Baer. It was his symbol of sorts," Dov explained.

"They hung it with a confession saying it was retribution for hanging Dad," Berwyn explained. "They started a war using our father's name."

"That explains why they're being so quick to hang us." I hadn't meant to speak out loud. The men looked at me and suddenly I felt like a child who had spoken out of turn.

"So, what are we going to do?" Dov asked, deflecting their looks from me. "If we don't fight, we're siding with the officials. If we *do* fight, we're taking respon-sibility."

"We have to draw a line somehow. We need to find a way to show it was Lowell, not us, who started this violence. But we also need to protect our people," Silas reasoned.

"Exactly," the taller of the two men said.

"Auluria, you know Lowell best," Berwyn started.

"Are you sure about that?" I muttered. He ignored me.

"What can we do? What is his weakness? Did he ever say *anything* that could help?"

I tried to think back to my time with my cousin. Most of what he said to me was about lessons on my training. He usually didn't discuss his plans with me, just what I needed to know to carry them out.

I must have looked like I was trying too hard to puzzle something out and was failing because Dov inter-rupted my thoughts.

"I'll work with her. Keep trying to figure out a way to show them it wasn't us."

He pulled me away from the group and took me to the far corner. Everyone moved away and gave us space to work.

"Sit back, Auluria." He motioned me to move back. "Just close your eyes and go through everything. Conversations, training, even things your...*handler* said."

There it was. His jaw clenched and he couldn't look me in the eye. He was still angry about Shadoe.

"Dov," I started to say.

"It's fine, Auluria." But his voice said he was anything *but* fine.

"I never wanted to be with him."

"I know, Lowell paired you. I don't blame you for that."

"But you're angry," I pushed.

His head snapped back up to look at me.

"Of course I'm angry. I hate the idea of him touching you. He has no right to hold you in his arms or kiss your lips." His voice became angrier. "Every time I think of him being near you I want to destroy him. You didn't love him—you didn't even care for him—and for Lowell to throw you together like that..."

His face was hard, so different from Berwyn's anger, but upsetting nonetheless.

"Lowell had no right to treat you like that. He had no

right to control your life. What would have happened if you hadn't escaped? Would you be married to a man you didn't love, or even like? What would you have had to do in that life? Right now, at this very moment, if Lowell's plan had succeeded, you could be married to that guy, ruling your cousin's empire, not even realizing all the damage you had caused."

He was right. I was a part of causing the damage.

"Auluria, that life was never meant for you. And if I ever see your handler again, I'll destroy him myself for going along with Lowell's plan."

The look of disgust on his face made my insides turn. Until Dov put it in perspective, I hadn't realized how horrible things had been for me *before*. I never agreed with Lowell's plans for a marriage between Shadoe and me, but it was worse when I thought about the intended outcome. Having it as a far-off possibility was one thing —it was easier to cope with if I pushed it off in my mind —but when confronted with the fact that Shadoe and I were to be close, the way I hoped Dov and I would one day be close, it was too much.

I wanted to reach for Dov's hand, but I held back.

"He didn't touch me, Dov," I said, trying to calm him.

"He kissed you." His eyes bored into me.

I lowered my head and whispered, "Yes."

He didn't respond.

"I didn't know you then, Dov. I would never let him touch me now and I had no choice then."

"It doesn't matter," he said quietly. *But it did.*

Of course, it did.

"We have work to do," he redirected.

I swallowed as I wrapped my hands around my knees against my chest and closed my eyes. I thought back over the last few years of never really knowing Lowell. I pictured his light hair and grey eyes, and the smile that never quite reached them.

When we were younger, he used to watch me with fascination, as if he were studying me and trying to decipher my thoughts. *Why* did I reach for the butterfly? *How many* times would I try before I realized I couldn't do something? *How long* before I gave up. *What* made me stop playing? *Why* was I motivated to win?

I realized Lowell was *always* studying me. He watched me with calculated movements, learning from my every decision.

I remembered how he manipulated situations to see my reaction. He'd give me something and take it away. He'd assign me impossible tasks just to see how far I'd go and how frustrated I'd get. I remembered my mother pulling me away from his games once, scolding him for upsetting me.

He challenged everything I ever did.

My breathing deepened as my thoughts proceeded. I

remembered when Lowell first brought me into his fold. I was amazed by the people he had collected.

We never stayed in one spot for very long. We led a nomadic life, constantly moving from one place to the next to avoid detection. He let me travel with him when we moved. We'd often have dinner together. Frequently he was joined by one of the girls that threw themselves at him, and I quietly ate while listening to her talk. None of them stayed for long, so I never worried about learning their names unless I worked with them.

One day, two years earlier, Lowell had brought a chicken and demanded I kill it for dinner. He placed it in my hands and it trembled beneath my grasp. Lowell told me what to do and waited for me to follow his instructions. I couldn't bring myself to do it. The look he gave me frightened me. I had disobeyed him, the first time ever, and he was furious.

He took it from me and snapped its neck. I tried to stay calm until he left, but the moment he was gone I retched. I hid from him that evening, not wanting to see his face. Shadoe gave me a passive look the next time he saw me, having heard that I couldn't do what had been asked of me.

Shadoe tried to teach me to do it several times after that, but each time I refused. I couldn't bring myself to be so callous. I still had nightmares about that moment.

I remembered one day, after a long and exhausting

day, Lowell came to sit by me on the porch of the small house we were staying at. I rocked in a chair while the breeze teasingly played with my hair. I had just lifted my face to the sky, letting the wind brush over me and I heard Lowell take the seat next to me. I left my eyes closed as he rocked back and forth.

"Auluria, you know I have great plans for you, don't you?" he asked, almost tenderly.

I nodded, still unwilling to relinquish the small freedom that the breeze and my closed eyes gave me.

"Together, we're going to stop the government. We're going to take back power and they won't be able to hurt us again. You'll marry Shadoe and you will both be my second in command. My little cousin, my right hand," he said almost inspirationally.

"That's nice, Lowell," I murmured, opening my eyes to look at him. I gave him a small smile. I believed he was doing the right thing.

"We're close," he grinned. "We have a plan in motion. You're a part of it, Auluria. You're going to be grand."

I shuddered as I thought of his plans for me. If I had known how sick and twisted he was at the time, I could have ended it right there. There was a knife sitting in my boot. With one flick of my wrist, I could have stopped all the bloodshed.

"He never cared about me," I said. "Just what I could do for him."

"I know. I'm sorry, Auluria," Dov started.

"No. He didn't *care* about me. He only wanted what I could do for him. *This is about power.* He wants the power. So, let's give it to him." I grinned.

I could see him processing my words.

"You want to draw him out and let him think he won." He began to smile. "But how?"

"He needs to think he beat us. So, we let him know where we are—*which obviously can't be here*—and when he comes to watch us lose, we confront him. Lowell has never been able to resist watching his plans fall into place," I said.

"Now the trick is how to get the right people there to witness it and how we can escape," Dov concluded.

We explained to Berwyn what we had come up with. We agreed it was a good concept, but we had to flesh out the details.

"He will never believe *me* again," I said, "so that won't help."

"How else can we get him to find out?" Silas asked.

The men and Eden tossed around some ideas, none of which would work.

I took a deep breath, knowing my suggestion would not be well received.

"I know how Lowell thinks. But I also know how Shadoe thinks. If we can find the relative area that Lowell's group is in, I know how we can make this work."

"No. If Shadoe is involved, you will not be part of it," Dov protested.

"He's not going to hurt me, Dov. He was supposed to *marry* me."

"And *you betrayed* him…for me."

The corners of Silas's mouth tugged up in a nearly unnoticeable grin. I focused on Dov.

"And that's part of my plan. He hates you too."

"I doubt he hates you," Dov interjected, but I ignored him.

"If we can be where he is, he'll find us. He always does. And he'll follow us back to wherever we set up camp. He'll bring Lowell straight back to us. Lowell has always liked playing with the mice he catches in his traps."

I don't think the group appreciated me comparing them to mice.

"Let's say this works," Eden started. "What then?"

Berwyn explained that we would need witnesses… enough that Lowell couldn't kill them all. One of the men laid out the plan for getting the guards there. We were going to contact them and tell them of our plan. We would ask them to come, knowing that they would plan to betray us. We made an escape plan, a secret get away route that we could use when the chaos ensued, one that we could destroy behind us. Lowell would try to fight his way out, but would only succeed if he didn't try to take on all the men.

Shadoe and his men would likely be with Lowell, eager for revenge, and I only slightly regretted their part in the plan. I had no doubt Lowell would survive, but his men may not share the same fate. Shadoe would fight, but if necessary, he would die for my cousin.

Berwyn, Eden, Dov and I would all be there, waiting for Lowell's game to play out. I wasn't eager to face my cousin or be the cause for his downfall, but I wanted to put this behind us.

We decided the next day we would go to the place Berwyn told us about. It was a small cave that Griz kept for emergencies. He had shown it to his sons a handful of times before his death, in case they ever needed to run.

There was a hidden tunnel in the back. Once we slipped through, we would set off a chain reaction, dropping stones in front of the entrance. When we were far enough down the tunnel we would set off an explosive that would demolish the tunnel, prohibiting anyone from following us. At the far end of the exit, Silas and the men would be waiting, our reinforcements, if necessary.

Once we had escaped, the group would stay underground for as long as we could before resurfacing. The group would then move to other safe houses, making our way to the camps. The ultimate goal would be to set the men and women at the camps free. Our hope was to move on, beyond where the government could reach us.

But it all hinged on exposing Lowell and escaping. The next day came too quickly, and with it, disaster.

Chapter 17

"I don't like that you are doing this," Dov said. "There's no reason for you to be a part of this. It's *us* that he wants. You and Eden should stay."

"You think I could turn on him like that and he'd just let it go? Dov, be serious. At this point, he might want *me* more than he wants *you*. Besides," I continued, "if he really is mad at me, he might use you to get back at me. It's better if I'm right there beside you. You can save me and I don't have to worry about him hurting you worse just to get to me."

He shook his head but held his tongue. I was grateful not to have to argue my point again.

Berwyn and Eden walked ahead of us. Eden look

scared to death. Berwyn touched her arm, trying to steady her.

Silas walked alongside of me, keeping me close between him and Dov. A few other men walked near us in a group, ready to take their place at the exit.

"Are you ready for this?" Silas asked.

"Confronting Lowell?" I clarified. "No. I don't ever want to see him again. But I'll be fine."

"I'll be right with you," Dov said, putting his arm around my shoulder. I moved closer to him. It felt good to be talking with him again.

We left Silas and the others half a mile away at the exit to the tunnel. Berwyn and Eden walked through the exit of the tunnel to beat us to the cave, staying hidden. Dov and I took the long way around, moving slightly less carefully than usual.

Our men had discovered word of Shadoe's spies in the area, so we hoped it wouldn't take long to find him. We walked with purpose, though we made several big loops to ensure he saw us.

I caught sight of one of his warning symbols on a tree. When he was young and first training his men, he developed a system with them based on rotating symbols. He hadn't bothered to change it since the abdication of my position with them. I knew he was near.

Dov and I moved toward the cave. If I hadn't known where to look, I may not have noticed Shadoe following us. I could tell Dov noticed too. We led him back to the cave and disappeared.

Eden ran to tell Silas to put the plan into motion. One of the men with him would go through his contact and reach out to the guards. Our people had already connected with them and told them of our plan, so all we had to do was tell them the location. Silas would send one of the men to tell the contact to get the guards. Everyone would arrive soon and it would all be over. One way or another.

I rested my head on Dov's shoulder, his arms wrapped securely around me. He set his chin on my head and we stood, waiting for the inevitable.

"We're sure this is a good idea?" Eden asked.

"No, it's probably a terrible one, but what else are we supposed to do?" Berwyn grumbled.

With each passing minute, I became more and more nervous. I worried about every little possibility. What if Lowell didn't come? What if he showed up with all his people?

What if the guards didn't care about Lowell's group and they just came for us? What if one of us got hurt in the fight? What if we had lost before we had even begun? The thoughts were relentless.

The barrage of notions flitted through my mind. I couldn't shut my brain off.

"Hey," Dov whispered. "You okay?"

"Yes," I said, looking up at him. "Just having trouble not over thinking this."

He bent down to me, kissing me softly on the lips. It happened so fast I almost didn't realize until after he pulled away. He gave me a sheepish smile and said, "Does that help?"

I grinned back. It was the first time he had kissed me since he found out that Lowell had sent me. I wished he would do it again.

He waited a few minutes before adding, "Now *I'm* having trouble focusing."

He looked at me expectantly and I obliged, reaching up to grab his collar. I pulled him toward me for a slightly longer kiss. He pulled back and gave me a lazy half smile. He was happy. So was I.

"Well, if it isn't my dear cousin and her *lover*. I'd say that's about enough, *missy*. Get over here *right now*," Lowell commanded, walking into the room.

"Back off, Lowell." Berwyn stepped between us.

"She's *my* responsibility, Berwyn, not yours. And I

want her back." The hardness in his voice made my hair stand on end.

"You will not touch her," Dov said, pulling me closer.

"So, young…so naïve. Don't worry baby Baer, you'll learn with time," Lowell smirked. "Isn't that right, Eden?"

I must have looked confused, for he added, "What? They didn't tell you, dear cousin of mine? Eden was supposed to be mine, but I had some trouble holding on to her after she was abducted and turned her back on me."

"That wasn't my choice, Lowell," she spat back at him. "And if I'd known about your little group I never would have married you anyway."

"But you chose to join another group, didn't you?" Lowell said spitefully.

That explained why Eden looked so shocked when he had spoken to her the time we planned to run into Lowell in town.

He looked around the room. "What a nice place you have here."

"Griz built it," Eden defended her father-in-law's hiding place.

"Ahhh, yes. Dear old Griz." He lowered his hands to his sides. "I like what you've done with the place. Do you like what I did with his name?"

Shadoe stood next to him, eyes intently focused on me. I couldn't read his expression. It may have been a mix of anger, determination, resolution, and maybe…jealousy? He couldn't possibly have been jealous of Dov…he never truly cared for me, so it made no sense.

He flinched as I ran my hand up Dov's arm and rested it on his chest. I tucked my elbow against my body. I always found closing in on myself to be comforting.

Berwyn looked like he was ready to hit Lowell. Eden placed a hand on his arm, calming him.

"Why?" he growled, low and fearsome.

"Why?" Lowell repeated in a mocking tone, his voice echoing off the walls. "*Why?* Because your father destroyed me, *that's* why. We could have crippled the Society and taken control of the country, but no! Your father had to have a *conscience*. He didn't like violence… only stealing.

"And when I tried to leave, he made it impossible for me. He destroyed any chance I had at succeeding." His face calmed, almost looking serene with his decision. "So, you see…he had to go."

Berwyn launched himself forward, lashing out at Lowell's face, but Shadoe was too quick. He raked something metal across Berwyn's arm. It came up streaked with blood. I saw the talons protruding from Shadoe's knuckles. It was as if he was wearing bear claws. Five bloody marks ran down Berwyn's arm.

He stumbled backward.

"So why?" Dov spoke up, stepping away from me,

keeping himself between me and my former confidants. "Why attack us now?"

"Because, *baby Baer*, I'm about to have what I wanted all those years ago. We're taking the government down and we'll be in charge," he bellowed, confident and strong. "And I *hate* your family. Your father destroyed me, your brother took my place as leader of the group, and you...*you* turned my perfect little agent against me. So, you see Dov, not only will I destroy your family, but I will thoroughly enjoy watching you hang for it."

He looked around Dov to me and added, "Last chance, Auluria. Whatever *I* do to you will be a lot better than what the *Society* will do to you."

"Lur, take it seriously," Shadoe warned. "We'll be more merciful than they will. And we can protect you from the Society better than *they* can." He almost sounded worried, like he was trying to will me back into the safety of being his charge.

"No," I answered. I saw Shadoe visibly deflate at my answer.

"Lur, please, reconsider. I'll keep you safe." He meant from Lowell. He meant Lowell would discipline me, but he wouldn't let him kill me. I didn't care.

"So, what? You launched an attack against the Society, and planted Griz's medallion and then framed my husband?" Eden shrieked, redirecting the conversation where we needed it to be.

"That, *miss*, is precisely what I did," Lowell said stepping toward her menacingly. "And there's nothing you can do about it. They're on their way already."

"Actually," Berwyn said, regaining his footing after reeling from the strike he had taken, "they're already here."

The guards, dressed in their dark uniforms, burst into the room. Lowell turned alongside Shadoe and the two of them lashed out at the men. The people they had with them weren't quite as fast and went down quicker.

Dov, Eden, Berwyn and I ran to the hidden exit, setting off the rockslide and blocking the doorway. Berwyn staggered, his feet slowing.

"Berwyn?" Dov asked.

Berwyn fell to his knees, only steps away from the exit we had just blocked. We only had a moment to reach the point where we could set off the explosive.

Dov ran to his side, dipping under his arm and pulling him forward. I slipped under Berwyn's arm on the opposite side and helped to carry him along. Eden ran ahead to prepare the blast.

The moment we reached Eden she set off the charge, causing a rippling boom to echo off the walls.

"What's wrong with him?" Eden nearly sobbed.

"Looks like there was poison on that thing Shadoe hit him with. We have to get him back…now!" I answered.

We raced through the tunnel, carrying Berwyn as best

we could. His feet gave out completely and we dragged him through the dirt walkway.

Eden ran ahead, bringing two of the men back with her. They took Berwyn from us, allowing us to run alone. We raced to the end of the tunnel, breaking free into the refreshing air. With the chaos and danger, a distance away, I finally felt we might have a chance.

The last thing I saw before the explosion was Lowell being attacked by two guards. I no longer felt I owed him my allegiance. I had absolutely no doubt that it wouldn't be the last time I saw him.

Chapter 18

We ran toward the closest of the safe houses, the men dragging Berwyn along. I clamped my hand around Eden's arm and forced her to stay upright as we struggled along the path.

When the path split, so did we. The men took Berwyn to a safe house for medical attention while the rest of us kept running. Dov and Silas repositioned themselves so that Dov was guiding me and Silas looked after Eden. She sobbed as we left Berwyn fighting for his life.

It was eerily silent in the woods. No birds, no crickets, no frogs. Something felt wrong. I tried to keep a careful watch, letting Dov pull me along, but I couldn't seem to focus on what was bothering me.

Dov and Silas kept turning to look behind us, watching for signs of the oncoming guards. I imagine Lowell and Shadoe kept them busy for a few minutes, long enough to give us a brief head start, extended even longer by using the tunnel.

The moment I opened my mouth I knew it was too late. I screamed my warning anyway, but the last words were ripped out of my mouth as we were catapulted into the air by a net strung from the trees. The air rushed from my lungs as we bounced wildly up and down.

Eden had just missed being swept up in the net. Silas's arm was ripped from Eden's hand as he was caught up in the ropes. The guards were on top of Eden so quickly we hadn't even had time to see her reaction. They forced her to her knees and bound her hands behind her back. Fear radiated from her eyes.

"No!" I screamed as they kicked her back, sending her tumbling to the ground.

"And who do we have here?" a strong, tall man called out.

"Let me go!" Eden yelled viciously, struggling against the man pulling her upright again.

"Don't touch her!" I chorused, causing the men to turn their attention to me.

"You must be the one." He pointed at me. "We've been looking for you, *missy*."

At the sound of that name, I realized Lowell had told

them about me. He specifically sent them after me. Whether they captured him or not, he wanted me to know he had won.

The men cut us down, surrounding us to prevent escape. There were too many of them to fight. Surrender was our only option. Once we had fallen and struggled to our feet, Dov gently placed his hand on my shoulder and pushed me to my knees. He didn't want me to fight. I looked at him, begging for some sign of rebellion, but his eyes had lost their light.

"No," I whispered, pleading for him to not ask me to do this.

"Please," he whispered back.

I sank to my knees and the men roughly tied my hands behind me.

"I was told to be gentle with you," my guard said once the boys had been secured.

I saw Dov and Silas tense, straightening their spine and lifting themselves as high as they could, knees planted firmly on the ground. Neither spoke.

Their guards pulled them to their feet, not caring to be gentle with them. They marched us forward, back the way we had come.

"Where are you taking us?" I asked in a monotone voice.

"To interrogation," one of them answered me. I hadn't expected an answer.

"And then to die," another added, laughing gleefully.

The others joined him in the celebration. They knew who we were. They knew what our capture meant.

My guard jabbed me in the back, nearly causing me to fall forward. Dov clenched his jaw, but he continued to stay quiet. When I righted myself, I intentionally changed my gait, giving me just enough time to "accidentally" step on my guard's foot, hard. He let out a yelp and grabbed my arm. Spinning me around, he slapped me across my face.

I tried not to shriek, but I couldn't hold it back. I whimpered as he pulled me close. "Don't you ever do that again, *Missy!*"

He pushed my shoulder, turning me away from him and propelled me forward. I could feel the side of my face swelling. I refused to cry.

Eden threw her head back, crashing into her guard. He saw her moving and caught her around her waist before she had fully moved and he clung on even after the blow. She lifted both feet and sent them crashing into his knees. They buckled beneath him and he pulled her to the ground with him. Two guards rushed to his aid, plucking Eden from the moss-covered ground. She struggled against them, but they held her in place.

Before Dov and Silas could do anything, I saw the blade. "Stop! No!" I shouted. "They'll stop, don't hurt them!"

A young boy put his hand on the older man's forearm and brought the knife down. In that moment, he stopped our massacre. He glared at us, hatred in his eyes, but I silently thanked him anyway.

I confirmed our compliance for the rest of the journey, assuring them we wouldn't try anything else. Dov, Silas, and Eden agreed reluctantly.

We walked with our heads down, bent low as our captors had demanded. When we reached the tree line, we were told not to make eye contact with anyone in the town. The guards formed a barricade around us and marched us through the city.

Finally, we arrived at a stately building. We were escorted inside where we found ourselves standing in the middle of a large indoor courtyard.

"The Baers," an amused voice boomed, deep and solid. "I see you've decided to join us."

We all looked up at the same time. The man sitting before us was probably older than Griz would have been if he were still alive. His graying hair was parted in the middle, combed to each side. His short beard framed his face, the whiskers sticking out at all angles. He wore a robe of vibrant reds.

"I am Magistrate Canton and *we* have been looking for you for a great many years, *Mr. Baer.* Since the day your father killed all those people."

"That wasn't my father who did that," Dov protested.

"I told you he would lie," a voice from the shadows called.

I turned to find Lowell, hidden in the dark confines of the overhang. He was bound and being watched by several guards.

"He would say anything to save his neck," Lowell continued.

"Lowell killed them, Sir," Dov said, jerking his head toward my cousin.

"It doesn't matter to me who did what. You're all going to die for it. The Society wants you gone and since it was my men who captured you, I'm the one who will get the credit for ridding the world of the likes of all of you." He rose from his chair and walked toward us.

He walked to Eden and lifted her chin. She restrained herself from biting him, but just barely.

"Tomorrow you'll all be interrogated. The people want answers. This will go on for several days. In a week's time, there will be a lavish ceremony held in your honor. Well, in honor of your deaths. Public execution will be a fitting end to you all."

He walked past the boys to me. He cupped my chin in his hands and bent down in front of me. The man tilted my chin up and inspected me before speaking.

"I've been told you are quite the nasty one, girl. Betraying your lover, betraying your family, betraying your country." He clucked his tongue at me. "We really can't trust you, now can we? What shall we do about that?"

He paused to think.

"I know. We have a special plan for you." He stood and backed away from me, smiling.

"Now, off to your cells. The interrogators will be here in a few hours and you wouldn't want to be too tired for your questioning, now, would you?"

His laugh echoed off the courtyard walls and followed us down the hall. I was sure I heard it follow us down into the cold stone chambers we were hidden in.

Water dripped down the sides of our cells. Eden and I sat in one small cell together while Silas and Dov were held in the cell next to ours. We were isolated from the rest of the prisoners.

The bars were strong enough that we couldn't bend them, no matter how many times we kicked them. They were close enough together that not even Eden could slip out.

I sat near the bars, my back against the wall. On the opposite side of the wall, Dov sat, mirroring me. We stretched our hands as far as we could through the bars and around the walls, holding onto each other.

Eden took up the opposite corner wanting her space. Her tears had long since dried and now the anger had taken a hold of her. If any of us had been able to break through the metal bars, it would have been Eden with her rage spurring her on.

"I'm so sorry you got caught up in this," Dov said softly to me. There was no privacy but there were things to be said.

"It isn't your fault," I said. "In fact, it's more my fault than your fault."

"Let's not do this," he begged. "Please, let's not talk about that."

"What else are we going to talk about, Dov? We're going to die within a week. Tomorrow they're going to separate us and interrogate us. What are the chances we'll ever see each other again?"

"We'll see each other again."

"How can you be so sure?" I questioned.

"Auluria," he said slowly, in a measured voice, "they want us to suffer. They want *me* to suffer. There's no better way to do that than to make me watch you being hurt and killed."

That horrible realization sunk in as he spoke the words. They would torture us just to make the other suffer.

"This is going to be bad, isn't it?" I breathed.

"I'm so sorry," he whispered, his voice catching.

"No." I squeezed his hand. "I don't want you to worry about me. Don't think about it. When it happens, promise me you won't watch. Promise me, no matter what, you'll look away."

"I won't do that, Auluria. I won't leave you to suffer alone."

"Dov, promise me."

"Auluria, you know he won't do that. He'll do whatever he has to do to make your suffering stop," Silas said from somewhere in the cell next to me.

"This is a nightmare," I said, letting my head fall to my raised knees.

"I'll protect you," Dov said softly.

"You can't, Dov," I replied, giving up. "And I don't want you to. I want you to take care of yourself. Don't worry about me."

"I can't do that, Auluria. You know that."

I sighed. I knew.

"We'll do whatever we can to protect you, girls," Silas confirmed.

"Silas, don't. Eden and I will be fine. You need to focus on protecting yourselves. Don't worry about us." I knew I would be fine. I wasn't so sure about Eden, but I knew if the boys could find a way to escape, they'd come back for the others or at least they would be able to warn the people that weren't with us. I wanted them to focus enough to escape.

"Auluria..." Dov started, clearly wanting to say something.

"I know," I breathed. "I know."

He tightened his grip on my hand. We both knew.

"Eden?" he asked. "Are you doing okay?"

"I'm fine, considering." Her voice was angry. Softening it, she added, "Are you okay?"

"Yeah."

"Dov," Eden started again. "I'm sorry."

She never said for what.

"Thanks," he replied.

"Silas…" I started, aware that we were beginning our goodbyes. "Thank you. For everything. For looking out for us and helping us and standing by us."

"Anytime, Auluria." He let out a short, hard chuckle. "I knew you two belonged together."

"Oh, is that right?" I questioned with a laugh. "It seems to me someone who looked a lot like you doubted that awhile back."

"I didn't doubt it," he retorted. "Just making sure you understood what it meant."

I laughed.

"You should have heard the way he pushed for us back in that storehouse, Auluria." I could hear the smile in Dov's voice.

"Yeah, I bet he was…really annoying." I smiled.

"Yes," Dov agreed.

"Knock it off." He joked, "I'm the one who got you two back together, and don't you forget it."

"Okay, buddy, okay," Dov replied.

"Are you ever going to tell me who that girl is, Silas?" I asked.

"Nope," he said.

"Dov?"

"Sorry, babe. I can't."

I squeezed his hand, but he still wouldn't relent.

Just then we heard the footsteps approaching.

Chapter 19

I was the first one taken. Two men pulled me kicking and screaming from my cell. I saw them lead Eden away. She didn't fight. In my thrashing, I saw Dov and Silas at the cell bars, reaching for us, but I couldn't hear them over my struggling.

We hadn't expected them to come for us so soon.

I was thrown into a chair, my wrists tied to the armrests, my feet fastened to the legs. I pulled against my restraints to no avail.

"Before we begin, there's someone who would like a word with you," the guard said.

The lighting was dim in the room, there were no windows, so it was flooded only by candlelight, most of which had burnt out. It was cold. If I was there for long, I knew I would begin to shiver.

"I told you not to betray me. I told you to focus. But you just couldn't listen, could you?" the sharp voice said.

His blond hair was matted with blood. The grey of his eyes was accentuated by the dark print from a fist surrounding it. His lip was split open, blood crusting over where it dribbled down his chin.

He was restrained, though not to the chair. He guided himself into the room, sitting across from me.

"What you did was wrong, Lowell," I said.

"We would have been just fine, cousin, had you not changed the plan. And not only did you disobey me, but you also sold me out. You blamed me for all this,"

"It was *your* fault," I interrupted.

If he hadn't been tied, he would have struck me.

"Well, now I suppose we'll die together. Mom would have been so proud we saw each other through until the end." His sarcasm set a fire in my soul. I strained against my bindings, hoping to lash out at him.

"But don't worry, I'm always true to my word. I'll see to it that your precious little Dov is to blame for all of this. I'll see to it he suffers. But you are still my cousin, so I'll give you a choice, Auluria." He looked up at the guard to make sure he still had time.

"There are two ways to hurt you both: either you get

hurt and he has to watch, or he gets hurt and you watch. Choose."

It was an impossible choice. I couldn't bear the thought of him being hurt; his handsome body being torn to pieces. But I knew how painful it would be for him to watch me. In the end, I couldn't take the thought of him in physical pain more than forcing him to watch my own pain.

"Hurt me," I said, looking down at the ground.

"What?" he demanded.

"Hurt me," I said louder, looking up at him. "Hurt me."

"All right then." He grinned that twisted grin I'd come to see often since being sent on my last mission. He glanced to the guard who nodded once. How Lowell had a guard on his payroll, I might never know.

"And not a word to Lover Boy"—he paused only slightly—"or any of them for that matter, or you'll only make it worse on all of them."

"Lowell," I yelped, trying to make a deal. "Make it quick for them. Draw mine out if you want, but don't make them suffer."

Lowell stood and walked to the door. "Goodbye, *missy.*"

I sat in silence after he left. My mouth felt dry and my throat was scratchy. This was the end of us.

No one else came for me. A guard took me back to the cell. Eden was already there. I caught a glimpse of Dov and Silas as I walked back into my cell. Both had taken a few punches while I was gone.

"Are you okay?" Dov raced to the front of the cell as soon as the men were gone.

"Yes." I quickly changed the subject. "Eden, are you all right?"

"Fine," she answered.

"They just asked her questions. What about you?" Dov supplied.

"Uh-huh," I mumbled, unwilling to answer.

"They're coming back in a bit for us," Dov said.

That worried me. I knew they would come back more broken than before.

Before anything else could be said, the guards were back for them. I watched as they dragged them away. Dov locked eyes with me and refused to look away, even as they strangled him back.

Eden came crawling over to me and leaned against the wall. We sat quietly until we were sure we were alone. She raised her head up to my ear.

"They didn't question you. What happened?" She used our hair to block our conversation.

"It doesn't matter Eden," I whispered back. She was an intuitive woman to have figured that out so quickly.

"Yes, it does. What happened?"

"*Lowell* happened. He has one of the guards in his pocket and he wanted to talk to me."

"I sat in a cell by myself. A man came in and asked two questions and then they dragged me back here and told me not to talk," she said. "What did Lowell want?"

"We made a deal. I think. I suffer…you all don't. Simple as that."

"Dov suffers. If he must watch you suffer, he suffers. It's revenge on you both."

"I know. But the more physical pain I take, the less he has to endure."

"That's brave of you."

"I couldn't let them hurt all of you. We're not normal, by any means, but I care about you all. I can't let you get hurt."

"I have news for you, Auluria. We're all about to experience the worst pain of our lives. When they're done with us, we'll be begging to die. That's how it works, and you, Dov, and I…we're the *special cases*. And Silas by proxy. It's going to be so much worse."

"They aren't going to be able to rescue us, are they?"

She shook her head.

I felt her shudder against me. It was a hard fate to accept.

The next time we were removed from our cells was to be brought before the Magistrate. He wore his shaded robe. It flowed out behind him as he walked. Dov and Silas were in chains in the center of the room as Eden and I were escorted in.

At the far end of the room, several moveable walls had been set up and a man stood by each. I fell hard as my knees were kicked out from behind me. I couldn't take my eyes from the partitions as I fell.

"And so, it begins. Welcome to your trial," Magistrate Canton formally announced.

High-ranking officials stood on either side of us. They were here to witness our pain. The magistrate smiled, looking down on us.

"Now…who's first?"

The guards lifted each of us to our feet and forced us toward the freestanding walls. The backside did not have a wall, leaving it an open entrance. In each makeshift room, there was a chair, a long table, and a small table with something under a piece of fabric.

Eden was pushed into the first room, terror on her face. Dov was given the next room. I was led into the third and Silas was taken to the last room.

We could hear each other, but we had no way of

seeing each other. I promised myself whatever happened, I would try to stay quiet for Dov's sake. I didn't want him hearing my screams.

I was led to the table. A man, my interrogator, walked in behind me. He forcefully pushed me against the table. As my back bent over, he scooped up my legs and deposited me on the metallic surface. With one swift movement, he strapped down my wrists and ankles. My skirt fell at an uncomfortable angle off the table, exposing my lower legs below my knees.

It was cold and I was terrified. I heard Dov struggling against something in the room next to mine. The voices of the interrogators started, but they barely waited for a response before they inflicted the pain.

Eden cried out first, her piercing shriek startling us.

"Eden!" Dov yelled out. I could hear him fighting the restraints.

I tried to hold still. I tried to block out the noise. Her shattering screams rocked me to my very core.

She quieted as they started to question her. She answered what she could, but she refused to give up the group. The pain they were inflicting was less, after the initial shock of trauma meant to scare her…and us.

Silas and Dov cried out as their interrogators turned on them. The Magistrate walked into my room, watching my reaction.

"Don't worry," he said, petting my hair. "Your time is coming. We just need him to be focused."

I watched as the man took out sharp utensils from under the fabric. He held them up, inspecting each one before setting them down. The light glinted off them.

I forced my tears back as I listened to my friends scream.

The sudden noise of the wall being moved frightened me. They only removed the wall that separated Dov from me. As the men unveiled him, I saw his perfect, beautiful face had been destroyed. His arms were covered in blood.

He looked to me, slightly dazed. His eyes registered me and it brought him back to an alert state.

"Don't hurt her, please," he begged.

"We're not," the Magistrate answered. "Not yet."

They forced me to watch as they mutilated Dov's body. Shallow knife marks ran over his chest and spilled around to his back. They took a long, sharp object and forced it under his skin, lifting it and piercing out in a second location. They twisted it and lifted it in the air, dragging the body part along with it. I would have retched if I had had any food in my stomach.

He had begged me to turn away, pleaded with me not to look, but I wouldn't look away. He focused his eyes on me, as if trying to remain calm for me. He tried to tell me he was fine in our silent way, but I knew he wasn't. I could see the damage they were causing.

Finally, they turned to me. I had never been so grateful.

"No!" he said, alert again. He struggled against the restraints, his wounded skin hanging off his arm in places.

"It's okay," I said. Over and over I repeated it as the man walked toward me.

Suddenly I was aware that I could no longer hear Silas and Eden. I prayed they had stopped to make them hear this.

The man held up the long tool Dov's interrogator had used to pierce his flesh. He dragged it up and down my arms. Back and forth from the tips of my fingers to my shoulder, across my chest, and back down the opposite arm.

When it punctured my upper arm, I thought I might pass out. I held back my scream, but I saw Dov's eyes widen in horror. With every entry into my body, I fought against unconsciousness. Lowell wanted me hurt, and if it wasn't good enough, they'd move back to Dov.

"Is this not painful enough?" the Magistrate asked, stroking his beard. "She's barely making a sound. See what else you can do."

"No!" Dov said, straining toward them. "Auluria, you have to scream. Stop holding back."

I couldn't. I couldn't do that to him. I had to take this punishment.

"Auluria, please!" he gasped as the interrogator began to saw off a piece of flesh from my upper arm. *"Please!"*

I felt the knife, dull and sharp at the same time. Blood rushed from my incision. I faltered.

With Dov's last scream for mercy, I released my pain. A blood-curdling scream that made even the Magistrate duck his head filled the room.

I couldn't bring myself to look at Dov. I knew the pain I'd see there. My interrogator smiled, enjoying the moment. He moved down my body, letting the chunk of flesh hang off my arm, not bothering to finish cutting it off.

He clasped my foot and ran his hand up my leg. Moving my skirt aside, he pushed his hand up along my thigh. I struggled to kick at him as Dov threatened him from his table. I could hear Silas and Eden yelling over the walls, begging for compassion.

He dragged the knife along my inner leg, careful to avoid the artery that would end my life too quickly. I screamed again, giving into their demands.

He picked up a small object, replacing the knife in his hand. When he placed it against my leg I didn't feel it at first. My flesh became warm and then instantly burned, the object searing into my skin. The smell of burning flesh filled the room as the object sizzled.

Again, and again, he placed the object against me. Tears were streaming down Dov's face. In between my screams, I shouted how sorry I was to Dov. He leaned to me, fighting to protect me.

Dov begged them to stop, to take my punishment himself. No one listened. Even Silas volunteered his flesh for my pain. I remember slipping into blackness.

Chapter 20

Days passed. The Magistrate decided to wait an extra few days before the execution to give us time to heal. My interrogator had done such a harsh job on me, I couldn't even stay conscious, though some of that was my own pretending.

Eden tried to care for me, but in our cell, there wasn't much she could do but sit with me. Even that was a comfort.

After a week, my scars were starting to heal. Dov and Silas said they were healing as well. Eden, thankfully, had taken the least abuse.

The dark burn marks would have been a constant, lifelong reminder of that day, had we not been scheduled for execution. It still hurt to touch them. Most of them ran along my legs, but he had managed to burn through my dress on my hip once, and he branded my left wrist; a twisted mark of darkly burned flesh as a constant reminder of our pending death.

They allowed us some bandages to wrap our bodies in. I gave most of mine to Dov to help rebind his skin to his arms and chest. My wounds, while painful, had not been as dramatic as his.

I listened to the sound of my friends breathing as they slept. It was the only time they were at ease. I prayed for it to be easy for them when the time came.

One night the guard informed us that the following day, the leaders of the Society would arrive. They would speak to us briefly before sentencing us and carrying out the hanging.

Five men gathered outside of our cells, watching us.

"So, this is the son of the Great Griz Baer," they sneered. "Not what we were expecting."

Dov didn't say anything.

"Where is your brother?" they asked.

"I don't know. Let me out and I'll go find him," Dov said, his voice dripping with sarcasm.

"And this is the wife?" they said, pointing at Eden.

She rose to her feet and walked calmly over to the bars. She placed one hand on the bars, leaning toward the men. Her free hand snaked out, catching one by the collar. She forcefully pulled him toward her, slamming his skull into the metal. His friends pulled him away and stabilized him.

I laughed. I couldn't help myself. In a place where everything was going so wrong, I found her small act of hatred to be hilarious.

I couldn't stop laughing. Everyone froze in horror as I continued to laugh. Eden stared at me, shocked at my response. After a moment Dov joined me. Then Silas picked up the chuckling chant. Even Eden turned back to face the men she had fought against and laughed. We couldn't stop.

Eden came and joined me on the floor and we laughed together, knowing our end was near. She took my hand and laid her head on my shoulder and we laughed until there were tears. The officials were so frustrated they finally left, causing us to laugh even harder.

Eventually, we quieted, and then the silent void crept in.

It was nearly dark the next day when they came for us. We had resigned ourselves to our deaths and walked into it with our heads held high. We did not give them the dignity of acknowledging them. We shrugged their hands off and walked ourselves to where the guards directed us.

Four ropes hung on four corners of a platform. Each had a trap door, but they also had the option to raise the ropes by hand, extending the death sentence.

I locked eyes with Dov, trying to communicate all the things left unsaid. I wanted him to know how much I cared for him. I needed him to know how much he changed my life. And I needed him to know I would die for him…though I didn't want him to know *that* was exactly what I was trying to do at that very moment.

A second, smaller platform stood to the right of the one we stood on. A single post rose from the center. Underneath it stood Lowell, awaiting his sentence. He glowered at me.

Looking at him, awaiting his death, hating me every moment for ruining his precious plan, I realized what he was. Lowell was a wolf, a vicious, menacing wolf. He played his part and wore many masks. And when he was ready, he attacked, maimed and destroyed. I regretted how long it took me to see him for who he really was.

We were escorted to our posts, each step more horrifying than the next. The rope grated against the soft skin of my neck as they positioned me to die. Our charges were read as the procession began, the tall man with a deep voice finalizing our lives. It seemed like an eternity went by as the officials read our crimes and told the people of our impending fate. The crowd consisted mostly of officials and guards, though there were towns-people in the back, forced to watch to remove any foolish ideas from them. Future uprisings would not be tolerated.

Dov's eyes nearly broke my heart. Those deep blue eyes that awakened me that first day in his house and caused my heart to melt every day since, watched me from our separate posts. He held such remorse in those eyes. Together we played out what our lives could have been, mourning the moments we would never have.

He swallowed hard, his throat bobbing with the effort. I held my tears at bay. I didn't want to lose this man I had come to care for so intensely. I didn't want to lose his smile or his laugh, his kindness and compassion, his integrity and character. The world would be such a wasted place without Dov in it to make it better.

The officials finally stopped and turned back to us. They took their places on seats near the platform. Ropes tightened around our necks, causing us to stand taller to alleviate the pressure. The guards pulled the ropes as tightly as they could before it was our turn. None of us could move. We stood, suspended in place, knowing it was coming.

The Baer family was supposed to suffer for their crimes. Eden was a woman so they would end it quickly for her. Dov would be made to suffer through my execution.

The others watched as my rope was pulled again. I was forced onto the tips of my toes. The restraints on my wrist were cut, giving me the freedom to clutch at the ropes around my neck as they lifted me higher.

I couldn't breathe. I felt the world swirling around me, as I was lifted bit by bit from the ground. I struggled to keep a foot on the wooden paneling to hold myself up.

Dov fought to get to me, but they held him in place. The others were still restrained and caught in their ropes, but they all tried to get to me to save their friend. Everyone but Lowell.

I felt my life slipping away. All the sounds were blocked out, everything slowed down. I felt the rope being pulled and I was off the ground. I tried to pull myself up, but I couldn't. I fought and I lost.

When I opened my eyes again I saw a white grey brightness floating above me. I moved my eyes downward, tipping my head back to its normal position to find I was in a pile on the ground. I gasped for air. The trees and grass came into focus even in the darkening hour.

I looked up and saw Dov's panicked eyes as he jerked his head for me to get up. He wanted me to run.

Chaos surrounded us. Guards were running at some oncoming foe. The officials were scrambling to find safety. I tried standing only to fall back down. On my second try, I managed to get to my feet and I staggered over to Dov as he violently shook his head.

I threw my arms around his waist, trying to lift him out of his rope necklace. Between his struggling and my near ability to lift him, he freed himself. Somehow, he managed to land on his feet. I raced to Eden, still stumbling from oxygen deprivation, and freed her. Dov had knelt in front of Silas, hands still bound and Silas stepped on his back to lift and free himself.

I tackled a guard who was running by the platform. Surprising him, I grabbed his knife with one hand while simultaneously, grabbing a rock with my other hand and pummeling it into his head, leaving him where he lay. I cut the chords around my companions' wrists.

"What is going on?" Eden gasped as we tried to run.

"Lowell," Silas said. "His people were here to save him."

"How ironic," I laughed bitterly. "Lowell sent us to die and yet he's the one who saved us."

We raced away from the guards and into the town. They'd find us instantly in the woods, knowing we'd run there.

"Be careful. If they were here to free Lowell, that means Shadoe's here somewhere." I trusted him even less than I trusted Lowell at that point.

We ducked around homes and buildings. People jumped out of the way as we crashed by them. Dov and Silas grabbed anything we could use as a weapon as we ran by it. Metal poles, bottles, anything we could use to defend ourselves, were collected during our run.

We were all still recovering from our wounds, so we moved slower than we would have liked, but we refused to let that stop us. Even Eden pushed forward, knowing our lives were on the line.

Everything blurred by me as we ran, but my training kicked in, forcing me to identify buildings and streets. Remembering my way back was something Lowell and Shadoe would expect of me, and while I didn't want to be what they taught me to be, I knew it was sound training. Should we need to escape or evade soldiers, it would be important to know where we had been. I took careful note as we ran, storing every dark building, every dilapidated side street, and every foreboding structure in my mind. Shadoe taught me well and I would use this experience to survive and help protect my friends.

Eden stayed by my side as we moved, racing past

people. We held up our skirts to avoid tripping, though I'm not sure how much good it did. Silas followed behind us as Dov led our race, pushing us to our limits and further.

We were out of breath when we finally reached the end of the town. Dov slipped into an alleyway between two dark buildings and we stopped to catch our breath. I felt like I could collapse.

"Are you okay?" he demanded as soon as he could speak.

He raced the few feet to my side and pulled me to his warm body. I leaned into him, my tears refusing to come.

"I thought I had lost you," he whispered into my ear. He kissed my head, working his way from the top to my ear. He kissed my jaw line through my golden locks. Pushing his forehead to mine, our noses touched as we breathed each other in. He was about to kiss me when we were startled by a noise.

Dov pulled away, grasping my hand and dragging me behind him. Silas and Eden ran with us as we escaped the alleyway, running from the sound. Together we scaled a large hill, the barrier between the towns. We crept down the opposite side and slunk into the unfamiliar area.

The four of us hid between buildings as people walked by, residing in the shadows. The sun had gone down and the moon was the only light to see by.

Our injuries forced us to slow our pace. Dov kept a

firm grip on my waist, still worried about my earlier suffocation. I had a hard time remembering what had happened before we ran.

"Dov, how did I get down?" I suddenly asked.

"What?" he asked, distracted.

"How did I get down from the rope? I was in the air. How did I end up on the platform?"

"Someone cut you down."

"Someone just randomly cut me down?" I repeated.

"I don't know who, Auluria. It was an arrow, shot from somewhere near the woods. It released you and then they attacked."

It made no sense to me but I didn't care. It happened and we got away.

"Here," Silas whispered, motioning us toward him.

We followed him into an empty building. It was small and dark. The place looked like one of the old shacks the government used to store the food they collected from the people. It was standing unused, only a few crates littering the floor.

"Look," Silas said as he broke into one. "Food."

He passed out the dried meat and we hungrily ate. Our captors had only given us enough rations to keep us alive in our cells. It was almost humorous that they wanted us to live long enough to be executed.

Food had never tasted so good...except for the picnic

Dov once made for us. We ate quickly, trying to regain our strength. Our flight was far from over.

"Where are we going?" Eden finally said.

Silas and Dov looked to each other. At some point, they had formed a plan without telling us.

"The wall," Dov said.

"The wall?" Eden asked in disbelief.

"You want us to leave?" I asked wondering if the boys had also suffered through the ropes cutting off their ability to breathe earlier that day that would cause them to decide on such a dangerous idea.

"Yes," he stated.

"But we don't know what's out there, Dov. Those people on the other side of the wall are the ones that started this mess in the first place. They tried to attack us, and now *because* of *them*, the Society is going after its own people. We have no idea what we're walking into on the other side of that wall." Eden protested. "Besides, what about Berwyn."

"Berwyn will find us," Dov said.

"You don't…"

"I *do* know, Eden," he interjected. "It was his plan all along. If we ever escape and can't go back, we go over."

"We don't even know if he's still alive," Eden choked.

"Berwyn is strong, Eden. He'll make it," Silas reassured her.

"How far away is the wall?" I asked.

"We still have a few towns to get through," Dov answered. "It will take a few days."

"What is our plan then?" I feared the wall, but I feared staying more.

"We need to sleep for a few hours. We should be safe here," Silas said. "We'll sleep in shifts. We need to leave while it's still dark though."

"I'll take first watch," I announced, knowing that if anything happened, the boys needed the rest more than I did. It would be easier for them to help me along than for Eden and me to drag the boys along.

After some protesting, they let me take the first watch. I spent the entire night replaying the day, knowing if the arrow had missed by even the slightest bit, I wouldn't have been awake to think about it.

Chapter 21

My feet dragged along as we left our hiding place several hours later. The sleep had helped a little, but I was still exhausted. My companions showed the wear of the past several days as well.

The early morning was quiet. It was cool against my skin and I wished I had a wrap with me. I shivered as we walked along the streets.

The sun had risen as we crossed over into the next town. This one, thankfully, was more spread out than the last. The distance between buildings was further which meant less cover, but it also meant less people.

We picked our way through the fields, now starting to

wilt and decay. We stopped by a small stream to drink water, a blessing during our journey. Dov helped me over the stream when we finished.

We found an area of tall grass late in the afternoon and chose to rest in its covering. We took turns sleeping again, always leaving someone to keep watch. The wind gently blew the grass towering over us, a wild mass of weeds growing in the bountiful land.

I rearranged my skirt around my feet and looked at the clouds that peaked between the stalks of swaying grass. The clouds moved quickly in the sky as I rubbed my hand over my knees.

"How bad is it?" a soft voice asked.

I turned to find Dov staring at me. He propped himself up on one elbow next to me on the ground and watched me.

"How bad is what?" I asked, unsure of his question.

His eyes fell to my legs. Last night he held my hand in his, his finger resting gently over the scar on my wrist, circling around it in a soothing motion.

"It's fine," I said.

"Auluria, you can tell me," he tried again, even softer.

I moved the bottom of my skirt so he could see my lower leg.

"See? It's fine."

"What you went through wasn't *fine*, Auluria," he said, moving to capture my wrist. He brought my burn to his lips and kissed it. "I'm so sorry you had to go through that."

"How are your arms?" I asked, motioning to his wounds.

"They're healing," he said. "The skin reattached and I didn't lose anything, so I'd count it as a victory." He tried to smile at me.

Reaching forward, I stroked his dark hair. I pushed back a piece that fell in his eyes.

"At least we match," I offered.

He smiled, more genuine and relaxed this time. I guided his head to my lap, stroking his hair as he drifted back to sleep.

It was evening when we weaved our way out of the grassy maze. We walked the entire night, not encountering anyone. We made it through the town and the town next to that, just entering a third as the sun rose.

"Hey!" a voice called harshly, trying to keep quiet.

We froze.

"Don't move," the voice commanded. "I'm a friend."

A man circled around us. His light brown hair was going grey and his clothes were old and worn from work.

He held a knife to us, still wary of the four strangers who were trespassing near his home.

"You're Griz's kid, aren't you?" he asked.

Dread washed over me. We had been recognized.

"You look just like him," he pointed at Dov. I took a step closer to Dov, wrapping my hand around his arm gently to avoid hurting him.

"Your dad helped me out once. You were just a boy. Let's see…Bernie or something, right?"

"Dov, actually. I'm the younger one," Dov surprised me by answering.

"And his name is Berwyn," Eden said spitefully.

"I heard they were looking for you," he said, still pointing his knife. "The way I see it, your father helped a lot of good people out of tough places in his day. Now it's time to return the favor. From what I hear, they aren't headed this way yet. Come on, you can stay with me for a bit."

He turned and walked away. Unsure of what to do, we looked to each other. Finally, Dov made the decision for us, and we followed him as he walked after the man.

His house was small, but it was nice to be in a real home again.

"My name is Barone," he said. "Are you hungry?"

We nodded and he started looking for something to feed us. He told us about how Griz had stolen food for his family and found supplies for Barone's sick daughter.

She had eventually died, but Griz had helped to prolong the life she had.

"So, you're the oldest son's wife," he said, pointing at Eden.

"Yes," she replied.

"And you're how old?"

"Twenty-three."

"And he is…?"

She sighed in frustration. "Twenty-four."

"And *you're* with *him*." He pointed from me to Dov. "But not married."

"No, we've only known each other for a little while," Dov confirmed.

"So, who are you?" He looked to Silas.

"I'm the friend, co-worker," he started before Dov cut him off.

"Co-*leader*," Dov corrected.

"…match maker, and all around good person to have on your team," Silas finished, grinning

"Interesting," Barone murmured.

He stood and walked toward the door. "I'm going to see what I can find out about the guards. Stay here until I get back."

"We can trust him, right?" Eden asked.

"I think so," Dov said.

"I think so too," Silas agreed.

"Okay, then we stay. But, only until he comes back with news," I said.

Everyone nodded. We took the time to change our bandages and inspect our injuries. Despite the deplorable conditions in our cells, we seemed to be healing better than we expected.

A few hours later Barone came back while Silas was on watch. He woke us as he heard the man approaching. I was just sitting up when he closed the door behind him.

"I have news," he stated.

We looked at him expectantly.

"They know you ran into the towns and not the woods. They're working their way through the towns looking for you. There is a reward being offered for your capture.

"I heard there are also men looking for you who aren't the guards."

"Our people?" Silas mused.

"Or not," Dov said, his voice concerned.

"I wouldn't wait around to find out. I heard the non-government men had a head start. They could catch up to you at any time. The Society folks aren't too far behind either.

"We should go," Eden said.

"Thank you for your kindness, Barone," I said, remembering my manners.

"Here." He stopped us. "Take this."

He scooped up a sack and filled it with the remaining food. I was certain it was all he had left in the entire house. "I owe Griz," he insisted, forcing us to take it. Something told me he would have helped us even if Griz hadn't helped that little girl all those years before.

Silas carried the pack on his back. His torture had not been as extreme as Dov's had been. I offered to help, as did Eden, but he refused. We moved as quickly as we could, standing out in the broad daylight. The afternoon sun cast harsh shadows against everything it touched.

A stray cat jumped in front of us, scaring us as we moved. Silas beat Dov to me and swooped me behind his back. Eden was several steps away, making me the closest one to protect. I was grateful that they were looking after me, but I was more than a little tired of being pushed to safety.

The cat wandered away, flicking its tail as it walked. It reminded me of a grey cat that used to visit me at one of our campsites a few years earlier. Every night, he'd come looking for my dinner and often I obliged, grateful for the company. He'd arch his back into my hand as I pet his sleek back. Once he was finished eating he'd run off into the night. I was never fond of cats, but I liked that one.

At the edge of the town, we found ourselves on a weed-infested road. We followed the pebbled path until the buildings came into view. Many of them were made from stone in this area.

The sun was setting once again and we decided to keep walking with the setting light. We wove our way around carts that had been left outside, blocking the walkways. Eden nearly tripped over a wooden bucket left in the road as she tried to skirt one of the carts.

We found ourselves along the edge of the town. The trees weren't more than thirty feet away. The group decided to take shelter in the woods we had come to trust. Just inside the tree line, where we couldn't be seen, we settled for a few hours of rest.

Leaning against Dov, I rested my head on his shoulder. Softly I placed my hand gently on his chest, hoping it didn't hurt him. He took the first watch as I fell asleep in his arms. The rise and fall of his frame was comforting as it lulled me into a deep sleep. He stroked my hair and murmured soft things in my ear. I dreamed of my childhood with Lowell, everything taking a strange new turn toward the reality I had only recently discovered.

Two hours later I was awake again, still leaning

against Dov as he slept. Eden would be next on the watch rotation, but for now, she slept peacefully. My mind wandered as I listened for any unwanted guests.

I thought back to the first day I had met Dov. He was so full of life, despite everything he had gone through. He took beatings to protect people. He saved those he could. He cared for me. How I had even possibly stumbled into his life was beyond me. He would never know how truly changed I was because of him.

I thought of Berwyn and Eden and how much they too had changed since I had come to know them only a few short months before. I admired them in some ways. I pitied them in others.

The moving grass caught my attention before I heard it. I reached out and shook Dov and Silas awake. They snapped to attention just as the men came into the small clearing.

"Well, if it isn't the *golden girl* and her *golden boy,*" Marty sneered.

Chapter 22

I was genuinely surprised to see Marty alive. I had been certain he wouldn't survive our last encounter. He had recovered better than I expected him to, though Jake seemed like the one who was ready for a fight. Another boy their age stood behind them.

"Looks like you really *are* a Golden Girl, *Sweetie*," Marty said as he eyed my arms wrapped around Dov. "You're going to make us very rich men."

"There's a reward for you, you know," Jake supplied. "We figure you owe us. Now get up."

Jake started toward me and I kicked him hard in the shin before I had time to think it through. Dov was on his feet the moment after I struck Jake. He kneed him in the abdomen, forcing him to double over. Silas threw his weight against Marty.

Eden was furious over yet another intrusion and she took out her frustration on the third boy. Her fist made a sickening thud as it collided with the boy's nose. Blood poured down his lip as his hand flew to his face. Eden didn't stop though, she chased him several feet back, hitting and kicking with each step. Marty whirled around, grabbing Eden's arm before she could throw another punch and tossed her to the ground. Dov, defending his sister-in-law, kicked Marty in the back, sending him to the dirt as well.

I took the opportunity to pick up the sack the third boy had dropped on the ground. I searched through it finding several knives, rope, and some rations.

Leaping on to Marty's back, I wrenched his hands around, fastening them with the rope. Dov looked impressed as I twisted the rope and secured it. I did the same with Jake and the other boy. We tied them to a tree, preventing them from leaving.

The four of us took off with their knives and rations in tow, leaving our rivals behind.

"How did they find us?" Eden asked.

"They were very motivated," Dov said. "I bet they tracked us this whole time. They probably found a way to watch the execution too."

"I'm sure they did," Silas said. "You okay, Eden?"

"Yeah," she panted, "just getting.... a little...tired."

I was tired too and I had more training than Eden ever did. Shadoe had demanded that I be ready to hold my own if a mission went sideways. He ran drills with me until I wanted to complain to Lowell. I never did.

"We probably should have knocked them out before we left," Silas said.

"We gagged them," I offered.

"It's nice that they planned on gagging us when they caught us," Eden commented making me smile.

"We need a plan for when we get over the wall," Silas changed the subject.

"We don't even know what is out there, how could we possibly make a plan?" I questioned.

"That's true, but we need some kind of idea about what we're doing. What happens if we get over and find ourselves in danger over there too? What are we going to do?" he replied.

"What happens if everything the Society told us is a lie? What if there is nothing? *Or* what if it's somewhere *safe*?" Dov countered.

I interrupted, listing off steps in a clipped voice.

"We need to stay together, assess the situation as we go, try to agree on a plan, and once a plan is made, we stick to it," I said too hastily. *"There. Plan made."*

"Sounds like Lowell did a number on you," Silas said, glancing at me from the corner of his eye.

"Shadoe, actually. Lowell didn't handle my training," I replied.

"I *really despise* that guy," Dov muttered.

"I know," I sighed.

"We *all* know," Silas and Eden said at the same time, prompting Dov and me to turn to them.

"How much farther is the wall, anyway?" Eden asked again.

"We should reach it by tomorrow afternoon," Dov said.

Eden sighed as she panted. We were all tired of running.

We sat behind a stone wall on the outskirts of the town. Everyone was breathing heavily as we sank back against the stone. Eden had stepped in a hole, twisting her ankle. The boys had to help move her over to the stonewall, preparing to carry her over. Silas bent, lifting her into his arms as he handed her to Dov on the other side. Dov set her down and we joined them.

"It will be fine in a few minutes," she assured us as she tested the injury. When she was done, we took a seat on the ground, using the stonewall as a covering to protect us from sight.

I had no doubt that even if she *wasn't*, she would push through it. She took Dov's hand in hers as we sat.

Silence stretched between us, not for lack of things to say, but because we were still so close to the town. The wall was only a short distance away, a half hour's walk from our resting place.

I was itching to start again, but I knew it was important to give Eden a break. She rubbed at her ankle. I could already tell it was going to swell.

"Can I wrap it for you?" I asked quietly. She nodded. Dov handed me one of the wraps he had taken off a few hours earlier from his arms. I bandaged the wound for Berwyn's young bride.

"We're close," she said, her voice lifting.

"We're close." I smiled back.

Within a few minutes, Eden decided she wanted to try walking again. Silas checked the area to make sure it was clear. Dov helped Eden to her feet. Sitting on the edge of the stonewall, she swung her legs over and righted herself on opposite side, back on the path we had started on, no longer needing the veil of the stone barrier.

I followed her over and waited on the other side for Dov. We could hear the noises from the town not too far away, but we stayed as far from them as we could, even if it added a few minutes to our journey.

Eden limped, gradually working out the pain in her leg. Eventually, she could walk closer to her normal walking speed. She stayed tucked between Silas and Dov in case she needed to lean on them for support. I walked behind her, keeping the group in my sights, watching behind us for any signs of followers.

With each step, I grew more optimistic. Each foot further was one step closer to the wall and the freedom it promised. Whatever freedom we found on the other side, I was willing to accept it. Whether we were to find ourselves truly free or on the run yet again, I was prepared to take that step.

Even the sky seemed more blue as the clouds floated silently by. Hope was a funny thing, the way it changed your outlook down to the very colors you saw. It pierced and stabbed at my heart, echoing "you're free, you're free." It quickened every heartbeat. It made each step lighter. Hope was a funny thing.

"There," Dov said, pointing ahead.

I stretched up to look around Eden. There, in the distance, so far I could barely distinguish what it was, stood a small black line stretching across the horizon. The wall.

Chapter 23

I smiled.

It was real. I could see it. If I could have run at that moment I would have. I would have run and thrown myself at the wall and leapt over it and run. I would have run as far as I could and never looked back.

Instead, we inched toward the wall. Each step was more torturous than the last, for we could finally see the finish line of our journey but couldn't reach it yet.

"Look," Dov said, pointing away from the wall.

Tall walls rose into the air. Guards were everywhere, forming a human wall around the fortress we could only distinguish because of their uniforms.

"The camps," I said. "Which one?"

"That's a boys' camp. They train them there to fight," Silas explained as if it was all new to me.

"How many boys must they keep there?" I asked astonished at its size.

"More than we'll ever know, I imagine," Dov said sadly. "Between the boys they *take* and the boys they get from the breeding program, there's no telling how many are in there. We don't even know what age groups that one houses."

As we walked, we saw a line of tiny dots being marched from one building to the next. The compound was comprised of several large buildings surrounded by a fence. The bottom part was a wall, holding them in and preventing their escape. Metal rose high, like an iron gate, on top of the stone.

The dots were taken into another building just as a second string of dots exited a different structure. They were stopped off to the side, we assumed for training. I counted at least thirty boys in each row.

We followed the line of the hill and descended too low to see the camp. I felt like I was abandoning them. They had no idea we had witnessed them that day, but I wish they could have known someone knew them and would remember them.

"We'll come back for them one day," Dov said quietly. "We won't just leave them there."

Dov; a heart of gold.

I wrapped my arm around him, hoping he knew I admired that golden heart that always put others first.

He wrapped his hand around my hair, pulling it down slightly. I tipped my head to accommodate his grip, but I didn't mind the adjustment.

We were so close to our escape. I could almost see some of the larger detailing in the wall. I felt the mood shift in the group as we drew close.

Something heavy clinked off Dov's back as we walked. He lurched forward as it clattered to the ground. The knife's metallic rattling drew our attention. Someone had thrown a knife at Dov and by some miracle, the wrong end slammed against him.

He dropped down and claimed the knife. We turned, trying to identify our attackers. Dov's grip tightened around the knife as I reached for the one in his belt we had acquired earlier.

They appeared so quickly, as if they came out of the wind itself. They were less in numbers than we expected would follow us, but still a surprising number. They stalked toward us, ready to fight.

"Silas!" Dov shouted, as if initiating some silently made protocol.

Silas moved into action, taking Eden and moving her away from us. Dov ushered me in the opposite direction. We were splitting up. I lost sight of Silas and Eden as we ran. Dov kept himself between me and the guards as we ran at an angle from them.

I prayed the distant trees would give Silas and Eden some covering. We were familiar with the woods, more familiar than the guards were. Perhaps if they had a head start, they could bury themselves within the confines of the greenery.

Dov and I ran toward the camp. It was still far off in the distance and I couldn't imagine we'd find refuge there. The camp guards would join in the pursuit and we'd be dead within minutes. The area was expansive and open.

My tall companion pulled me back toward the town, championing our race. His hair was disheveled as he turned to look over his shoulder. He was frustratingly handsome, even then, as fear gripped us both.

The Society's man had thrown his knife too early, alerting us to their presence and giving us the advantage. It might have been our only hope for survival. He gave us the gift of distance.

Time stretched out as we ran back toward the town. The group had split, sending a smaller number after us. Even so, if they caught up to us, there was little chance we would win.

We pulled carts into their path, throwing the small objects we could find at them. They pressed onward, only allowing our distractions to slow them a little.

Crashing through the town, we changed course often, hoping to misdirect them.

"Stay here," Dov whispered harshly as he pushed me to the ground.

"No." I pulled myself back up. "Together. Captured or not."

I wrapped my arms around his neck, fastening myself to him. He embraced me and begged me to listen to him.

"No," I insisted.

I watched as he deflated in my arms. He would not win this battle. I would not leave his side.

He leaned to me and kissed me, the kiss I had waited so long to have once again. Dov placed his hands on my hips and pulled me close. His kiss was rough and harsh and passionate. Heat radiated across my body as his breath feathered over my cheek and neck. My vision clouded for a moment, swirling around us in this stolen moment.

"Auluria."

"Dov." We breathed in the same moment.

Dov pulled back first, pulling my wrist with him. The guards had run past our hiding place and this was our only chance. Freedom was just beyond the town buildings, through the fields and past the wall. Liberty was heartbeats away.

With my hand in his, I felt like we could make it. I put all thoughts of everyone else out of my mind and focused only on the steps ahead of us. Dov pulled me along, his stride lengthening my own.

We made it down the hill before we were spotted. I heard them approaching. Dov heard them too, his grip tightening on me.

"When we get there, I'm going to put my hands out for you. Step in them and I'll boost you over. I'll follow right behind," he added before I could protest.

"Okay," I gasped, short of breath.

"It's the only way we'll make it. Once we get over, we must run. As soon as your feet touch the ground, go. I can catch up to you."

I knew it made sense; he was faster than me and could easily overtake me, even if I had the lead. This time I would do as he asked, without question and without the hesitation that might get us killed.

I registered the set of footsteps that approached faster than the others, even over our own noise. It came so near I knew they were on top of us.

"Get a move on, Lur," he shouted as he ran up behind me.

He maneuvered himself to my free side, running his hand along my back. I felt his grip tighten around me and propel me forward. I nearly lost my footing.

Between Dov and Shadoe's strong guidance, I was running faster than ever as they nearly carried me to the wall.

"Shadoe," Dov growled, his eyes turning fierce.

We were only feet from the wall now, and I felt Dov slow as he prepared to lift me over. The wall wasn't what it appeared from a distance. Up close it was more of a large metallic fence. Rocks lined the bottom on both sides, keeping it in place. There were holes, allowing air to pass through from one side to the next. Its frame was large. The top was flat, strong enough to hold a person on top. I decided it must be in case the government ever needed to use it to defend the land; it was a perch for soldiers.

"I was the one who cut you down, Lur. It was my arrow," Shadoe said, loud enough for Dov to hear. He was trying to gain our trust.

While Dov slowed, Shadoe removed his hand from me and launched himself forward. He threw himself at the wall, clinging to its high grips. He scrambled to the perch just as the guards caught up to us.

We were trapped between the metal wall and the human wall. The guards sneered at us, weapons ready. We must have been wanted alive or they would have killed us already.

Dov pinned me against the wall behind him, protecting me.

"You can't save her, Dov," Shadoe shouted. *"She's not yours."*

"Yes, *she is*. She'll *always* be mine," Dov shouted back. My heart swelled.

I was his.

In my peripheral vision, I saw something fly through the sky, coming from behind me. Shadoe had thrown an explosive device behind the guards, not close enough to *us* to hurt me, but enough to disorient the guards.

In that moment Dov turned. He bent before me, cupping his hands. I grabbed his shoulders and set my foot in his waiting fingers. He lifted me and I watched the top of his dark hair leave me. I reached up as Shadoe grasped my arm, pulling me to the perch alongside of him.

"Go!" Dov shouted as the guards ran toward him.

I struggled to get back down to help him. Shadoe threw me to the ground on the opposite side of the high wall. I landed hard, knocking the wind from my lungs.

Dov turned around one last time as I regained my footing. Through the openings in the metal wall, he shouted to me.

"I *will* find you!" He turned to Shadoe. "Get her out of here!"

He no more trusted Shadoe than he trusted the guards attacking us, but he knew it was the safest option for me in that moment. Dov knew that I knew his reservations about Shadoe helping me and that I wouldn't let my guard down. My best chance for survival was with only one opponent on the far side of the wall. Dov faced our attackers alone. One raised his baton, about to bring it down over Dov's head. I screamed as Shadoe pulled me away, refusing to let me turn back as Dov fought to keep the guards from me.

I was on my own with a man I had never loved and no longer trusted. Dov was alone, at the Society's mercy. Eden and Silas were out of my sights. No one knew what had become of Berwyn or the groups in the safe houses. I didn't know of Lowell's fate.

In those short few months, I had learned to love the Baer family. I had lived with them, shared their food and their home. I had talked with them and grown to know them. And yes, ultimately, Dov chased me away, forcing me to leave to *save me*, just like they say I was chased away from the people I had come to know.

I was the girl who couldn't be saved. He was the man who couldn't help but save me.

The wall, with all its promises of protection and freedom, stood uncaring as we were all dragged away to our own separate, desolate isolations.

But I was Dov's and he was mine. And somehow, I'd find a way back to him. No matter the cost.

Shadoe violently dragged me along.

No matter the cost.

ACKNOWLEDGMENTS

My beautiful readers, thank you so much for going on this journey with me. I hope you don't hate me too much. I know my beta readers spent quite some time live-texting comments to me…mainly yelling, some tears, and some happiness…so I can only imagine what you are thinking right now.

Before you go getting too upset with me, don't worry —I know there are unanswered questions. I promise you, you will find out how Goldilocks got her name early on in the second book, but that's all I'm telling you. There's so much more to her story, and we'll be exploring that in books two and three, as well as the prequel. I can't wait to share the rest of this journey with you!

Special thanks to my amazing beta readers! You were so incredibly helpful and I absolutely loved the live text reactions to what you were reading. I will always cherish the screen snaps of those conversations!

To my mom and dad, I know it was a bit surprising when I dropped *"Hey, I wrote some books and one of them looks like it is going to be published!"* so thanks for rolling with that and being supportive!

To my little sister, Susie, thank you for giving me permission to not be nervous during the early stages of all this and for listening to me while I was talking myself through it. You've definitely improved on your secret-keeping skills since we were kids!

To Alexis, I have no words to express how much our friendship means to me. You've done so much for me and for Reading Transforms and I cannot thank you enough. This book would not be what it is without you and your stunning interior artwork. I am in awe of all you do.

To Jenny, the first person to call Dov bae. I'm so grateful for your live messages as you read Golden, it was so affirming and an amazing experience. I'm sorry I *"broke your heart in pieces"* and made you yell *"why"* a lot. Actually…I'm really not sorry at all, Cupcake. *To Option A, my friend, to Option A!*

To Charlotte, thank you for your friendship, Peaches! You've been so wonderful and so supportive. One day we will cause complete chaos when we meet half way. I'll bring the floaties, you bring the math.

A big thank you to Awnna Marie Evans, my lovely friend and the first person who tried to find Auluria and Dov a home, thank you from the bottom of my heart for believing in Golden. Your jokes always make me laugh. I'm so thrilled to have been able to work with you and

I'm so grateful we met! I truly appreciate your confidence in me!

I'm so grateful to have found a caring and supportive home with Crescent Sea Publishing. With all of the ups and downs in this industry, I'm so grateful there is a steady rock of people who are upstanding, compassionate, and professional in every way.

To my amazing street team, The Robins, thank you for all of your hard work and effort. I truly appreciate everything you have done to help me get the word out about *Golden*! Special thanks to Yentl, Elissa, and Jess for all of your help!

To my fabulous readers, thank you for going on this journey with me. I cannot wait to tell you more about Auluria and Dov in the rest of the series.

Thank you, thank you, thank you.

Keep reading for a bonus scene from Dov's perspective, and the first chapter of Locked, the sequel to Golden. You'll also get a sneak peek at both of the Golden prequels that tell Dov and Auluria's stories before they met (and meet some characters that didn't make it to the series!) as well as find out how to get bonus scenes, play an interactive game to help Auluria get ready for her mission, and more!

Stay inspired,

-K.M. Robinson

Above the sounds of the crackling fire and people running to save themselves, a voice pierced the noise. Auluria stood next to me, shoulder hunched as she drank in the smoke-tinged air.

"That's not one of ours," Silas said as he approached us.

I turned back to Auluria, quickly telling her to say there before spinning to run back inside. I couldn't let someone die inside our storehouse, even if they were the enemy. I heard Silas wrestle Auluria back. She cried out for me to stay, but I couldn't let that stop me.

Smoke billowed out of the storehouse, clouding my sight. It burned my lungs, the tears pooling in my eyes were a physical manifestation of the smoke curling around my insides and squeezing.

"Where are you?" I called, trying not to inhale too much smoke. I ducked my face under my collar.

"Here," the boy coughed.

I moved in the direction that I heard the voice. He was somewhere nearby. The orange glow of the fire lit the smoke up, creating a hazy sunset look. It might have been lovely if it hadn't been so dangerously hot.

"Where?" I yelled again, hoping I had made my way closer.

"I'm here," the boy shouted, sounding weaker. "Help me!"

"I'm coming," I responded, moving as quickly as I dared. I tried to avoid the coughing fit, but it did me no good.

"Please," the boy cried, "get me out of here!"

He struggled under the weight of far too many supplies. The boy had stayed behind to raid the storehouse, despite the fire. Youthfulness likely led him to believe he had something to prove, though I doubted his boss would be happy.

A beam had fallen, catching part of his collection of prizes. It pinned his leg down at a dangerous angle. He had to be in pain.

"Get the beam off me," he pleaded.

Picking up one of the bags he had left scattered on the

floor, I wrapped it around my hands to protect them as I lifted the beam. I winced when I felt the sharp pain in my shoulder from the punch I had just taken. The wooden beam creaked as I forced it off of the boy.

"Go," I instructed, gritting my teeth as I held up the weight of the board.

He struggled to stand. The kid was tangled in everything he had collected. My eyes traced over everything, looking for the source of what held him down. Using all the strength I had left, I tossed the beam as far away as I could, missing his leg by a few inches.

I dropped to my knees as he coughed again, pulling bags of supplies and weapons away from him.

"I need those," he protested, trying to collect the objects I discarded.

"You're welcome to them, but that also means you'll be trapped here," I warned him. "I can't get you out if you're tangled like this. You need to let me help you get out."

The fire crackled, hissing in the boy's ear. His eyes grew bigger than the apples that rolled out of the bag I tugged on. He clawed at his shoulders, trying to remove the bags he was caught in.

Together, we managed to free him as the flames drew closer. I pulled him to his feet. He stumbled forward, his leg buckling beneath him. He swayed, likely from lack of oxygen.

"Come on," I said, ducking under his arm. He shifted his weight onto my shoulders as I dragged him toward the door. We had only been twenty feet away, though the smoke made it seem like a mile.

The air hit me when we stepped outside, setting off another coughing fit. I let the boy go as he perked back up now that he was out of the smoke. Like a cornered rabbit, he took off, limping away as quickly as he could.

"Let him go," I gasped, waving my hand to Silas. "He's a kid."

Silas nodded, watching the boy run off.

"We need to separate. Go!" Silas directed.

Auluria moved to my side, sliding under my arm to assist me. My breath caught as she wrapped her arm around my waist and I prayed the jolt that ran through my entire body blended with my already-staggered breathing.

She guided us to the trees, putting as much distance between us and the storehouse as possible. I tried to focus on anything that wasn't the scent of her hair, allowing me to be incredibly aware of where we were.

"What's going to happen now that the storehouse was destroyed?" Auluria questioned.

"There are more storehouses. We only lost that one. We'll be okay." I realized how much I was depending on her in that moment, leaning the majority of my weight on her shoulders. I straightened, letting my arm rest casually across her. I didn't want to put too much strain on her. I smiled to let her know I was grateful.

Walking with her was wonderful. It felt meant-to-be. When she turned to me to speak, it seemed as natural as if we had been doing it our entire lives. I waited for her to talk.

"Dov?" Her hesitation confused me. "Why did you do that?" Run back in?"

"He needed help."

"You didn't know who he was, only that he was trying to hurt us. But you ran in anyway." She looked down at the ground, intently studying the leaves we were walking over.

"Auluria," I said softly, turning to look at her. "It's about doing what is right. Yes, he was fighting against us, but that doesn't mean he should die."

"It doesn't mean you should die *for* him either," she snapped.

"*I'm fine*, Auluria." I tried to alleviate her growing fear. She didn't respond.

"Auluria," I faced her as I spoke, growing quiet. I had to know. "Why did you brush me away earlier?"

For someone who didn't seem to care much an hour before, she was awfully worked up. Still, she said nothing, forcing her eyes to remain fixed on the ground between us.

"Auluria, why have you been avoiding me?" I dared to step closer to her, staring at her downturned eyelashes.

When she didn't answer, I couldn't take it. I stepped forward, wrapping my hand around her shoulder as I pulled her to me. My feet moved on their own—*the traitorous things*—propelling us both toward the closest tree.

I knew I need to be careful. Auluria needed the space to decide once and for all on her own if she wanted me or not, but she also needed to know that I had made up my mind about her. I wanted her.

Everything about her was beautiful; her concern for others, her laughter, her history, the fact that she needed me, and those gorgeous lips that kept calling to me. I wanted to take her into my arms and protect her.

She looked so tired, as if she had carried the weight of the world for too long and one kiss would take it from her. I wanted to take her worries from her and carry that burden. I wanted to see her smile.

I waited, searching her eyes.

She stood, frozen.

"Tell me to stop," I whispered, moving a little closer, begging her to give me permission.

Her eyes grew wide, lips parting into the tiniest smile as she realized what was happening. Just as quickly, her face iced over and she turned away.

"Hmm," she squeaked. Her shoulder rose and fell with heavy breaths. She was as nervous as I was.

"Tell me to stop," I said again, unable to help myself from grinning at her unexpected response.

She mumbled again, refusing to look up from the forest floor. Her face flushed red and I knew I was winning her over. She was stunning when she blushed.

"Look at me." I tried to banish my smile. We both knew that if she convinced herself to look at me, it would be all over. "Tell me to stop."

I shouldn't have sounded so desperate, but I also didn't care. The most beautiful woman I had ever seen was a heartbeat away, blushing furiously, only seconds away from kissing me. I didn't care how I sounded—I just wanted her lips on mine. I needed to know who she was when she was with me.

"Tell me to stop," I whispered.

She stared at me, looking so deeply into my eyes that she had to have seen every part of me.

"Don't stop," she finally said, spurring me into action.

She was sweet, and everything right with the world. Her kiss burned through me. I couldn't breathe. I couldn't think. All I could do was tangle my hands in her never-ending hair.

I lurched forward when her hands touched my waist, surprising me. She was so warm. Everywhere she touched etched bolts of lighting through my skin. Auluria's hands moved over my chest, making me flinch into her. They finally rested on my collar as she pulled me closer.

She matched my fervor as we kissed. Each time I moved closer, faster, more passionately, she responded, her body arching into me like a vine crawling toward the sunlight.

I couldn't breathe. When I realized she couldn't either, I pulled back just far enough to give her a break. I hovered an inch from her lips, waiting for her to give me some indication of whether she wanted to continue or if it had been a momentary lapse of judgment.

LOCKED: BOOK TWO IN THE GOLDEN TRILOGY

Goldilocks didn't run away. Dov Baer forced her over the Wall to protect her and now she's returning with an army to rescue him.

Unsure if anyone survived the brutal attack inside the Society, Auluria is forced to work with her former handler, Shadoe, to raise an army and stop the government from murdering everyone she cares about inside the Society. She's willing to do whatever it takes to get Dov Baer back, but the far side of the Wall holds as many dangers as the Society does.

Auluria's plans could fall apart at any moment, and she

risks betrayal with ever new conspirator she takes on. Her allegiances are shifting—but so are everyone's as the battle lines are drawn.

Now available!
Learn more about Locked at
lockedinfo.kmrobinsonbooks.com

FORGED: A GOLDEN TRILOGY PREQUEL NOVELLA

Goldilocks was innocent once, but her cousin's plan to turn her into a killer has changed that.

Before Lowell sent Auluria on a mission for his master plan of destruction, before Shadoe trained her to be a vicious and deceptive fighter, before she ever met Dov Baer and his family, Auluria was a young girl merely trying to survive.

When Auluria is brought into Lowell's fold after the death of her aunt, she's placed under the supervision of Shadoe, a cruel and careless mentor to teach her to be a weapon in her cousin's war. As her training continues, she finds herself in growingly dangerous situations, all leading to her greatest mission yet: to destroy Dov and Berwyn Baer and become the deceptive fighter that no one will survive.

Now available!

Learn more about Forged at

forgedinfo.kmrobinsonbooks.com

**TEMPERED: A GOLDEN TRILOGY PREQUEL
NOVELLA**

Before Dov lead a rebellion, he was a son and younger brother working to protect his family.

When the Baers discover the Society has called for their father's execution, they won't stop until he's safe, but their former friend has other plans. Forced into the open, the Baers try to protect their people from destruction at the merciless hands of the Society, but even *they* don't have the power to stop what is coming.

After the unthinkable happens, the brothers are forced to choose sides and take on roles they never wanted, but a new arrival changes everything and throws their world into chaos.

Now available exclusively in the Golden Boxset/Omnibus!

Learn more about Tempered at

goldentrilogyinfo.kmrobinsonbooks.com

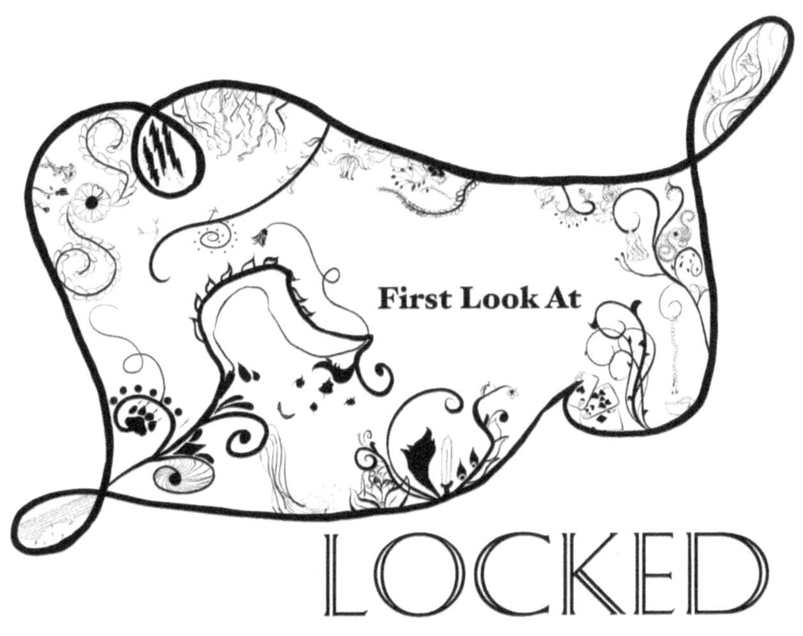

The moments between *knowing* the pain is coming and actually *feeling* it are the most agonizing. As soon as I heard it—the low, vicious growl—I stopped moving. I held in my gasp, as I had been trained to do.

Before I could turn to confront my attacker, I heard the collision as body met body. The wolf that had been crouching behind me flailed in the grass. It hissed and snarled as it tried to attack Shadoe.

He held the beast back, trying to strangle it. Without thinking, I picked up a large branch and brought it down on the gray wolf's head, silencing it. Shadoe made sure the job was done.

It had been a week since Shadoe and I escaped over the wall. Dov, the man I cared for, was still trapped somewhere in the Society. He gave himself up to save me, as he had been doing since the day I met him all those months ago.

Shadoe, my former handler, and I had been traveling together since that day. I didn't trust him, but we still work as well together as the day we started training. I relaxed enough to work with him without fearing for my life.

The day we escaped, I learned a great deal of information from Shadoe as he attempted to convince me not to run. Every day since, he tried to show me he was not a threat. We both worked for my older cousin Lowell, following his every command. His mission was to take down the Society by framing Dov Baer, his older brother Berwyn, and Berwyn's wife, Eden, along with their entire group. Knowing I could never be a part of that once I met Dov, I betrayed Lowell.

Shadoe remained loyal to Lowell, despite the fact that he was gone. Just before our escape, the government was going to hang us. In an effort to save Lowell, his men unintentionally gave us the opportunity to escape. When the soldiers finally caught up with us, we split up. Silas and Eden ran toward the woods. Dov and I ran toward the town. Shadoe found us at the wall and helped Dov to save me. The last thing I saw was the soldiers capturing the man who stayed behind to protect me.

Shadoe and I had rabbit meat, having saved our meal from the wolf. A meal of anything more than tiny birds was more than I could ask for. My former handler and I set up camp in the wastelands that lie between our nation and the foreign nations that attacked our people. With our camp being only a few miles outside of the closest foreign town, we had the perfect opportunity to spy on them while staying far enough away to keep from being discovered.

Each day, we crept toward the city. Each day, we got a little closer, pushing our luck and challenging them to notice our approach. The next day we planned to go into the city. I prayed it wouldn't be our last.

"Are you ready Lur?" Shadoe asked me.

I tucked the last bit of my long, golden hair under my wrap and nodded to him.

Shadoe and I carried sacks of food we had gathered to trade. We decided the best thing we could do was disguise ourselves as traders to get around the city without much notice. Some of the rabbit meat was tucked away in our bags, ready to be bartered for supplies. I was grateful we could hunt in the wastelands.

"What do you have, dearie?" A woman clutched my arm and held up several strings of beads.

The glittering crystals caught my eye as they shimmered. For a moment I was lost in their beauty.

"They're beautiful, but not today, thank you." I shook her off.

"We need more weapons." Shadoe muttered.

Shadoe had always been practical. For as long as I'd know him, he always made the dependable choice. Shadoe had been assigned to me since the day my cousin brought me into his fold. He had been my trainer, my partner, and even the man I was supposed to marry. Together, we were to lead as Lowell's next in command.

I glanced around, looking at the goods for sale. This town was much freer than where Shadoe and I came from. People came and went as they pleased. There was still an oppressive feeling over the town, but the fear was not as great. I concluded it must be because they were so far away from the people controlling them.

"Shadoe…" I nodded to a nearby man.

He eyed the short man before stepping over to speak with him. I stood near, my back to his. I pretended to scan the area for trades, but really, I was watching for oncoming attacks.

I imagined they must have been hunting us by now. The Society was furious with me. They may not know Shadoe, but *I* had escaped. They would be coming for me. Over the years I worked with Shadoe, he had trained me well; our reactions to each other came instinctively.

We walked away with several knives, having traded for the rabbit meat and several small birds. I put a knife in each crumbling boot, grateful to have it securely against my skin. My hand brushed over the knife in my belt.

I watched as children ran through the streets. They reminded me of the little ones from the storehouse. I hoped they were all safe under Berwyn's watch.

I still didn't know of Berwyn's fate. He had been poisoned during our plan to show the government it was Lowell who had attacked them, rather than the Baers. I still hadn't worked up the courage to ask Shadoe what he dosed Berwyn with. My sight bounced to Shadoe's hip where the dangerous metal claw hung, just out of sight under his shirt.

Shadoe nudged me and I looked away from the children's game. Just inside a small doorway sat a row of boots, ready for sale. We cautiously approached the illuminated doorway, warm with candlelight, even in the day.

"Welcome. Welcome." An older man eyed us. "Freshly made boots, perfect for long journeys and hard labor."

His eyes swept from my wrapped hair all the way down to my boots. He grimaced at the sight of them. They were the same boots I had had when I started Lowell's mission all those months ago. Somehow they survived every attack and murder attempt. They served me well, but I was in desperate need of a new pair.

"What do you have?" he asked, and Shadoe showed him the remainder of our trade items. "Not enough, but for the pretty lady, I'll take it."

I shook my head at Shadoe. It was way too much and we hadn't finished gathering our supplies yet. I started to walk away when I heard the man speak again.

"Which pair would you like?"

I turned to see Shadoe handing everything we had left to the man.

"No." I shook my head again.

"Be practical, Lur. You need this. We can come back another day."

I tipped my head at him, trying to read him. On one hand, I couldn't imagine Shadoe ever paying such a steep price for something as simple as everyday boots. On the other hand, I really needed them. I hadn't complained, but I knew he could tell that it was getting too bad for me to continue in them.

Sighing, I reached down to inspect them. I tried several on before selecting a pair. I used my skirt to block my knives as I tested them. The man never knew I had them safely hidden around my ankles.

"Thank you," I said as we left.

"You needed them," was all he said.

Shadoe had always been a man of few words…at least to me.

We hunted again that afternoon. I never had the stomach for killing, so I helped Shadoe track, but allowed him to take them down. It made me sick each time, but I knew it was the only reason we were able to survive.

The sky was dark that night. The clouds blocked the moon, allowing us slivers of passing light as we lay on the ground next to the fire. On our journey we had seen several nomadic groups roaming about, so we felt safe enough to have the flames at night.

The days were growing short and the air was getting cooler as summer slipped into fall. The leaves dropped off of the trees and swirled around our feet.

"Tomorrow we'll go back again. We need to be seen. The more familiar they become with us, the more they will let their guard down." Shadoe said absent-mindedly.

"Shadoe?" I asked. "What's the plan?"

He looked at me as if I was crazy. "The plan is to get information, Lur, you know that."

"I mean the long-term plan. We escaped, but all those people are still back there. What are we going to do?"

"Auluria." He demanded my full attention. "We're not going to *do* anything. You're safe. Now we just have to survive."

Now it was my turn to look shocked.

"Shadoe, I'm not just leaving them there. I'm going back for them, whether you help me or not. It's just a matter of when and how."

I couldn't read his expression as he gave me a strange look.

"The guards took him, Lur. If they didn't kill him on the spot, they have surely hung him by this point."

I felt like I had been punched in the gut. Not even the pain of the torture I had received only weeks earlier compared to the notion of Dov being dead.

"He's not dead. He can't be." I said quietly.

Shadoe sighed at me and rolled over, ending the discussion.

But I didn't care. I would find a way back. I'd save Dov and Eden, Silas and Berwyn. I'd save all of the Baers' group. I wouldn't give up on them.

I brushed my hair back with my cold hand and forced the tears back into their deep wells.

By morning I had a plan. I'd learn my way around the city. I would find alliances if I could. I'd find a way to provide for myself, and then, if need be, I'd slip away from Shadoe and run. I knew it was very likely that he'd find me and drag me back away from the wall, but I had to try.

The town was full of people again. They bumped and jostled into each other as they walked. I watched carefully for every move they made.

"Hello again, dearie," an old lady said—the woman with the beads.

This time she carried a small cart behind her. "Help an old woman, dearie, and I'll let you have one of these." She held up a sparkling necklace.

"What do you need?" I asked kindly.

"I need to be across town." She looked down to her cart, heavy with bottles, jars and crates.

I nodded to Shadoe, indicating he should let me be. He branched off and went to trade. I picked up the handles and followed behind the woman.

"What's your name, dearie?" she questioned me.

"Au..." I caught myself. "Lur. My name is Lur."

"That's an unusual name, dearie. *Lur.*" She grinned as she tried out my name. "I'm Necesta. As you can see, I'm a bit of a medicine woman. Nothing other-worldly, mind you, but herbs and natural remedies. And the beads, of course." She chuckled to herself.

"You seem to be quite experienced." I remarked, trying to keep the conversation going.

"Oh yes, dearie. I've been doing this since before your parents were even born."

"Where are you taking all this?" I asked.

"Across town where I set up shop once a month. If people need me, they find me, but I try to make myself available in different locations when I can," she croaked, still chuckling.

I could tell as she walked that she was stronger than she appeared to be. I had no doubt she had been about to haul the load by herself. It made me wary.

Once we arrived, she asked me to help set up. It was almost like a small shack, similar the ones the Baers had in back of their house—only this was missing a side. The front had been removed, leaving it open to the world. There were several chairs and a table waiting.

She set out a few things but left most of her work in her cart.

"Sit, dearie, you could learn a thing or two." She winked at me.

I obliged out of curiosity, but my hand sat on the knife in my belt as I leaned away from her.

Almost immediately people started making their way

toward the shack. Necesta called out ingredients for me to fetch for her. I examined each one before handing it to her. Watching, I waited as she set a young boy's broken arm. I helped her as she wrapped the hand of a man who had lost a finger, barely stomaching the blood.

Within a few hours, I felt strangely at peace around the woman.

"Necesta, thank you for letting me help you today. I've truly enjoyed it." I said. "Let me help you take your cart back."

I stood and picked up the handles. She nodded and we walked together back to her side of the city. Most of the cart's contents were gone, making the trip lighter.

"Where's that friend of yours, dearie?" she asked as we drew close to the street we met on. "Is he your lover?"

Her question nearly pulled me to a halt, but I caught myself and continued with only a slight hesitation in my step.

"No, he's not. He's a friend."

"I thought so. You didn't seem too worried when he left your side. *Him*, on the other hand, *he likes you*."

I gathered that Necesta was a woman of many talents. She was very perceptive, even if she was a little off.

"You'll both come to dinner, and then I'll pay you for your help."

"Oh no, Necesta, you don't have to pay me, I enjoyed it. And we don't want to impose…"

"Oh, nonsense, dearie. Go find your companion and let's get on with it," she demanded, scuttling into a small house.

Shadoe appeared, as if on cue.

"You were watching," I said without turning to him.

"Of course," he grumbled.

"Did you get anything accomplished today?" I asked.

"Yes." He seemed cross. "I stayed close in case you needed me, but I didn't watch you all day. You're trained well enough to take care of yourself. I just wanted to be sure you were all right; this *is* a new place, after all."

"Necesta wants us to stay."

He raised his eyebrows at me.

"She's feeding us. Just don't be rude." I said stomping off toward Necesta's door.

Shadoe followed me. The house was small, but the warmth of the fire was like heaven. She pointed to the table where she had already started setting out food.

"So, young man," Necesta started. "I have already met *Goldilocks* here, but I haven't had the pleasure of meeting her *young male* companion yet."

"I'm Shadoe, ma'am." He introduced himself as she bustled about the room.

"Ma'am," she mocked. "*Ma'am.* I may be an old grandma, young man, but you will call me Necesta, understood?"

"Yes," Shadoe confirmed rigidly.

"Yes?" she prompted, hands on hips.

"Yes, Necesta."

"That's better." She proclaimed, "Now, tell me. Where are you two from? It's not around here, that's for sure. And it's not from *our* country… Now don't worry," she said glancing at us, "no one else knows that. I'm just a perceptive old lady who's been around long enough to know who's from here and who ain't."

Shadoe and I were both horrified but managed to keep straight faces. I felt him stiffen, preparing to run if needed.

"Relax, young man, I'm not telling anyone. I'm only saying if you and your pretty lady friend were to have come from over that wall"—

She pointed in the direction of the wall—"then I'd just be obliged to tell you that there are those of us who wouldn't mind it. That's all. *Apple?*"

I sat stunned for a moment before reaching for the red apple in her hand. *How had she known? Did she know who I really was?*

"You aren't the first to run, dearie," she said, eyeing me.

"*You… ?*" I couldn't stop myself in time.

"Yes, dearie. I was once just like you. I jumped the wall and escaped. I found refuge here, though hardly anyone knows it. Don't worry; I'm on your side. Tell me, how has it been?"

"How did you survive?" Shadoe interrupted, unwilling to give her any information.

"Same as you will. I made friends. I learned to blend in. I made myself important." She nodded as she started to eat. "You'll find this place, while still controlled by violence and fear, to be a much easier place to live. Only, though, because we're so far removed from the capitol. Once they want something from us, which is still often, it can be very deadly. On days like today, when there is no oversight, we're free." She smiled thoughtfully.

I was beginning to like this woman. She was a no-nonsense, down-to-business, incredibly perceptive person. I had no doubt she was a good person to know in this town.

We finished our meal without upsetting Shadoe any further. We thanked Necesta and walked back to our campsite. Shadoe checked behind us every few steps the entire way back.

"I like her," I announced. "I think she's going to be helpful to us."

I touched the necklace around my throat. I insisted Necesta keep it, but she forced me to try it on and then pushed me out the door. I took it off and put it in my pocket.

"Keep it on, dearie," she had said, "so they know you're one of my friends. It will keep you safe here."

The next day when we went back to the town, I would wear it for her to see. Its jewels sparkled in the firelight before I dropped them into my pocket.

"We'll be careful," I said, "but I think we can trust her."

THE COMPLETE GOLDEN TRILOGY

Did you know the complete Golden Trilogy is now available with all three books and two prequel novellas?

The ebook boxset and printed omnibus contains Golden, Locked, and Edge, as well as the prequel novella, Forged, which tells the story of Auluria's training before Lowell sent her on that deadly mission to destroy the Baer family, *and* an exclusive bonus novella, Tempered, which tells the events in Dov's life before he met Auluria—including what happened to his father.

You can only access Tempered and an exclusive note from the author through the boxset/omnius.

For more information, please visit
goldentrilogy.kmrobinsonbooks.com

preorder swag, giveaways, and more, so watch the social media pages carefully for the next scene giveaway.

K.M. Robinson also has bonus scenes and extras from all of her books on
newsletter.kmrobinsonbooks.com

Sign up now for weekly emails with special bonuses, extras, live broadcasts replays and upcoming dates, events, coloring pages, games, introductions to new authors+live broadcasts with them, and more.

WORLD PORTALS

Ready to learn exclusive facts about The Golden Trilogy and other K.M. Robinson Series?

World Portals are now available on www. kmrobinsonbooks.com

Learn behind the scenes facts, watch videos, play games, check out our book filters, find out where to get bonus scenes, view fan art, and get access to other secrets we've hidden away inside the World Portals on the website.

The World Portals are constantly changing and information is being taken away and added all the time, so check back frequently for new content!

GOLDEN MISSION INTERACTIVE GAME

Auluria is being sent on one last mission before Lowell and Shadoe send her to destroy Dov and Berwyn Baer and she needs your help. Are you ready to assist Goldilocks and locate the Baers?

This interactive, choose-your-own-adventure game is played through Facebook messenger so you never miss a mission. Played over the course of one-two days, you and Auluria will go on several missions to discover the location of her next target and then you can go back into the story and see how your actions lead up to everything in the book.

PLAY THE GAME

at

goldenmission.kmrobinsonbooks.com

Auluria will meet with you few times for different missions over the course of a few days, with gaps of time in between so you can "complete the missions" and report back. She will be in touch!

Have fun running missions to help Auluria find Dov and Berwyn and then go back in the story to see how your choices directly affect them in the story.

BONUS FACEBOOK FILTERS

Want to get your hands on some incredible Facebook filters for Golden? Now you have the ability to get filters for the story, characters, etc right inside your phone.

You can use these on your photos, profile pictures,

videos, and live broadcasts. All you have to do is like my author page and they will automatically show up in your filters!

I've even taken these clips and put them on Instagram Stories by saving them to my phone and uploading them to Instagram.

Visit www.facebook.com/kmrobinsonbooks to grab these filters for your photos, videos, and broadcasts! Bonus points for tagging me @kmrobinsonbooks so I can see how you're supporting The Golden Trilogy.

ABOUT THE AUTHOR

K.M. Robinson is a storyteller who creates new worlds both in her writing and in her fine arts conceptual photography. She is a marketing, branding and social media strategy educator who is recognized at first sight by her very long hair. She is a creative who focuses on photography, videography, couture dress making, and writing to express the stories she needs to tell. She almost always has a camera within reach.

Visit her at her website: www.kmrobinsonbooks.com

CONNECT ON SOCIAL MEDIA

facebook.com/kmrobinsonbooks

instagram.com/kmrobinsonbooks

twitter.com/kmrobinsonbooks

Get free excerpts and full novels from K.M. Robinson at excerpt.kmrobinsonbooks.com

ALSO BY K.M. ROBINSON

The Golden Trilogy

Book One: Golden

Forged: A Golden Novella

Book Two: Locked

Book Three: Edge

The Complete Series Boxset/Omnibus with Tempered: an exclusive bonus novella

The Jaded Duology

Book One: Jaded

Book Two: Risen

The Complete Series Boxset/Omnibus with exclusive epilogue

The Siren Wars Saga

Book One: The Siren Wars

Book Two: Darker Depths

Book Three: Beyond The Shores

Origins of the Siren Wars: Prequel Novella

Book Four: Forbidden Waters (coming soon)

The Legends Chronicles

Along Came A Spider: A Prequel Novelette

And They'll Come Home: A Prequel Novelette

The Archives of Jack Frost Series

The Revolution of Jack Frost

The Redemption of Jack Frost (coming soon)

Stealing Steam Series

Book One: Lions and Lamps

Book Two: Pistons and Prisoners

Book Three: Railcars and Rulers

Top Hats and Telegraphs: A Prequel Novella

The Complete Series Boxset/Omnibus with Vambraces and Victories: an exclusive bonus novella

Virtually Sleeping Beauty: A Novella Retelling

The Goose Girl and The Artificial: A Novella Retelling

The Sinking: A Little Mermaid Novella Retelling

Cindrill: A Cinderella Assassin Novella Retelling

Sugarcoated: A Hansel and Gretel's Witch Novella Retelling

JADED: BOOK ONE OF THE JADED DUOLOGY

If the only way to stay alive was to convince your new husband not to murder you and make it look like an accident, could you do it?

At eighteen, Jade shouldn't have to be forced to marry the son of her father's enemy as part of a revenge plot for a failed rebellion. When she's thrown into the life of being the wife of the Commander's son and heir, her only hope for survival is convincing Roan Diamond to actually fall in love with her so that he doesn't kill her on his father's wishes.

While a dutiful son, Roan shouldn't have to trick his new wife into believing his family accepts her, but as the only one in a position to make the country believe Jade is part of their family, he will do what he has to before his family murders his young bride and makes it look like an accident to get back at Jade's father.

358

With half the country trying to protect Jade and the other half oblivious to the atrocities committed at the Commander's hand, it's a race to see who will win at a deadly game of cat and mouse.

One chooses life. One chooses death. In the midst of chaos, only one will succeed.

Now available!
Learn more about The Jaded Duology at
jadedinfo.kmrobinsonbooks.com

THE SIREN WARS: BOOK ONE OF THE SIREN WARS SAGA

War has hovered around the kingdom of Scylla for generations ever since the original sirens left the mer collection generations ago after nearly drowning the human prince. Over the years, select mermaids from the royal bloodline have been trained as spies to work for the reigning kings and queens, keeping the collection safe from sirens and humans.

Celena and her partner, Merrick, work covertly for the royals—not even her twin brother knows. When they discover the sirens have broken through the barriers the mer set up to keep the sirens out, Celena and her friends must race to the old kingdom of Metten to stop them from starting a war within their borders.

When she's dragged to the surface, Celena realizes that the war above the waters is as deadly as the one below the waves—and sacrificing herself may be the only way to protect her family.

The Siren Wars have only just begun.

Available now!
Learn more about The Siren Wars Saga at sirenwarsinfo.
kmrobinsonbooks.com

deadlier, and he knows he can't trust the girl who snuck into the competition this year...but Cyra might not survive his ruthlessness either in a game where only the lion's heart can win.

All wishes require sacrifice, and someone is going to pay the price for the Stourbridge.

Available now!
Learn more about The Stealing Steam Series at
lionsandlampsinfo.kmrobinsonbooks.com

ALONG CAME A SPIDER: THE FIRST PREQUEL NOVELETTE TO THE LEGENDS CHRONICLES

Little Hacker Muffet
sat on her tuffet
destroying her cords and Way.
Along came a hacker named Spider,
who sat down beside her
and frightened his opponent away.

When Fet, one of the most skilled hackers in the Legends, discovers her best friend and leader of her group has been abducted and held for ransom, she must escape unnoticed and find Peep before it's too late.

When Spider, a new recruit training to join her hacker

ring, slips out with her and claims to have a plan to save her friend, Fet is forced to bring him along. As she discovers he's not who he claims to be, she faces grave danger and learns just how deadly a spider bite can be.

Now available!
Learn more about The Legends Chronicles at
acasinfo.kmrobinsonbooks.com

VIRTUALLY SLEEPING BEAUTY

To *wake her up, he has to enter the game and help her beat it...*

Surely the class president wouldn't illegally over-juice to stay in the virtual reality game citizens are allowed to play for four hours a day, but when Royce's aunt calls in a panic because her goddaughter hasn't left the game yet, his only option is to go inside the game and drag the girl out.

The golden knight quickly discovers the princess' absence in the real world isn't of her own doing—*she's trapped inside the game by unknown forces*—and if she can't escape soon, she could die for real outside of the game. He's even more shocked to discover that Rora outranks him inside of the game, which means she'll have to fight to *protect herself* from the evils locking her inside a dangerous world.

Can Rora and Royce work together to outsmart a vicious queen and evil magician, and defeat digital dragons, or will Rora slowly fade away until there's nothing left but an empty shell and the game ranking she will leave behind?

Now available!

Learn more about Virtually Sleeping Beauty at vsbinfo.kmrobinsonbooks.com

THE REVOLUTION OF JACK FROST

No one inside the snow globe knows that Morozoko Industries is controlling their weather, testing them to form a stronger race that can survive the fall out from the bombs being dropped in the outside world—all they know is that they must survive the harsh Winter that lasts a month and use the few days of Spring, Summer, and Fall to gather enough supplies to survive.

When the seasons start shifting, Genesis and Jack know something is going on. As their team begins to find technology that they don't have access to inside their snow globe of a world, it begins to look more and more like one of their own is working against them.

. . .

Genesis soon discovers Morozoko Industries, but when a foreign enemy tries to destroy their weather program to make sure their destructive life-altering bombs succeed in destroying the outside world, only one person can shut down the machine that is spinning out of control and save the lives of everyone inside the bunker—Jack.

Now available!
Learn more about The Revolution of Jack Frost at
jackfrostinfo.kmrobinsonbooks.com

THE GOOSE GIRL AND THE ARTIFICIAL

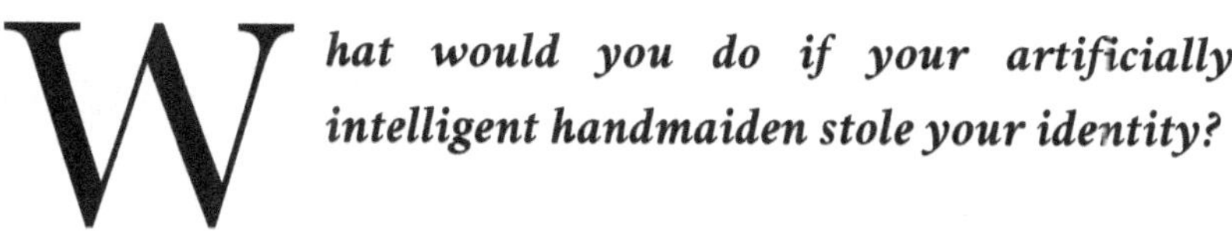

What *would you do if your artificially intelligent handmaiden stole your identity?*

Threatened by her Artificial, Arta, Princess Goselyn is forced to switch places and pretend she isn't human when she reaches Prince Corinth to negotiate a treaty they both need to be able to take their respective crowns one day. If she doesn't comply, her Artificial, controlled by her evil cousin, will not only kill Goselyn's mother, but Prince Corinth and his father as well.

Can the quiet princess outsmart a machine created to be more intelligent than she is, all while surviving the other

Artificials and robots working against her in the foreign palace, or will Corinth and his father find out and destroy her chance to save them all?

Learn more about The Goose Girl and The Artificial at
goosegirlinfo.kmrobinsonbooks.com

THE SINKING

The sea witch wants to silence her, but not for the reason you think.

When a quirky older woman pawns a fancy seashell necklace at her mother's antique shop on the pier, Cara doesn't think much about the story the woman spins about the wearer turning into a mermaid.

On her way home, she accidentally drops the necklace into the ocean and is swept out to sea where she meets— a merman who volunteers to take her to his mother, the sea queen, to help her get her legs back.

. . .

Cara soon learns that it's Quay's eighteen birthday—a day that has been a curse for his family—and is meant to be one for her too. Now she must fight to survive the sea with Quay at her side.

Fans of The Little Mermaid will love this twisted take on the beloved story.

Now available!
Learn more about The Sinking at
thesinkinginfo.kmrobinsonbooks.com

CINDRILL

 inderella is an assassin out to murder the prince...*but he's hunting her too.*

The nanobots Cindrill's master gives her to use as a mask allow her to slip into the ball wearing a face that isn't hers, but when the assassination attempt goes sideways, Prince Davin doesn't understand why her face changes when he injures her, slicing her foot open around a unique pair of shoes as she runs away.

When Cindrill runs into the prince the next day without her nanobot mask on, he doesn't recognize her, but immediately decides her skills will be useful on his hunt for the would-be-assassin woman who nearly killed his father and his fiancée the night before.

Both are tasked with the job of murdering the other, but things don't quite go as they had planned when Cindrill's master and Davian's fiancée interfere as the two try to decide whether or not to kill the other.

It's hard to recognize a woman when she uses technology to change her appearance, but Cindrill is going to use that to her full advantage as she destroys the prince. ***Will either survive?***

Now available!

Learn more about Cindrill at
cindrillinfo.kmrobinsonbooks.com

SUGARCOATED

Hansel and Gretel's witch was actually on their side...

Annika's job is to create a cake to match the candy-colored rooftops, nightly firework shows, and daily parades ending in unexpected executions for the mad king's ball, but her true mission is to sneak a thirteen-year-old assassin into the palace using her gift of illusions.

Hansel's job is to protect his little sister, Gretel, once she assassinates King Levin and ends the destruction in Candestrachen, using his power over light to rescue the young girl from the chaos her influence over life and death will create.

. . .

When the entire forest reconstructs itself under Gretel's command while trying to save herself from a king's guard, Hansel and Annika must put their feelings aside and ensure their plan holds true—even if it means one of them has to sacrifice themselves to protect the mission.

Her illusions were meant to save her....but not everyone will survive the assassination attempt.

Learn more about Sugarcoated at
sugarcoatedinfo.kmrobinsonbooks.com

BLOOD IS SILENT

Red Riding Hood is a circus aerialist and the wolf is ready to cage her.

Sienna has grown up working for the circus, dangling off her signature red silks every night. Her grandmother has been known to wander off to train new acts for their boss, but when Sienna tries to find her to bring her back to the show, she doesn't expect the dashing and dangerous Elijah to join her.

When they finally find Grandma Ida has been transformed deep in the heart of the woods, Sienna will stop at nothing to save her—but the wolf has her right where he wants her, and she won't be able to escape his claws.

378

She was told not to go into the woods alone.

Now available!

Learn more about Blood Is Silent at
bloodissilentinfo.kmrobinsonbooks.com